The Adventures
of the Chicano Kid

and other stories

Max Martínez

Arte Público Press
Houston, Texas
1982

Acknowledgements

"La Tacuachera," "Memorias," "Doña Petra," "Faustino" and "Monologue of the Bolivian Major" were first published in *Caracol;* "The Adventures of the Chicano Kid" and "Portal" were first published in *Revista Chicano-Riqueña.* All of the stories, with the exception of "Doctor Castillo," which is new, and the two that appeared in *Revista Chicano-Riqueña,* have never been published before in their present, final form.

Cover design by Narciso Peña

This volume is made possible
through a grant from the Texas Commission on the Arts.

813

M 385a R

Arte Público Press
Revista Chicano-Riqueña
University of Houston
Houston, Texas 77004

218489

Library of Congress Catalog No. 81-0601

ISBN 0-934770-08-5

Printed in the United States of America

For Freda Bleeck Martínez

CONTENTS

The Adventures of
the Chicano Kid

A Dime Novel

Chapter One (In which the Chicano Kid undertakes a magnificent entrance
into the hamlet of Santo Gringo, and of his reception)

There is no sun that gently laves with golden showers quite to match that
which radiates so splendiferously upon the terrain and the creatures of God
who inhabit the southwestern region of the United States. It is indeed a sun
which gilds the people and the imagination. It is the lofty, the majestic, the
omnipotent Hyperion that casts his glow upon the Southwest.

The shadows of the morning, lengthening toward the west, engendered
from the east, had all but dissipated when the Chicano Kid rode into the
village of Santo Gringo. In appearance, in majesty, in magnificence, in
splendor, the Chicano Kid is, to all but the most stultish of mind, a fit rival for
the lofty Hyperion.

It was a time of sadness in Santo Gringo, a sadness which swept the
territory, leaving it barren of joy and mirth. The morning gently perched itself
upon the rooftops of houses and dwellings that long ago verily deserved the
signification of home. But that was before the Gringo invaded the territory.
Yes, the sun did indeed rise only to shine upon the misery of the doleful
Chicano barrio. The velvet blues, the fiery oranges that kissed upon the
horizon went unnoticed, as they did each morning, by the denizens of this
village of scorn, of abject poverty—reader, if you could only see it! Surely you
would be overcome by sympathy and pity. Only the hardest heart of stone
could not but melt at such a piteous tableau.

The clarion call of the martial roosters, grateful to have survived yet
another evening of battle for the entertainment at the fighting cock pits,
arouses the inhabitants of the village, of the barrio. The people of the barrio
rise, dress, relieve themselves, breakfast meagerly, as has been their custom
since their ancestors, the Aztecs, discovered the right path to civilization and

grandeur. For these people, these noble sons of the desert, these lineal descendents of the majestic Aztecs—oh! lift up your spirits, dear reader—for these people, today will have the appearance of all other days, but truly such an appearance will be illusory. Yes, yes, the day will beckon yet more contemplation of misery, of deprivation, of oppression. The harsh, brutal, cruel life they have known since the coming of the Gringo despoiled this arid paradise, will present itself in the quotidian treadmill of sameness. Indeed, the single change these barrio dwellers ever experience is the variety in the cruelty of the Gringo, such cruelty as only the Gringo can yield with his fancy and his imagination in complete abnegation. Trust your spirits to soar at their most liberated will, follow sojourner along this voyage of narration, for, indeed, this miserable existence, if existence it be, is coming to an end. For these noble sons of the desert, destiny is attendant only upon the slowness of the pen.

Into their midst, at this very moment, in fact, there is coming a stranger, one of their own, one with the dark, mestizo features, one with the noble physiognomy of the sun. It is the return of one who had been their protector in earlier, gentler times, one whose family is well-remembered for wisdom, for grace, for kindness, and he, as the inheritor of these traits will surely not disappoint our expectation and will, in due course, reveal these very same eleemosynary characteristics.

There will come into their midst, a champion, a bronze knight of the sun, one who without a trace of reluctance will take up the mantle in the cause of justice, truth and liberation. How fortunate indeed are sometimes the accidents of history. How we must marvel at that fate, though it may cast those it ought to care for the most to the deepest depths of degradation. How wonderful I say it is to have fate return in the guise of our hero to make ample and just restitution for decades of profound neglect. For indeed, at this very moment, though the poor, abject, dwellers of the barrio will not know it for several hours, the true, gentle and stout-hearted knight of the desert: The Chicano Kid, is in their village. Misery, be on your guard!

The cause of this misery is none other than the nefarious Alf Brisket, arch-enemy of the Chicano Kid, despoiler of his sister, usurper of his patrimony, the scurrilous scourge of the Southwest. The days are already numbered for this vile, this evil, this vicious, viper of a man. He will no longer spoil the beauty of nature with his presence. Today, if our predictions are consistent, will be a sad day for the nefarious Alf Brisket. His cruel and vile deeds will be avenged, the sweet and dulcet tresses of Justice will again flow in the gentle breezes of this golden land. Her face will once again turn upward toward Helios and, not as has lately been the case, toward the deplorable depths of Hades. Persephone returns permanently to her mother of the earth.

But, let us pause momentarily in our discourse and simply submit to the dazzling and majestic entrance of the Chicano Kid into Santo Gringo. It is a sight so magnificent in splendor that we ought not for even a moment jeopardize our appreciation of it. The pertinent details of our narration must be held in abeyance. I take this liberty in the hope I have thus accrued to myself the confidence of the reader and he may rightly trust that once this impoverished description of the Chicano Kid is presented, our tale will resume in its proper trajectory.

Odysseus did never appear so majestic! Achilles never so valiant! Zeus himself was never so awesome. Oh, reader, if you could only see the jet black stallion prancing in the mid-morning sun, the musclar rippling of its shoulders, it is enough to send Michelangelo throughout the Carrara quarries in search of Nature's inert copy. The spry, energetic prance! This charger, this courser, so worthy indeed of the most valiant knight errant of the West!

And you, dear reader, are so much more fortunate than the characters who people this inspiring narrative, for it is truly a pity that the sultry mid-morning sun has driven so many of these doleful inhabitants inside. This sleepy hamlet of Santo Gringo will be deprived of this wonderous sight which, surely, were they to see it, how they would treasure it in their hearts forever. How they would spread news of it among themselves, how they would journey at great expense to limb and pocketbook to spread the news about the countryside. How the rustic bards and balladeers would tune their instruments, and with Nature as a guide, begin the spontaneous elaboration of his magnificent sight in song. It is, to be sure, the veritable stuff of legends. The Lone Ranger, the Cisco Kid, the Durango Kid, Roy Rogers, Gene Autry, Zorro, Matt Dillon, John Wayne—mere ruffians by comparison!

The wide-brimmed Charro hat, the national chapeau of the bronze people of the sun, swept upwards at the edges with the mighty force of a raging sea, made—nay, sculptured—from the finest felt, embroidered with the richest silver from the mines of Oaxaca, especially selected by management itself for its purity and lustre. And of the remainder of his attire? Attire is hardly the word! Dare I even speak of it? The poverty of language overwhelms this, your humble servant, when he tries to describe the manner of the Chicano Kid's dress. Were I Homer, Virgil, Dante, Shakespeare, Goethe and Rod McKuen all in one, I could not do justice. Were all the languages of the world whipped together to yield the butter of the human soul, it would not be enough. What care I for words! In the Panavision of my mind, I see so clearly. I can only say, gracing his limbs, a black outfit, of the finest wool, each strand gathered with utmost care from the most heavily guarded and virgin of English sheep. Virgin English maids before the loom, weaving as they utter silent novenas. This, too, is embroidered in silver, large brilliant buttons the size of Big Mac's. The boots of highly polished, impeccable calf-skin, the toe and tops inlaid again with metal the color of moonlight. Reader, I, with all honesty, cannot go on. It is futile to attempt to describe the clothing of the Chicano Kid. Were not the tale of such import, I would send me to a monastary. I beg of you, indulgent reader, to allow me the small luxury of composing myself that I may continue with the force and vigor our tale requires.

It is in front of the village saloon that the Chicano Kid glides to inertia. How like a powerful statue he sits upon his steed! It is with the grace and indolent celerity of a ballet dancer that he alights from the horse, the music of his jingling, tinkling, tinny spurs accompany the first encounter of the Chicano Kid's feet with the soiled earth of Santo Gringo. Though the spurs may jingle, though it be music for a thousand ears, though a symphony could be written to describe what the heart feels and the mind cannot say, the Chicano Kid does not hear music, there is no symphony in his life. There is only a heavy burden in his heart, a burden so heavy it would have driven a hundred lesser men to despair and the grave. This burden which the Chicano Kid feels so heavy on his person—need I say it, dear lector?—may only be lifted by the death of the vile, the evil, the vicious Alf Brisket—the very name fills my pen with contempt! Until that day dawns upon our hero, until we too accompany the soaring of the Chicano Kid's heart, there will be no music in the Chicano Kid's life. However, that day is almost upon us. The musician of the soul rehearses his funereal dirge for the last time. The faint strains of gaiety are discernible in the secret recesses of the soul for the optimist who can will his imagination to anticipate the just conclusion to our narrative.

The interior of the saloon is cool, still retaining the coolness of the previous evening; for it is dark inside, as dark as the deeds which transpire nightly within. Reader, how often have you heard of the rectitude of the Gringo? How often have you been assailed by the righteousness he labors so diligently to fabricate? How well do you know the base hypocrisy that dwells beyond the appearance so meticulously and deceptively presented to the world? However, inside these especially constructed locations, these saloons, these monuments to the baseness of which men are capable, it is here that the true and evil nature of the Gringo is allowed to roam freely. The true Nixonianism of the Gringo is released. It is here, in these public houses, that the Gringo may, without fear of retribution, escape from his hypocritical mask and give free rein to his latent, yet ever-ready debauchery and licentiousness. A Puritan by day, a Libertine by night! I perhaps have alarmed the reader, perhaps it is true that the reader at this point may be trembling with apprehension, for it is indeed an unfit place for our hero, the wonderful Chicano Kid, to enter.

But, fear not, dear reader, the purity and innocence of our hero has not been corrupted. He has not been soiled in the least, though he has entered many, many similar places in his quest for justice and liberty in the American West. Would that evil did not seek refuge in such places! However, the Chicano Kid must go forth to right the wrongs of this world wherever evildoers lurk. Temptation and sin have yet to sway this prized possession of his mother's womb away from the path of the true way and the way of truth. The saloon in Santo Gringo, though filthier than others into which he has entered to seek justice, will not tarnish our hero. Verily, he is made of sterner stuff.

A white man, a Gringo, sits behind the bar of the saloon, reclining on his elbows in a stance reminiscent of the decadent Trimalchio and redolent with the fetid odors following the spoilage of the Banquet. The man's face is fat and sweaty as if perspiration continually oozes from his pores. As the Chicano Kid nears he is able to see the pools of sweat and grease which well in the pores, with only an occasional oasis of a black mole sprouting thick, coarse black hairs. Genuinely porcine features! This man, this Gringo, this bartender, is an individual whose sweaty, oily, greasy, fingers stain the very glasses he is attempting to clean, but stained glasses, even stained windows, do not stand in the way of Gringo debauchery!

The dazzling, awesome, magnificent appearance of the Chicano Kid discomposes the rude, rustic, vulgar, fat man behind the bar. This cheap, unforgivable imitation of Trimalchio perceives, yes, he perceives, even through the film of ignorance and the drooping eyes of a dullard, that this is no ordinary mortal who deigns to grace the white man's pigsty. The Chicano Kid, standing near the bar without touching it, is indeed a pearl before swine.

The fat, oily, greasy man, a sorry excuse to represent any race also perceives the mestizo features of our hero—the almond eyes, the bronze skin, the black, straight hair—but, the fat tub of guts ignores the superior carriage of the Chicano Kid, the graceful, delicate, catlike movements. Lo, my dear readers, the Chicano Kid is in the presence of a racist. Yes, indeed, this fat tub of guts, ever mindful of his duty to racism and to the arbitrary duty to separate the sons of the desert from the sons of greed, feels compelled to make clear to the Chicano Kid that he is not welcomed in a place so low, so base. Little does this ersatz Trimalchio know that were it not for the crimes against man and nature which have their execution therein, the Chicano Kid would certainly be elsewhere.

Reader, let me propose a reasonable, though unlikely proposition. Suppose the Chicano Kid, in all his magnificent splendor, were to indicate his willingness to avail himself of your hospitality. Reason, good taste, and that common courtesy which is reserved among equals, dictates that you consider it an honor, an enriching experience, to be sure, something to treasure among your best and most pleasant memories. Ah, but such is the nature of the Gringo. Little good does it do to talk about it. Such is the baseness with which he regards others, particularly those to whom he has caused the most grief. Ah, but now, the oiled, highly polished, hand-made, silver-inlaid, calf-skin boot is on the other foot. The Chicano Kid is about to redress those grievances. However, as you have witnessed, the fat man behind the bar is fortunate to recognize the rising of the sun. He does not know he is in the presence of the bronze avenger of the West. This ill-chosen, misfit, spokesman for Gringo depravity, this lard-bucket behind the bar will question the dignity of our hero. So does he live in the darkness of ignorance that he does not see the light of truth and justice. It is indeed a sorry event which follows next, a dolorous turn in our story, but fidelity requires the telling of it. I would not be worthy of the reader's trust were I to ignore it. Furthermore, it is perhaps best to tell it since it is conceivable the dignity of the Chicano Kid's character will be revealed. It is but the prudent investment of the Chicano Kid's capital for the profit of the reader.

It is the Chicano Kid who speaks first. Those of his station do not wait to be addressed. Readily do they perceive the base station of those such as the bartender. We shall hear the modulation of his voice, the crispness of his vowels, the graceful turn of the phrases. Seldom has a hero either in history or fiction revealed such magnificence in so short a speech. And, for the reader's depository of information, our hero speaks in a tongue foreign to him. Yes, indeed, the Chicano Kid acquired the language of the Gringo late in life. It was not he who learned it at his mother's breast, yet it is he who speaks it so much better than even the most educated of the Gringo—inasmuch as education and Gringo may be a contradiction in terms, but the reader shall be the judge of that. So perfect is the inflection of the Chicano Kid's speech that were it not for the mestizo characteristics which inform his physiognomy, it would be impossible to distinguish him from the most articulate of Gringos, with the exception, of course, that no Gringo could devote the entirety of his being to truth and justice.

"Serve me a cup of coffee, please." Pause for a moment, reader, and consider the phrase just now uttered by the Chicano Kid. He does not ask, he does not say, "will you serve me a cup of coffee." The Chicano Kid fully expects to be served a cup—not an indefinite amount, such as some, but a cup—of coffee. The assurance, the self-confidence, the precision of the Chicano Kid's speech. The Chicano Kid knows exactly what he wants. In addressing the fat man, the Chicano Kid is gracious, affable, but also with just the proper degree of authority in his voice lest there result either of two outcomes: in the first instance, the individual whom he is addressing breaches the barrier of courtesy and becomes too familiar; in the second instance, the individual whom he is addressing becomes so awestruck and overcome with fear and trembling that he is unable to carry out the mission thus assigned to him. No, the Chicano Kid instinctively knows the precision of speech required for every situation. It is only when the individual he is addressing does not pay due attention to the manner of the Chicano Kid that his words are misinterpreted and calamity follows, usually to the detriment of he who misunderstood.

"We don't serve greasers in here, Meskin," expostulates the corpulent, oily, petroliferous bartender. However, anyone present would have detected the statement delivered not without some slight hesitation, a certain quaver, a tremor, resonating the vocal apparatus of the voice. Some individuals, to be sure, are born to the servant class, destined from the first breath breathed outside of the body that bears them to be subservient before those of yet a different class, those born to rule and hold dominion over lesser men. The bartender, repugnant though he may be, instinctively is reminded by those recesses of the brain about which our modern scientists can only speculate, that the Chicano Kid deserves the utmost self-abnegation from such as he, and yet, dear reader, and yet the vicissitudes of human behavior require on these occasions the expostulation of the well-rehearsed cant of racism. Nevertheless, the oily bartender is uncertain as to his own behavior toward the Chicano Kid.

One of the character traits which inhere in the bronze people of the sun is a certain graciousness, a certain politeness, a certain affability, a certain equanimity in the face of adversity and disdain. It is something that in other times was quite unnecessary, a time when mutual respect for human life and an orderliness in social intercourse ruled the day. Since the coming of the Gringo, the best order and the best exchanges in human relationships have given way to disrespect and sullenness, humans behave little better than those creatures undistinguished by rational faculties. The Chicano Kid, as the best specimen of his race, revealing the highest level of rational behavior to which a human may aspire, does not become angry, nor does he in any way demonstrate his displeasure. Such outbursts, such brief, though significant, moments of emotional discomposure, are not to be given vent in the presence of the lower order of human beings. No, not at all. The Chicano Kid remains even-tempered, affable, regarding the greasy bartender as only a pesky inconvenience, paying to him no more attention than one would an obstreperous fly, although it is readily admitted that a fly's *raison d'etre* is the irrtation of human beings and only fulfills that function for which it was placed on earth. The bartender should know better. The Chicano Kid replies with a smile.

"Fat man, I make a habit of not killing insects." After having uttered these words in such a way as to have his true intention remain ambiguous and yet investing the utterance with sufficient authority as to affirm his superiority over the base bartender, the Chicano Kid inspects his fingernails, as if at that moment it were imperative that he ascertain their cleanliness, as if by simply regarding the bartender it were possible for his fingernails to become soiled. The Chicano Kid continues in modulated, though not forced restraint. "Just serve the coffee and go about your business. I have nothing to do with you."

The assurance, the confidence, the aristocratic bearing reflected in the Chicano Kid's words, all combine in the cumulative effect of the bartender's tremor. By now, primordial instinct, prehistoric messages stored in the brain of this human lice, come to the fore. The bartender now knows he has seen the face of greatness, of that human superiority, that human hierarchy, which God ordained at the Creation lest His labor go unfulfilled, lest His best Design for man languish under the dominion of those whose faculties compete unfavorably with the best creatures of nature. Yes, the true, unmistakable, unavoidable message passed on by generations upon generations of servants leaves its indelible imprint upon the consciousness of the bartender. He cannot but experience, perhaps for the first time, the lowliness of his nature, the baseness of his being, the obviousness of his inferiority.

"Mr. Brisket aint' gonna like you being in here. He ain't gonna like you coming in here like a white man. He don't like any Meskin in here. He might just go on and fire me. I might lose my job, you understand, mister?" The adipose folds adhering to massive quantities of surplus human flesh tremble and shake the very foundations of the saloon. Beads of perspiration erupt through the layers of oil and grease which blanket the bartender's face.

"I understand, cowardly fat man, that you will serve me the coffee. I will not order you to serve me again and I also know you will hurry to do so." The Chicano Kid stands upright, perfectly perpendicular to the curvature of the earth. He does not observe the fat bartender; he knows the bartender dares not take his eyes away from the majestic bearing of his countenance. "This Brisket man may take away your employment, but I will shoot away your feet. Hurry on your feet, while you still have them. Get the coffee." The cold, icy, unflinching glare of the Chicano Kid finally meets the face of the fat bartend-er, piercing its way through several generations of his menial ancestors.

"Yes, sir!" So saying, the fat man serves the coffee, his hands atremble, spilling most of the brown, steaming liquid on the bar. The Chicano Kid, still not displaying any annoyance, still not revealing the least emotional discom-posure, signals gracefully for the nervous bartender to place the coffeepot on the bar. The greasy Gringo hands deposit the container on the wooden surface. The Chicano Kid finishes pouring the coffee, moving the cup and saucer to one side while the still nervous and trembling bartender wipes the bar with a soiled cloth. The coffee, as may well be expected, is not of the consistency to which the Chicano Kid is accustomed. In fact, a sampling—and this only with great daring—would reveal it to be hardly fit for human consumption. Of course, reader, we must remember that the patron of privilege in this establishment is none other than the Gringo himself, and he, not particularly discriminate in the finer things in life, considers this odious brew the best in the hamlet. You may well wonder the reason the Chicano Kid should endanger his person. Fatigue, dear reader, fatigue. He has been without the comforts of civilization for several days, on the trail, with no one but his trusty steed for companionship. This brew, this coffee, although our hero would have preferred better, will suit his needs until that day when his patrimony is restored and he again has those efficient and loving servants, members of his own race, who, though they be servants, do not relinquish human dignity and worth and who sincerely consider it an honor and a pleasure to be in the service of such a kind and humane employer. Yes, readers, the members of the Chicano Kid's race recognize as well the hierarchy of the human race, they know we may not all be within the ruling class and they gladly submit to their fate but with the understanding that though they be servants on earth, once within the Glory of He who created us, they will sit equally with the Chicano Kid and share equally in the fruits that accrue to us when we journey into eternity.

"You might cow that yella fat-belly, Meskin, but you ain't gonna back me down! When you turn around, go for your gun!"

The sound of the nervous, impetuous voice, came from the end of the

14

saloon, some dark corner which gives refuge to the darkness of men's souls. So frequently since the day he was dispossessed, since he became of age, has the Chicano Kid been at pains to answer such calls for no other reason than Death has some inscrutible, undecipherable manner of drawing those it will to its bosom. Each case, prior to this one, the Chicano Kid answered the call of the would-be challenger, each time participating in the challenger's appointment with the Grim Reaper. But, now, after so many years of sending so many Gringos to their final Satanic embrace, the Chicano Kid is weary of his ad hoc mission. The killing of Gringos no longer satisfied his taste for revenge. No longer did he perceive the face of Alf Brisket in every itinerant cowpoke he was forced to send to hell. The blood of so many who did need killing weighed heavily upon our hero. No, he would not perform the deed justly reserved for Death itself. If the owner of the sound at the back of his head was bent upon suicide, it would not be he, the Chicano Kid, that would become the agent. The Chicano Kid was saving himself for Alf Brisket.

"You don't want any trouble, son," said the Chicano Kid, weariness in his voice, fatigue upon his limbs.

"Ain't no greaser ever called me son, go for you gun."

Such is the impetuousness of callow youth. So fervently and unthinkingly do they court death. Little does the figure from the corner of the saloon realize the closeness of death's embrace. But, reader, pause a moment. Consider the nebulous figure now addressing the Chicano Kid. It is cowboy, of the Gringo persuasion, having barely said farewell to his teenage years, and now so willingly intent upon foreclosing his future. It is youth, indeed, dear reader. Recollect, if you will, your own youth, remember the heat and passion of youth in your own lives, how willingly you would have forsaken this life in the name of honor and valor. Such things as old age places into perspective, youth submits to instinctively. And there is justice in it, as well. For it is far better to die young in the flames of passion for some noble cause than it is to venture timidly into old age with the knowledge that valor beckoned and was denied. However, this is no noble cause which the cowboy aspires to defend, it is nothing but the sustenance and maintenance of racism, the furtherance of racial discrimination, the result of which has been the dispossession of the bronze people of the sun. While we may indeed admire the flame and the passion of youth as it springs in this young man, prudence requires that we acknowledge forthrightly the ignominy of his cause. We need not fear any danger for the Chicano Kid, the individual who most concerns us, for he has been in countless similar situations and has yet to emerge with but a scratch in his victory. We forewarn the reader that if the cowboy does not desist and withdaw his intemperate challenge, the hearth of old age shall not warm his body.

"I'll kill you if I have to, young man, but there is no need to. You are young, let it be. Withdraw now and go into an old age." The Chicano Kid still has not turned to face his challenger. Nor will he, unless the cowboy persists in his determination to die at such a young age.

"Don't give me no darned sermons, greaser! I aim to waste a bullet on you."

So weary is the Chicano Kid of killing the Gringo, that he must try one last time to keep from killing yet another one. It is true he has not turned around, knowing that were he to turn, the explosion of hot lead would resound throughout the dingy, dark saloon, knowing as well, that were he to turn, yet another Gringo would face his Maker perhaps without the sufficient coinage of good deeds on earth to open for him the gates of that Eternal Paradise. The Chicano Kid is about to utter his last words to the still living cowboy. Let us listen and not know the want of having failed to hear.

"I don't want to kill you."

"You ain't gonna kill me, you a Meskin. Meskins don't kill white folks, it's the other way around, ain't you heard? Well, if you ain't, I'm gonna make you learn the hard way. And if you don't turn around real soon, I'm gonna shoot you in the back. Yeah, that's right, I'll shoot you in the back. Backshootin' is more Mexican style" The Chicano Kid tenses, every nerve of his splendid person coils, taut in the expectation of imminent peril. Had he the time, the Chicano Kid would sigh in dismay, perhaps even pause to reflect on the utter inability of some individuals to recognize the futility of challenging someone such as himself. But, there is no time now. The moment is for action only.

Instinctively, as if he had eyes in the back of his head, the Chicano Kid wheels on one heel, pistol in hand. The thunderous explosion rattles the glasses on the bar and the folds of the bartender's fat. The bartender, needless to say, is awe-stricken at the swiftness and dexterity of our hero's draw. Certainly, the blink of an eye is slower than the celerity with which the Chicano Kid palms the handle of his revolver, aims without fixing his eye, and discharges the lethal projectile from within the exploding chamber.

As the haze of smoke begins to clear out of the saloon, moving on little cat feet through the doors, windows and cracks in the walls, the loud, dull, thump of the dirty cowboy making an unexpected encounter with the wooden floor is heard. The Chicano Kid blows the remaining smoke away from the barrel of his six-shooter and replaces it in its proper, leather and silver inlaid receptacle. During the brief encounter, the Chicano Kid had not placed his coffee cup upon the bar. The cup remained in his hand throughout. So sure of his movements, so steady of hand, arm and eye, was the Chicano Kid that the contents of the cup were not disturbed. Truly, dear reader, the entire exchange wherein one life was threatened and another dispatched to the greater beyond, indeed, during the entire exchange, there was not one untoward movement which would have caused even a ripple on the surface of steaming liquid.

There are still a few seconds of life in the dirty cowboy, a few precious seconds which another individual, mindful of his proximity to his Maker, would have put them to the use of reconciliation with the Supreme Creator,

16

but, no, such is not the case with this piteous, misguided tool of Gringo ignorance. He will not spend his last conscious moments as a resident of this earth making peace in preparation for what is to come. He will not see the error of his ways. He will journey to the dark beyond, where eternity awaits, cursing still the people to whose dispossession he has contributed.

Incredulous, the eyes in concert with his voice, utter: "Meskins ain't supposed to outdraw white folks! I can't believe I been killed by a Meskin!" With these, his last words, the dirty cowboy expires on the filthy floor of the saloon.

The Chicano Kid strolls, slowly, gracefully, to where the corpse of the dirty cowboy lies. The soft, light, feather steps hardly disturb the funereal silence of the saloon. A contrast indeed to the raucous din which characterizes the ambience of the establishment. This evening, perhaps, the noise will be a bit more subdued, certainly not out of respect for the slain cowboy, but in apprehension of the fate awaiting the vile, the vicious, the villainous Alf Brisket. There is some sadness in the eyes of the Chicano Kid. He speaks to the soul departed from the still warm individual now inert upon the floor. It is a lamentation perhaps in supplication to He who made us all that the judgment soon to be rendered be not severe. For, inasmuch as the Chicano Kid has been the agent who dispatched the young, impetuous, dirty cowboy, he harbors no personal ill will toward the deceased. He may justifiably refer us to his attempt to avert the lethal confrontation. Yes, dear reader, the Chicano Kid, wise beyond his years, judicious as Solomon, understands all too well that not all Gringos are bad, not all of them evil, that there is no causal basis in the genetic inheritance of the racist, oppressive attitude they display toward the bronze people of the sun. The Chicano Kid knows it is a habit acquired not long after the flush of innocence evanesces from the rose-cheeked spring of boyhood. They learn it from their fathers and pass it to their children. The cycle continues, unbroken except for a few cultural mavericks, those hardy individuals who insist upon judging their fellow human creatures by using a more humane measure, preferring instead to consider individuals as good or bad individually and not grouping them together indiscriminately. However, reader, and this is as certain as the sun rises to grace the land with its golden glow each morning, these vile customs are soon to be forfeited. It has been just a few short years since the Chicano Kid began his journey of justice, righting wrongs which through that particular quirk of human nature are sometimes perceived as right. The Chicano Kid has journeyed far and wide rooting out the evil lurking in the hearts of men. He has roamed the West in search of evil Gringos, always prayerful that they, the vicious oppressors, will have a change of heart, knowing that all too often he must dispatch the evildoers to another world wherein they will not have the benefit of artifice and fabrication, wherein they must stand before the Ultimate Tribunal and answer to the demands of Universal Law. Let us listen as the Chicano Kid speaks over the dirty cowboy's body.

"It is not entirely your fault, young and misinformed representative of your race. It is in the nature of youth to be brash and intemperate. Only years and experience mature and restrain the surgings of youth. But, alas, perhaps it is better this way. By killing you now, you will not live to mistreat my people anymore as I know you would have. I also know I would have had to kill you sooner or later. Rest well, young man, go to your Final Judgment, for you knew not what you did and I know not where you go."

What a magnificent benediction, so worthy of this hero of the West!

The Chicano Kid remains quiet, contemplative, over the body of the dirty cowboy. Perhaps he continues a silent prayer for the departed. So fair and just is this exemplary specimen of the bronze people of the sun that the shooting of another human being weighs heavily on his heart. He is not at all elated over the result of his agency, nor is he particularly conscious of having survived a momentary menace to his own life. As if waking from a dream, the Chicano Kid becomes conscious of the bartender, meekly trying to interrupt his solitude.

"Say," began the fat bartender with great temerity, "you all don't mind if I go tell the sheriff about this, do you? He's gotta find out about it and come after you."

"I don't mind at all. Of course. It is, after all, your duty. Just leave the coffeepot on the bar in case you do not have the courage to return and should I require more of this distasteful liquid."

"Well, listen, I ain't never seen shootin' like that, and I'll be sure to tell the sheriff about it. And, it'll probably take him an hour or more to get a posse together to come after you. So, I calculate you have time to drink a couple more cups of coffee. You could even get away, if you had a mind to."

"I have business in this town."

"All right. But, I just oughta tell you that ain't no Meskin ever killed a white man in this town before and the sheriff and Mr. Brisket ain't gonna like it. They ain't about to start lettin' Meskins kill white folks. It just ain't right."

"There is a time for everything. All things must change."

The fat bartender, not understanding the full import of the Chicano Kid's last statement, waddles out of the saloon in the direction of the sheriff's office. The weight of his enormous belly, hidden by an apron surely the size of a bedsheet, is a heavy burden on his knees.

Meanwhile, the Chicano Kid glides as if floating on air to a nearby table, casually draping his limbs over a chair facing the door. As is true of the pure heart, death is a difficult matter to contemplate. A bright flame of hope, visible only in the dim recesses of his heart, forestalls an inchoate depression which invariably overcomes someone who has taken the life of another. Indeed, the Chicano Kid is weary of killing gringos, tired of Death as a silent, ever-present partner. It is his wish now that he kill no more until his inevitable meeting with Alf Brisket. He must reserve all of his strength until that inevitable meeting, he must store all of the energy possible for that fateful

18

encounter, the terminus of his lonely journey in search of justice.

It seems only moments, but the quickness of his hearing perceives bootsteps on the wooden porch outside the saloon. He must not kill again, he must not loose the lethal lead from his revolver of justice. He must refresh himself, for the appointment he has sought for so long is almost upon him.

Four men enter the saloon. Two are armed with shotguns, two have their handguns drawn. The one in front, a vulture-like creature, has a tin star on his breast. The Chicano Kid sighs in dismay although it would have been difficult to notice it from his external appearance.

The men spread out in front of the Chicano Kid, in a semi-circle, aiming their weapons at him. The Chicano Kid does not seem concerned, he continues to sip his coffee as though he were still alone. A brave soul, indeed!

"All right, Meskin! We got you covered. Make one move and we'll blow you to hell!"

. . . to be continued.

Faustino

I

The truck clang-banged over the bumpy dusty road which half-circled the house. Faustino held on to the wheel, partly to steer, partly so he would not bounce out of the cab. He maneuvered the truck recklessly but expertly around the house, coming to a noisy, clattering, dust-filled stop beside the withered, unpainted tool shed.

His face was a blurred image through the film of dust and splattered bugs on the windshield. Faustino was smiling, almost laughing, exhilarated by the ride. His smile revealed a set of even, white teeth offset by the dark sunburned brown of his face. He raced the engine a few times feeling the cab sway back and forth. He hooped and hollered and yelled as though he had just declared his independence. The sound of the popping mufflers, like distant gunfire, made Faustino shudder with glee. He felt good.

He switched off the ignition, feeling his body continue to quiver and shake as the motor sputtered rebelliously and was finally stilled, emitting a vicious reptilian hiss from its bowels beneath the rusting hood.

Faustino did not step down from the truck immediately. He slouched a bit and reached inside the breast pocket of his denim jacket for the crumbled blue bag of Bugler cigarette tobacco. After smoothing the half-empty bag, he opened it, buried his thumb and forefinger in the contents, pinching enough of the stringy brown tobacco to roll a cigarette. He smoothed a crumpled cigarette paper, cupped it in his hand lengthwise to accept the tobacco. Satisfied that the paper was in proper position, Faustino began to cautiously sprinkle the pinch of brown strands, bending his head, his tongue draped over his lower lip, oblivious to all else, intent upon rolling a perfectly round smoke.

Faustino was very proud of the way he rolled his smokes. He manipulated the paper and the tobacco so that he spilled only a few errant strands, rolling it continuously, twisting it, squeezing it, smoothing the lumps; inspecting it all the while, until the degree of roundness and firmness was achieved.

The cigarette finished, he looked at it one last time before he gingerly licked the glue-coated flap of the paper. He wet his tongue-tip, slid it out of his mouth, touched it to a corner and smoothly ran it along the glue. That finished, he twirled it between his forefinger and thumb, proud of his workmanship. Satisfied, he twisted one end to contain any loose tobacco and stuck the other end between his dark maroon lips.

Faustino relaxed, leaned back on the cracked, imitation leather seat, allowing the cigarette to dangle from a corner of his mouth. He searched for a match, first in the jacket, then in his jeans, brushing some tobacco strands from his lap as he did so. He found a match, raised a thigh, touched the head of the match to the canvas material of the jeans, and slid it forward in a swift, violent motion. The match did not ignite the first time he did so. He repeated the arched motion several times until it caught fire.

The match-tip flared into a yellow flower, then subsided to a steady flame producing a sulphurous stench inside the cab of the truck. He touched the flame to the twisted end of the cigarette, inhaling deeply, drawing the smoke into his lungs with a long, laborious gesture.

The exhalation through his nostrils was abrupt, fierce, almost as if he expelled a noxious gas. Positioning the cigarette comfortably in the corner of his mouth, he was ready to step down from the truck. Through the dim haze of the windshield, Faustino could be seen with the smoke swirling around his head.

So intent had been Faustino on the ritual of rolling his cigarette that he had not looked to the backyard of Buster's house, in front of which he was parked. As he grabbed the door handle, he chanced to peer through the dusty windshield toward the ranch house. Mrs. Crane, Buster's wife, was in the backyard, hanging the contents of an aluminum washtub on the taut wires of the clothesline. Faustino had seen her before often enough, had noticed her, had been aware of her presence, but never without Buster at her side or within range of her. Now Faustino noticed her as something other than a faceless, shapeless, voiceless extension of her husband. Mrs. Crane appeared different to him now.

Faustino thought better of stepping down just yet. He released the door handle and settled back on the seat to enjoy his smoke. He continued to observe the woman under the clothesline facing away from him. Her actions were monotonous, single-minded, repetitive. Stooping to the tub, straightening to the line, shaking the article of clothing, pinning it to the wire. Then again and another, then again and another. As she stooped, on the downward motion, her long brown hair fell along the sides of her face, shielding the narrow profile she gave him. As she did so, the hair fell in a long, graceful swing, almost touching the rim of the tub. Then, suddenly, the hair would erupt, shudder out of its stillness, and became wild in the wind as her head jerked upward and Mrs. Crane stood erect. Once again, the hair glided softly around her neck and shoulders, smooth, flowing, finally becoming feathery still in the sun.

Faustino only briefly noticed the woman's hair. Of more interest was the outline of her buttocks under the thin housecoat she wore. When she bent over, the housecoat draped itself snugly over her back, ballooning in front. It expanded, flowed and flushed itself over and around the buttocks like a multicolored waterfall. The housecoat slid between the flesh of her buttocks as they parted, then the material was sucked in as she stood up, imprisoned, the swallowed part becoming a thin, jagged, puckered line. It would burst forth and become instantly smooth when she lifted her arms to the clothesline.

Faustino did not know her first name. Mrs. Crane was all the address required of him should he ever have occasion to talk to her. Although he did not know her first name, Faustino was not at a loss, thinking to himself, the sound of his words exploding in his head, *ay, mamacita, güerita, empínate más!*

Buster Crane and she had been married for a year. Rumor among the hands had it that she came from San Antonio, but Faustino would have no business asking about such a rumor. The affairs of his employer and of whites in general were not the concern of Faustino and the other Chicano ranch hands.

¡Qué nalgas, güera! Muévete un poquito más para ver mejor, que no se hace nada. ¡Mamá, mamá, me meo!

From the talk in the fields and the few times he had seen her, he calculated she was at least ten years younger than Buster. That Buster looked so much older than she would be enough to start rumors. Now, as Faustino noticed her, as if for the first time, she did look young to him, pretty in a gringa sort of way, but not too pretty.

He saw that she was already becoming stocky, heavy around the hips, with the thick thighs and bulging calves common to Anglo farm women of European peasant stock. Buster, on the other hand, was balding, his once-young ruddy face already losing its battles with age as if it was no longer a battle and age pranced about proudly over the lines and crevices and puffiness of the vanquished gringo face. Buster had a perfectly straight back, no buttock line. In front, his thin chest swelled at the bottom into a full flowing belly which spilled over his belt, cozily snuggling his accustomed large belt buckle in its folds.

¡Chingao! ¡Chingao! ¡Qué cura! ¡Qué puerta! ¡Si te empinas un poquito más, mamá, qué sonrisa me darás!

Faustino yelled inaudibly, feeling the tightness in his temples. He became agitated in his seat, squeezing his thighs together, curling his toes.

Because of the difference in their ages, Buster had to suffer a great deal of good-natured, but irascible, joshing on account of his wife. The ribbing came from those who knew him well and who felt confident of their equality with him. Casey, the ranch foreman, was largely the cause and instigator of this field sport at Buster's expense. Others present might join in but they would be just a little more restrained than Casey. Casey had a special relationship with Buster, allowing him privileges which no other ranch hand could enjoy. The ranch had been started by Buster's father and Casey. Since the old man's death, Casey felt himself to be a second father to Buster.

If the Anglo hands joked at all about Buster's marriage, they did not do it to his face. The Chicanos, who largely made up the work force on the ranch, never joked about it out of respect for the sanctity of the man's marriage. The whores and loose women to be found in the Gonzales bars were fit topics for ribald conversation, but not a man's wife. Besides, if Buster had been known to fire an Anglo hand for such an impudence, there was no telling what he would do to a Chicano for something similar.

Mrs. Crane turned from her laundry to notice Faustino sitting inside the truck. A faint smile crossed her lips, almost a smirk, which said nothing at all, which gave no indication that she knew he was there, had known he was there, watching her, had been watching her. She placed her hands on her hips, stretched her bones, pushing her breasts forward, before continuing her work.

When she stooped over the next time, she seemed to go slower and lower than necessary, allowing the housecoat to ride up higher over her hips. Faustino could not be sure, but it seemed she raised the housecoat with her elbows, briefly, fleetingly, mysteriously. This time, he saw more than before. There flashed before him a thin, white glimpse of her panties as a comet streaking across the expanse of pink universe.

Faustino had not had such a cura in the few moments he had been watching her. He could not have missed one as he had not blinked at all, his eyes wide, clear and intent. The possibility of a cura did not allow for blinking.

He could not be sure, could not be certain that she was not now performing for him, that she had made him an audience and she, conscious of being seen, knowing his eyes were draped over her body, prepared a slow, long, undulating movement. Faustino continued to watch, unable, unwilling, to leave the truck at that moment, frozen in his vision, unconcerned about the errand that brought him to the house.

Mrs. Crane, instead of rapidly bending down as before to pick up a garment for the line, anxious to finish the chore, now measured and calculated her movements, doubling at the waist, lingering over the tub, lifting first one garment, than another as if she required long, thoughtful deliberation on which article to hang on the wire.

Faustino's throat swelled. He tried to swallow, his mouth, throat, dry. He felt an uncomfortable, dry, rasping sensation as he swallowed. His jaw slackened to relieve the pressure on his teeth. He had no other conscious thought except the vision of the slightly over-weight woman in front of him.

Faustino's father had worked for Buster's father, and with the passage of the ranch to Buster, Faustino, who had been born on the place, grew up to work there, it being the only world he had ever known. Faustino, without thinking it, without so much as admitting it, felt an obligation to his father's memory, to the memory of Buster's father, who had been a good man, to continue to work on the ranch, for Buster. He had a strong sense of tradition in the best way of tradition which does not require the saying of it or the knowing of it, it being what is done and what has always been done.

Faustino had a sense, something as palpable as the callouses on his hands, that he belonged on the ranch, that he belonged to the ranch; that he must give of himself and of his labor to it; knowing all the while but never thinking that he did not own the land, that he would never own the land; that finally the land was neutral, that what happened upon it was something else; that his devotion to it was one-directional, that Buster used him, that Buster hired his sense of obligation, his sense of tradition, his sense of loyalty in the same way he hired his body to plow the fields, to care for the stock, to mend the fences, to do the hundreds of tasks that kept the ranch going, that made more work for the hands, that made Buster a profit.

Faustino lived with the exploitation without ever knowing it for what it was, accepting the wages he earned, accepting the fact that there was no further obligation on the part of his employer toward him. And Faustino knew that the money, the wages paid for work completed, the wages withheld on account of rain or because of the slack seasons of the year the money was never enough. He knew that the money only sparingly provided for his needs and the needs of his family. That the Chicanos were paid only when they worked and that the Anglo hands were paid weekly whether there was work or not, did not bother Faustino. He had accepted his position in the scheme of things, he recognized his situation. Except for the hardships which befell him and his family from time to time, he was content with his life, with the life he had been born to lead. He did not concern himself with the rest.

Faustino loved the ranch, he knew every inch of it. Since he had been old enough to be placed on the payroll, at the age of eight or nine, he had sprinkled his sweat over every square foot of the ranch. He was satisfied to work for the low pay and the long hours because it was his home, the only home he had ever known, and it was his wish that it be the only home he would ever know. All of this in spite of his not owning a single clod of earth over which he stepped, a single tree against which he peed or rested, a single drop of the water in the streams from which he drank.

Buster owned the land. To him it was property, the subject of a compact between him and other men that they not trespass upon it. To Buster the papers he kept locked away in the bank were proof of his ownership, they bestowed title to him and his heirs, should he have any. Beyond that, it was only a means to provide for himself and his wife.

Faustino had a special relationship with the land. He had risen from it, he had grown tall on it; and because the land belonged to Buster, because the land *was* Buster, Faustino felt an especial allegiance toward him. The two were interwoven, threaded through the black richness of the land, interdependent, and finally joining to become an indistinct shape, inseparable from one another.

Buster perceived the scheme of things differently. To Buster, the fact of

Faustino's birth on his ranch meant that he could expect more from Faustino, extra work for which he did not have to pay. When Buster spoke of Faustino, he spoke of him as his nigger, his Meskin, and there was a ring of authority in his voice, a self-satisfied sense of proprietorship, a pride and a satisfaction that comes from a bond so strong that one human being can claim ownership of another. And this bond is further cemented when the one owned cannot, will not, break the bondage, when he who is owned dare not, for reasons petrified in the bond, annul and rupture the perverse union.

Buster knew of, realized, his hold on Faustino, a hold connected long before either of them knew of it, and he used him, exploiting his skills and knowledge of farming and ranching; paying him half the salary he paid the lazy and incompetent Casey, and less than he paid Anglo high school kids who worked summers.

Casey, who attached himself to Buster parasitically, exploited the friendship with Buster's father, using Buster in the same way Buster used Faustino. And Casey, knowing he could not ranch, knowing he had neither the will nor the skill to hire working hands, remembering his two ranching starts ending in bankruptcy, clung to Buster, playing upon Buster's weakness in the memory of his father, retelling the anecdotes of the beginning, the friendship begun as roughnecks, the stakes they pooled, omitting the buying out the one of the other, the years together, the forging of a ranch, an identity, where once there had been only brush, mesquite trees and rattlesnakes. And just when Buster, in the throes of a grown man's tantrum made up his mind, decided once and for all, to fire Casey, to force Casey away just as he would any meddlesome hand, to rid himself of the spectre of his father who loomed still over the terrain in a constant disapproval of all that Buster did, Casey would interpose the spectre of the father between him and Buster, make flesh through his words what Buster most hated and what he most feared. Because the memory, the spectre of the father that stretched the length and breadth of the ranch, was larger and more powerful than Buster could contain or deny. It was as if Casey was indeed the father, spoke in the cadence of the father, brought the father's wishes from a tomb that Buster was too weak to seal once and for all. And Casey would stay, year after year, not relishing his power over Buster, never over-playing his hand, never taking more than he needed. Buster resented the hold Casey had over him, he hated knowing it, feeling it, giving in to it.

Faustino, at the urging of María, his wife, had approached Buster to ask about more wages for working Saturdays and Sundays. Faustino had gathered his strength, had summoned his courage, had brought himself to the full force of what he was, formulating the words over and over again even before they became speech, assuring himself, reassuring himself, the words finally clear and unmistakable and irretrievable. Buster had heard ingratitude and impertinence; had become indignant, furious, and had yelled, mentioned, questioned Faustino's presence as part of the ranch, the rent-free house, the work always available, the paycheck always on time, the loans secured by work undone. Faustino had taken the step backward, ashamed, angry; had recognized the tenuousness of things, had sensed but did not know the injustice of the refusal, had turned and left with an apology unsaid.

Home again, he faced the house he had to enter, he thought of the wife he had to face. Faustino, bitter at his failure, kicked in the door, the question in María's eyes hitting him between his eyes, and he, taking out his fears and frustrations and bitterness, blackened María's eyes. He resolved never to ask Buster about wages again. No matter what Buster chose to pay, the hope of more was not worth what he had gone through.

Buster did try to be nice to Faustino, did on occasion yield to a sense of distant responsibility toward him. Perhaps it was because he had grown up with Faustino, the two of them playing together as children. Buster would visit Faustino and María, early in the morning, the day following a holiday, to bring a left-over turkey dinner or a piece of baked ham, poured indiscriminately, disdainfully, into a brown paper sack in the same way that scraps are gathered and tossed to dogs baying at the kitchen porch. The meat would be coated with creamed corn, gravy, peas; sometimes, a half-eaten piece of bread would be tossed in. Faustino and María would thank Buster politely, agree with him that it was good food, that it always was good food; neither of them knew how to be rude, not to Buster, not to anyone; they did not know how to refuse; and they would wait until Buster's pick-up turned onto the main highway, see the top of the cab sink beneath the roll in the land, and then they would feed the scraps to their dogs without making comment to each other, not acknowledging what it was they did for fear of offending an unseen, unhearing master.

Mrs. Crane gradually, languidly, came up to her full height, bending backward a little, holding a blue work shirt in her hands. She shook the garment, spread it wide between her arms, examined it. She knew Faustino's eyes were on her as are a worshipper's eyes riveted upon the sacrificial victim before the altar. Raising herself on tiptoes, making the offering before an imaginary tabernacle, she pinned one shoulder of the shirt to the line, then the other. As she did so, the housecoat rose up, loose and billowing around her upper thighs. The wind made it flap suddenly and again Faustino caught a glimpse of her white underwear.

While he had been looking at Mrs. Crane, the cigarette in Faustino's mouth smoked itself, the ash-covered ember inching its way toward his lips. He had not felt its initial warmth and it was not until his upper lip was burned that he grabbed it quickly and tossed it out the window. Momentarily distracted, he opened the truck door, adjusted his trapped, erect, straining penis inside the tight Levi jeans before stepping down.

Once on the ground, with a determined effort, he forced himself not to look in the direction of the clothesline. Inside the truck he had been protected as if he really had not been there. Outside, he knew himself to be vulnerable to the distance he must keep between them. He could not stare at her as before.

26

In the open nothing would be between them and the brief pretense to which they both tacitly agreed was over.

Faustino walked directly to the tool shed a few steps away from the truck. The door was held in place by a length of manila twine. He tried to untie the two knots, having an unexpected difficulty as his fingers trembled and could not maintain their grip on the twine. Finally and feverishly he unsecured the door and entered the shed to look for the wrench Buster and Casey wanted.

It was musty inside the shed, with its odors of old leather, dust, grease and rusting metal bluntly and heavily snaking their way into his nostrils. He felt hot and sweaty. The shaft of light coming in through the door, along with slivers of light coming in through the cracks in the walls, helped his eyes adjust to the hazy gray inside. He pulled on the string attached to the light switch overhead. The impotent clicking signaled the bulb was burnt out. He found a block of wood and used it to wedge the door open in case the wind started up and shut it. He began his search for the wrench.

As he searched, Faustino thought of Mrs. Crane outside, a few yards away from the shed, hanging her wash. He wondered whether she continued in the same way now that she knew he was in the shed. He could still spy on her through the cracks in the wall. His erection was subsiding, he felt a drop of liquid moist against his thigh. He pressed the palm of his hand against his pelvic bone, squeezing the bulge of his crotch, numbing the residual erection.

His thoughts were centered on her wide, mottled pink buttocks and the white flash of her panties. She must have known I was watching, he thought, *curándome*. And didn't I see more of her, more of her ass *after* she saw me there? Didn't she change her position and didn't she perform for me?

There was a resurgence inside his trousers. the bulge grew larger, stiffer, more aching. There was nothing he could do to ease himself. To relieve the strain, he repositioned the tumescent organ, but that did little for the deeper, more insistent ache within. He made a sweeping motion in front of his face as if to wipe away his thoughts and he began to look for the wrench with renewed and frenzied interest.

He soon found the wrench, stuck it in his back pocket, and came out of the shed to a cool breeze that had started while he was inside the stifling shed. The sweat on his face, glistening blisters of moisture, was cooled by the gentle rushing of the wind and he felt better. The tension in his upper chest relaxed, the dryness in his throat eased as his body cooled. The flesh of his penis lost its tautness, becoming tangled in his loose underwear. He was about to smooth his clothing when he heard his name called.

"Faustino!" Mrs. Crane yelled in the thick, nasal twang of South Texas that he was accustomed to hearing from Anglos and which, had she not used it, would have seemed strange to him.

"Yes, m'em," Faustino said in a low, husky voice, unsure whether she heard him, but certain that having stopped his movement, having turned in her direction, she would know he had heard her. He stood with his hand frozen on the door handle of the truck, looking in her direction, his eyes not raised high enough to meet hers. Had he looked up, higher than is permissible, had he the temerity to face her squarely—something which Chicanos did not often do to Anglos—he would have seen her standing under a row of her underwear, a fluttering rainbow of colors and shapes, each with a pan-handled, wrinkled crotch. It was an erotic cross-bar under which Mrs. Crane purposely stood.

Faustino's eyes were fixed on the region of her knees. He was uncomfort-able at being called but he could not keep his gaze from devouring her deep, splotchy skin, the outline of her fleshy thighs under the material of the housecoat, the recessed, sunken, almost bashful V at the juncture of her legs as the wind pressed the housecoat against her; and he took in the steep, rising mound directly above the V, which impertinently curved upward, then slightly downward, finally disappearing into the folds of a beginning paunch.

Mrs. Crane relaxed one leg, bending it slightly foward, bringing her thighs tightly together as she did so in a slow, fluid movement unmistakably for Faustino, brazenly inviting him to look at her, appealing to his eyes as she repeated the movement several times before she spoke again.

"Faustino, com'ere a minute," she said at last, letting her tongue slip slowly out of her mouth, snaking it upward in the direction of her nose, wiping her upper lip with it. Her thigh continued to move forward and backward, her hips moving to and fro.

"The boss, m'em, he want this wrench," said Faustino, nervous, embarrassed, overcome by a sexual confusion he had never before experi-enced. In his world, it was man the aggressor and women, certain kinds of women, submitted. This was different for him. He told her again that Buster wanted the wrench, taking it from his hip pocket to show her as if to demonstrate the truth of his words.

Faustino sensed a situation he would not be able to control. Immediately, he felt a chill scurry throughout his skin like a lizard scurrying into a gopher hole. There was a danger in remaining, if only because he could not be sure what it was she had in mind. He did not control very many of the events of his life, that he knew, but he could sense trouble and he could control whether or not to participate in it. He was not in complete ignorance of Mrs. Crane's gestures, they being the source of his confusion. He knew that white women did not entice Chicanos, of that he was sure.

He pointed the wrench at Mrs. Crane, shaking it a little to be sure it caught her attention, wishing desperately that the wrench could speak and confirm the truth he spoke, that if she did not believe him, she would believe the inanimate object. Faustino lifted the wrench in the air as if offering it to her.

"I don't care about no wrench, Faustino. I said come here. I got somethin' for you to do." Saying that, she turned without waiting for a response, walking rapidly toward the house. She walked awkwardly trying to keep her houseslippers on her feet, losing her balance once when she stepped on a stone hidden by a tuft of grass.

A thought crossed Faustino's bewildered mind. Of course, he said to himself. She knows I was watching her, *curándome*, and this is her way of punishing me. She wants me to look at her while she looks at me. Like the time my mother caught me taking a piece of pan dulce and made me eat and eat and eat until I got sick, to teach me a lesson. But, he could not be sure that this was what Mrs. Crane had in mind. It was all very strange to him.

Faustino watched Mrs. Crane walk away from him. He started to follow her as she had ordered. When she reached the porch, she turned to the side to open the screen door. Just then, a gust of wind blew into her housecoat filling it out like the sails of a schooner. The two buttons holding it together could not withstand the force of the wind. The bind slipped as the wind died down, the cotton material gently coming to rest along the sides of her body. Mrs. Crane held on to the door not bothering to fasten the coat, not bothering to conceal her body.

Faustino trembled as he caught the glimpse of her naked, pendulous, bobbing breasts. She stood on the porchsteps looking at him. He took a longer, more leisurely look at her nakedness, down to her waist and below, the pink whiteness of her skin interrupted only by the tight white bikini panties she wore which seemed to be stretched to the point of tearing and which so compressed her flesh that the side panels produced an indentation in the flowing outline of her body.

"M'em," Faustino said, trying to recall her words from what seemed an eternity before, trying to make them echo inside his confused, struggling brain. It was the vision of the siren in front of him, its song echoing, bouncing off the flesh of her body, beckoning him to come closer, to obey. Faustino, like the mariners off Amphitrite, was powerless, beguiled, unable to turn away.

Faustino walked forward a little along a narrow path where grass would not grow. He stepped off the path to one side in the direction of the clothesline, his boots crushing some brown weeds and withered grass, victims of the late summer suns. He felt the hardpacked ground beneath his feet refusing to give and cushion his footfalls. He stood with the wrench in his hand, reluctant to go any further.

Mrs. Crane took one flap of the housecoat and covered her left breast, the other still exposed, its nipple beginning to swell. She turned and went inside the screened porch. Faustino did not, could not, avert his gaze until she was completely swallowed by the cavernous blackness of the house. He was afraid, confused by a dangerous desire, but he knew to obey.

The wind picked up again and opened the unlatched screen door. The gust twisted and swirled, slamming the door shut. The sound of it reverberated through Faustino's body as though a thousand bits of shrapnel were stinging him with hot pinpricks, forcing him from the trance he was in. He gripped the handle of the wrench, momentarily grateful for the hard reality of it. Faustino replaced the wrench in his hip pocket and continued to walk toward the house.

In a brief flash, he looked up in the direction of the clothesline and saw the blue, black, red, green, pink and yellow panties; some small, dainty, bikini-shaped, mere wrinkled wisps; others large, flowing, nylon parachutes with leg openings warped by the distended elastic. Some had large, wide puckered crotches, others flat and proud, smooth and pristine, and still others with crotches so thin they could not contain side-tufts of pubic hair. A few had shrivelled, wrinkled, dark brown crotches from menstrual overflows, worn monthly and then hidden as if they were a reminder of something unspeakable.

These, the monthly underpants, speaking of unproductive birth cycles, seemed in particular to stare at Faustino. They presented an image of defiance, unashamed and wanton. They were pinned side by side in another row, apart from the others. The crotches were aligned as though they were giving him a leering, obscene, brown smile, as if they were in possession of secrets they would not tell and which he would never know. Faustino walked slowly, deliberately, his gaze still on the line.

The panties waved in the wind, palpitating now rapidly, swaying, now gently fluttering like the guidon of some chivalrous regiment enticing its members to exotic adventures in far away never before heard of places. Faustino tried to recall if any of them resembled the underclothing that María wore, but he could not conjure up an image of his wife in underwear.

Faustino finally reached the edge of the porch steps. His head ached, his erection dissipated as his fear of the situation increased, looming as dark as the house he had been ordered to enter. His penis wilted against the cold but soothing emollient of thwarted secretions. He stood on the porch, the screen door at his face, reluctant to go any further.

Presently, she opened the wooden door and said, irritably, "Will you come in here!"

"I don't know, m'em," Faustino said, his reluctance tossed between them onto the wooden floor of the porch worn smooth by dust, wind and rain. He was grateful he was wearng his newer, darker jeans. The dark splotch of wetness to the left of his crotch did not show.

"Well, you have to come in the house, Faustino. There is something in here I want you to move for me because it's just too heavy for me to lift. I can't bring it to the door for you, you have to come in and get it."

"Yes, m'em," Faustino said, not moving, still reluctant to enter the house.

Faustino knew instinctively that it would not be possible for him to simply leave, to avoid entering the house, to hurry to Buster with the wrench. He could not trust Mrs. Crane. If he refused and she became angry, there was no telling what she would say to Buster, what story she would tell, what horror she might invent. Faustino wished to return to the safety of the fields, to his skill at work, where a man was judged according to what he produced.

He took a few steps forward and sideways, shuffling, trying to go toward the door and away from it at the same time. Mrs. Crane held it open for him; it was an invitation and a command. She released the door and disappeared inside. Abruptly, he swung it open all the way, walking past her into the kitchen.

Faustino could smell her perfume forcing its way into his nostrils, invading his sense of smell. As he stood in the middle of the kitchen, with Mrs. Crane further away from him, the perfume became entangled with the heavy cooking odors which clung just above his head as an invisible cloud.

Had he touched her at the door? he wondered. It felt as though he had, but he insisted lamely to himself that it could not be true, that the stinging sensation on his elbow was imagined, that it was caused by the confusion of the situation. Faustino was aware that he was very much alone in the spacious kitchen, that something cold and forbidding was nudging against him like the wet nose of his mare pushing at his bare back.

Mrs. Crane leaned against the wall, her hand on the doorknob. She held it, swinging it to and fro; played with it, letting it swing as if to slam shut only to break the contact; drawing it to her again, teasing it. She did not speak, she did not seem to be in any hurry. She shifted her gaze between Faustino and the broad expanse of South Texas outside.

Faustino waited for Mrs. Crane to show him what she wanted him to do. His mouth was open, his lower jaw loose as if he were unable to control it. There was a question on his forehead. There was worry there too.

Time seemed to freeze at a moment lost to him, even though he had been in the kitchen only a few seconds. The ongoing processes and rhythms to which he was accustomed suddenly stopped. He stood outside of the cycle of his life, marking some other time, not his own, strange and new to him. The anticipation he felt, the anxiety that made his flesh crawl, all of it was not in time; in drawing its being, its movement, from some other extra-temporal dimension where he the subject was not the knower of the world, rather, he was something to be known, but not yet understood.

Faustino felt a panic compressing the muscles of his chest, crushing his ribs, drawing his belly tight. He felt the tips of his fingers tremble, he felt an itch crawl inside his arms and legs. This he felt whenever he sensed a rattlesnake nearby, long before he saw it. The question on his forehead remained and he waited.

Gradually, the weight of the panic eased. A peaceful and cleansing flush spread throughout his body, opening his pores, his tension evaporating like the film of sweat coating his skin. Faustino began to feel some control of the situation. He started to relax. His eyes started to survey the kitchen, careful to avoid looking directly into Mrs. Crane's eyes. She was still by the door, biting her lower lip, not moving except for the hand swinging and stopping the door. Her face was only partially visible to him on the periphery of his vision. She stared at an object outside, something she could not distinguish and which caused her to squint.

Looking around the kitchen, Faustino realized it was the first time he had been inside the house. For all the years and in all the years he had worked on the place, Buster had never invited him inside. He usually came by on Fridays to pick up his paycheck when Buster did not distribute checks in the fields. It was understood that Faustino and all of the Chicano hands would stand at the foot of the porch steps while Buster remained inside reviewing the days worked in the ledger he kept before determining the amount due in wages. It was not a matter of concern to Buster that the Chicanos stood outside waiting for him in all weathers. When it was cold or it rained, Buster would invite the Anglo hands to come into the kitchen while leaving the cold and wet Chicanos to stand and wait or to scurry to their cars and trucks for shelter.

Faustino could remember standing outside at dusk in a cold rain, the wind cutting through his wool coat. He would be looking through a partially steamed kitchen window, seeing the Anglo hands inside drinking coffee, surrounding Buster, laughing with him, leaning over him, making all manner of obsequious gestures. Faustino did not feel what Buster did as a personal insult or that Buster diminished him in any way. All he remembered, all he could say happened, was his standing in the cold, listening to the tattoo of raindrops on his hat, peering through the blurred window into the warm yellow glow inside.

Faustino did not wish to be a part of the group of white-skinned men inside, he merely wished to be out of the rain and in the warmth. When he thought of quitting Buster, the few times he had thought of gathering his family together and moving on to another place, it was this moment that returned, cold and wet, clear and painful, filling him with a rage that, once subsided, made him gentle and loving toward his wife and children; and finally, when the pull of the land made contemplation of the matter useless, he was more respectful to Buster, atoning for having sinned.

There was a gringo odor about the house, an odor of stale, unimaginative cooking, odd and repulsive to Faustino. In his house, with few utensils and less money, there would be the smells of meals past which clung to the walls, giving the entire house a fragance of garlic, comino, chile, oregano; from outside, the impertinent smell of the chile pitín plants wafted in fresh and saucy. It was a reminder of meals enjoyed, lingered over, mixed with conversation, laughter and sometimes sorrow.

In Buster's house, the kitchen smelled heavily of air fresheners, detergents and other antiseptic fluids which were sprayed, poured and spread into and on every surface, every crevice, every utensil; their purpose to destroy any and every reminder that this was a house in which people lived, to erase the slightest suggestion of living. The stale odors would not be vanquished. The air fresheners tried in vain to route them, but they remained and combined themselves with the heavy, nauseous scent of Mrs. Crane's cheap perfume. All

32

of the indistinct but oppressive smells created a leaden atmosphere inside the kitchen which made Faustino at first gasp for air, his lungs constricting. It smelled of vomit.

Mrs. Crane walked past Faustino, suddenly roused from her trance. Slowly, lethargically, she began what seemed a long journey from the door to the sink. As she passed Faustino, she purposely brushed his chest with her shoulder.

She stopped in front of the sink, raised a forefinger to her lip. With her back to him, she bent over to inspect a grease can full of water as if by doing so she justified asking him in. Still bent over, she twisted her body, raised her head to face him. The housecoat came open, the mischievous button again slipping through the careless buttonhole. She brushed it back, pinning it to her hip with her closed fist, exposing her breasts. Her nipples were erect and thick, blood pink, set in a wrinkled circle of discolored skin about the size of tarnished silver dollars.

"Come here," she said, and all Faustino could hear was the sound of her voice in the room exploding around his head, coming from no certain direction. The buzzing in his ears prevented him from understanding her words; later remembering, vaguely, something about a leak in the pipes and something about a can used to catch the spill, and something about Buster emptying it each morning, and something about Buster having forgotten to do it. Faustino's attention was concentrated narrowly and exclusively on her gaping breasts, large, dangling, moving with each word she uttered, quivering like jelly as she struggled with her balance.

Mrs. Crane moved around to grip the handles on the can. Finding that the housecoat was in the way, she hiked it over her hips, bunching it in front.

"Come on," she said, "help me move this."

Faustino did not hear and did not move. Mrs. Crane pulled on the can, her breasts bobbing wildly as she did so. It was too heavy for her, but Faustino stayed where he was. His eyes were riveted on the broadness of her buttocks, his vision pinpointed on the double-crotch corona of the panties, noticing the bruised wet welts made by the elastic bands of the leg openings.

Small, curly, kinky tufts of dark brown pubic hair escaped the double layer of synthetic material. Underneath the panty-crotch, pressured by it, snuggled against it, mashed by it, her vagina reposed, surrounded by the canyon walls of her thighs.

"I want you to take this," her lips parting suggestively into a smile, "out," she said in conclusion.

She let go of the can and stood up, wiping her forehead with the back of her hand. The housecoat fell along the sides of her body, she pinning it against her hips with her fists.

Faustino walked over to the can. She had not moved away from it and as he stooped to grab both handles, his elbow, covered by the demin jacket, pressed against her breast. This time he was sure. She inched forward toward him, pressing his naked hand with her knee. She placed her hands on his broad back and began rubbing in wide circles.

He lifted the can off the floor and moved it away from under the sink drawing two steps backward. He set it on the floor again, secured his balance to get a better grip on the handles. Mrs. Crane came to stand in front of him, with the can between them. The juncture of her legs was directly in front of his head. She thrust her hips forward, the V of her panties inches away from his face. He could smell the concentration of feminine odors emanating from the region, a mixture of crystal secretions, urine, soap, deodorants and stale perfume. The underpants were much too small for her and Faustino could see pubic hairs overflowing the top ridge of the material. Through the webby lattice of fake lace, shoots of hair poked like porcupine quills.

Before he could right himself, he felt Mrs. Crane's hands move across his shoulders, caressing the base of his neck, lingering there, squeezing roughly, massaging maniacally. She had leaned over to do so, her pendulous breasts swaying easily, brushing his temples and cheeks. From a corner of his eye he could see the erect, purple, distended nipples. He felt a tremor go through his fingertips as she moved her hand up and down his neck swiftly, uncontrollably, urgently.

Mrs. Crane removed one hand, leaving the other like a hot comal searing his flesh. The free hand pressed against her breast, first one then the other, kneading them, mashing them against his head, pinching, tweaking the nipples. She moved forward, straddling the water can, rhythmically pumping her hips toward his face. Her smell was stronger. All he had to do was move his head upward and his nose would be buried in her crotch.

Faustino, still bent over, backed away as if crawling out of a low, narrow cave. He straightened slowly, shakily, maintaining his balance with difficulty. There was a tremor in the back of his knees. Desperately, he tried not to touch her, drew in his hard stomach to avoid contact with her body. She had matched him step for step and stood close to him.

She now placed both hands on his shoulders in imitation of beginning a slow dance. When Faustino did not move, standing there frozen, she slid her hands down his shoulders, along his hard muscular arms. When her hands reached his wrists, she tried to encircle them with thumb and forefinger, making rapid upward and downward motions. Then her fingers glided over the back of his hands, her fingers slipping between his fingers, making the same in-out urgent movements.

She drew him closer to her, the length of her body touching him. She moved her arms around his waist, pressing first her breasts against his chest and then her pelvis against his crotch. She released her grip on his waist only long enough to move the housecoat aside, pressing her naked flesh against the rough material of his denims. She now slipped her face against his shoulder and began to rotate her hips, pushing, mashing, bumping, her pelvic bone hard against the erection that swelled inside his jeans.

34

Mrs. Crane brought her hands around to Faustino's chest, brushed the jacket aside, hurriedly, nervously, pulling on the snap button on his blue checked shirt. She pushed him back, spreading her fingers, running them over the hairs on his chest. She inclined her head and began to kiss him, starting with his lower neck, her lips traveling an erratic, jagged trail over his chest pulling on the black curly hairs with her wet lips, gathering them in sparse tufts; her tongue darting out to pierce his brown skin, penetrating through to his muscles and bone; he could feel the tongue sliding over his entrails, teasing his maleness. Eagerly, hungrily, she tugged and bit his nipples, moistening them, flattening them with the flat part of her tongue. A low, hoarse moan started deep in her chest, rising up into a whimper, vibrating her lips, tingling the loose skin around his nipples.

Faustino was thoroughly aroused, wanting her but not wanting her, his tumescent maleness stretched beyond the point of prudence and fear, the confusion he felt becoming a counterpoint to the desire for the lubricious female enveloping of his member. He had allowed her to go far enough. The demands of his penis had not risen to the point where he would become the aggressor. He was perilously close but he still could not be sure it was what she wanted. He feared this might be part of an elaborate tease, that if he made a first move to join in what it seemed she wanted, she would laugh, push him away, throw him out the door. He stepped away from her.

He spoke in a pained voice full of phlegm. "I better go, m'em. I can take the can," he said, pointing behind her.

"Faustino," she started, her voice deep, husky, urgent. "Don't go. Not just yet." Her face was vulnerable, now as unsure as he was. "All those things people say about Buster are true. I know you've heard them. Everybody knows about it. He ain't a husband to me." There was a suggestion of a tear in her high-pitched voice as she lowered her head.

"I never heard nothing, me'em. I don't know nothing."

"Faustino, I'm telling you he ain't no good to me!" she said, almost snarling a threatening edge to her voice, insistent, unwilling to stop what she had started, her upper lip curling slightly.

"I need a man," she continued. "Right now! It's been so long. Faustino, please. I don't want to have to beg. I could be good to you, very good to you, Faustino. And this don't have to be the first and last time, you know. You could come visit me. I know you can do it. Nobody would have to know. Not Buster, not your wife, not nobody. I could fix it so Buster could pay you more money, or, I could give you some of my money. I have my own money. Faustino, listen to me, please."

With that, she stepped forward and grabbed his engorged penis through his tight jeans, the tautly stretched material preventing her from wrapping her sweating, trembling fingers around it.

"Jesus Christ, Faustino!" she yelled, leaning against him. "I want this! I want you to fuck me, Faustino."

35

Faustino pushed her away again. He felt her fingernails trying to scratch his penis.

"I got to get back to work, m'em," he said. "Mr. Buster, he wants this wrench real bad." He showed her the wrench once more.

"Oh, the hell with that god-damned wrench," Mrs. Crane said, yanking it out of his hand. She grabbed his penis with the other hand. She tossed the wrench toward the door where it fell with a dull clunk and at the same time she squeezed the erect throbbing organ in his jeans. The metal instrument slid on the floor and rested mute.

"I want this wrench," she said. She flattened her hand and pressed the palm of it in a circular motion over his penis.

"Maybe all you need is some encouragement. I saw you looking at me outside and in here. I know you want it, Faustino. I'll make you want it."

Mrs. Crane slid down to kneel in front of Faustino, keeping her hands behind his back, sliding them along his buttocks as she went down, resting them in back of his upper thighs, drawing his crotch to her face. She pressed her cheek against the bulge of his crotch. She shoved her chin between his legs, opened her mouth wide and tried to swallow cock, balls and bluejean. She pushed upward, mashing her nose against the base of his penis, her cheekbone against his pelvic bone.

She slid her tongue inside the flap of his fly, running it upward along the jagged copper teeth of the zipper. She took the zipper tab in her teeth and pulled down, bringing her fingers up to help.

Her mouth insinuated itself inside the trousers, moving along the underclothed shaft, her hands now in front of his waist, undoing the belt, tearing the waistband apart, pulling it down, her lips and teeth searching for the glans penis.

She took a mouthful of underwear and penis. She let go, leaving a wet round spot on his shorts. "I can't swallow all of it, Faustino," she cooed. "It's so big. You're so big, Faustino," she said in a little girl voice.

Mrs. Crane slipped a hand inside his shorts, cupping his testicles, gently scratching the tender patch of skin behind them. The sensation startled his throbbing penis and made it jerk. She then brought her hand around his balls and under the aching shaft, drawing it out. The penis, finally free of the cloth constraints, surged outward and upward, secreting a small drop of fluid which welled on either side of the seam of his foreskin. Mrs. Crane stretched the loose skin back, bending the stiff shaft, hurting Faustino.

"Stay here, Faustino," she said. "You can tell Buster you couldn't find the wrench. You can tell him it took you a long time to find it. Stay here, Faustino. He'll never miss you. I need you."

The tip of her tongue touched the moist tip of his penis, drawing an ever-increasing wet circle around the aperture. As the circle became larger, her lips touched it, lingering longer each time; she sucked on it more and more each time.

36

Faustino was unable to move; did not want to move; and he would have stayed standing still until she finished. However, she stopped abruptly, gave his penis a pat and stood up to face him.

"See what I mean, Faustino?" said Mrs. Crane, smiling, as if saying, I told you so. "Follow me."

Instead, Faustino backed away from her. He noticed the wrench on the floor and walked toward it, intending to pick it up. She followed him. Near the door, where the wrench lay, Faustino tucked his penis in, zipped up his trousers and fastened his belt.

Mrs. Crane came to an absent-minded stop. She was confident of her victory. Faustino, she thought, had a lapse of nerve. She tossed the collar of the housecoat back, over her shoulders, shrugging it loose, letting it slide down her back; it slid smoothly down the curves of her arms, noiselessly around the ample hips and thighs, until it at last came to rest in a soft billowing pile around her ankles.

Faustino had some difficulty breathing as he was assaulted by the fullness of her breasts, as he saw them in the door light; now not so mysterious, devoid of shadows, nothing hidden. Their udder-like massiveness flattened them against her torso. Mrs. Crane's were the biggest breasts Faustino had ever seen, much bigger than María's, bigger than the pictures in the girlie magazines Casey kept in his shack. He took another step toward the door and she stepped back toward the bedroom.

As the distance between them increased, the desire he felt earlier, the blind demand of his erection, his confusion, all of it became less intense. He realized that her breasts were entirely too large, too bovine, too evocative of nourishment than of pleasure. Her waist was narrow but the curve ballooned out to her hips. Mrs. Crane, standing in front of him naked except for her panties, was oddly shaped, disproportionate, outside of what he knew of the female body.

The suggestive glimpses he had caught of her, pieces of body, partially obscured, hidden and highlighted by shadow, had caused his arousal, had produced for him an unwanted erection. It had been the erotic thought of possibility, something created altogether in his mind, the fear and terror and confusion being as much a part of it as the physiology of it.

Looking at the nakedness of Mrs. Crane, Faustino felt as if he were looking at another woman. In the fullness of the light, he confronted the unadorned flesh of a woman who was not attractive in the least. Faustino became calm. He felt like smiling, laughing; he had now regained full control of his mind, his body, his penis, his situation. The danger which had hovered over him like a vulture was gone, there was no longer a threat, and he could now avoid trouble. She was repulsive to him.

Mrs. Crane was not aware of Faustino's thoughts; she noticed the change in him, the smoothing out of the brown face, the relaxation of his fuzzy moustache; she thought he was ready for her, having overcome his reluctance.

"Faustino," she said, "follow me." She kicked the housecoat away and turned, walking the full length of the kitchen to a small corridor leading to the bedroom. He watched her with an odd curiosity, feeling his stomach turn queasy. Her tumultuous hips quivered like flan, sending shimmers through the flesh and fat, up and down and around the clearly massive buttocks. Her tight bikinis slid over one buttock and disappeared in the crack between them. He was embarrassed and sorry for her. In another time, before her body started to sag in resignation, he might have gone through with it, he might have been unable to contain an orgasm.

She walked into the dim corridor. At its end, the bedroom door was open and the windows poured bright blinding sunlight into the room. She stopped in the frame of the bedroom door. Faustino could see her, his view only slightly blocked by the refrigerator. Mrs. Crane peered seductively over her shoulder at him and began the labored negotiation of the panties down her ample buttocks, a movement which she had to interrupt over and over again as the waistband rolled and became trapped in the flabby flesh. Faustino was morbidly fascinated. He could leave at any moment but he was fixed in place.

When she had pulled, twisted, rolled, churned, wiggled and teased the panties midway down her thighs, Mrs. Crane stopped. She took a sidestep with one leg, stretching the material of the bikinis which became a white rope digging deeply into her thighs. She then bent over so that her upside down face was framed by thighs, bikinis and the hairy V of her crotch. She smiled.

She brought her hands around, spreading her buttocks. Her vagina had been hidden primly under the thatch of thick pubic hair. As the skin stretched, its wet pink inside opened. A little above, nestled within a gash of dark brown, her puckered anus stared at Faustino. She remained in the position for a few moments. Faustino did not move.

She straightened, lifted one leg to shake it out of the bikini bind and kicked them away with the other leg. She went further into the bedroom. She stacked hers and Buster's pillows and reclined slowly in the center. She slid down off the pillow until her face was almost hidden by her breasts. After she spread her legs and raised her knees, she pressed her breasts together, her small pudgy hands unable to contain the ooze of breast that pushed between her fingers. She slid her hands down, combing her pubic hair with her spread fingers, lowering them on either side of her vagina. She parted the pubic hairs, searching slowly until she found the fleshy skin on either side of the vagina. Gingerly, she clasped the vaginal lips in her fingers, pulling them apart, exposing the inside that hungered for Faustino, that yearned for any man. She waited.

Faustino turned and ran out of the kitchen.

II

The truck came alive with the first turn of the ignition key. He narrowly missed a corner of the tool shed, but he swerved around the house and was quickly moving on the mile of gravel road leading to the highway. The road had not been graded or surfaced since Buster convinced a Texas Highway Department crew to do it on two weekends, using state equipment and materials. Faustino held on to the steering wheel as the truck leaped high into the air. Normally he would not have gone as fast, but he was in a hurry to get on the highway and as far as he could from Buster's house and Mrs. Crane.

The distracting noise and clatter of the truck had a soothing effect on Faustino, forcing him to concentrate on the truck and the road. He flew past the cattleguard, the front wheels of the truck going over the two-inch pipes embedded in concrete, only the rear tires thump-thumping over it. The truck slid briefly out of control on the loose gravel shoulder, the tires spinning a cloud of white dust before he jerked onto the smooth blacktop and felt the roaring hum underneath him. the black ribbon of highway undulated and snaked its way between the pale green-brown of the chaparral before piercing the horizon and going out of sight.

The smooth road and the steady hum of the wheels lulled Faustino, relaxed his concentration, the truck speeding forward by itself. He thought, *vieja chingada, nalgona.* The images inside Buster's kitchen returned, oscillating between clear and blurred, sharply in focus and then as indistinct phantoms. Against his will, the grotesque sight of her naked body pulsated in his mind, making his temples ache. His thoughts became images of the clothesline with the panties hanging like jagged teeth; a ghost-like flowered housecoat flowed and billowed about him; Mrs. Crane's body, hidden and mysterious, freely floated in and out of the housecoat, up and around the panties, fleetingly revealed itself, beckoning to him, inviting him into a black vortex.

As though overtaken by an uncontrollable spasmodic reaction, Faustino flipped the steering wheel, aiming the truck at the road shoulder. His body had tensed, his penis was rock hard pushing against his jeans. He braked, bringing the truck to a stop but did not turn off the ignition. He liked the feel of erotic vibration coming from the idling engine.

Chingao! he yelled at the top of his lungs, the sound of his voice rising with the heat from the black pasture soil. He gripped the steering wheel until his knuckles whitened. He felt his penis consuming, channeling, drawing, sucking all of his body's blood into itself, becoming larger, packed harder than he had ever felt it before. The engorged member throbbed and ached, straining inside his trousers, yearning for the denied release. *Chingao!* Faustino yelled once more, the sound exploding out of the cab of the truck, echoing and reverberating in the bushes, tumbling about the brittle chaparral, slithering into the brush where it became a whimper, finally dying in the short distance.

Voy pa' 'trás, he thought. *Se la meto, vieja jija de su chingada madre! Conmigo no juega. Le voy a enseñar. Vieja culera, de veras quiere coger, pos aquí mero. Aquí estoy. Se la meto. Se la meto hasta en el fundío.*

Faustino raced the engine into a deafening revolution, overheating it, straining the thick metal of the engine. He mashed the clutch and violently jerked the transmission into gear. He braced himself on the wheel ready to release the clutch and surge forward, his mind made up to return to the ranch house, no other thought on his mind, determined to relieve himself inside Mrs. Crane's white waiting body. The roar of the engine rattled away any other sensation.

Faustino lifted the shift level and released the clutch and eased up on the gas pedal. He knew he would not go. The soft, diaphanous, seductive image of her under the clothesline, unaware of being seen, gave way to a sharper image of the flabby Mrs. Crane in the kitchen, a lewd, repulsive mass of flesh abused by a man, knowing only that abuse, seeking to abuse in return, wanting to swallow his maleness, to negate the thwarted sexuality she had known. Faustino could not go back.

Still, his arousal lingered, his excitement remained; he needed a woman, a sexual coupling to restore the sense of himself to himself. His manhood had been threatened, challenged, made separate and apart from himself in a way he had not known before. He needed to be restored into a whole man.

It was true that Mrs. Crane was ready, available, nearby, in desperate need of a penis, any penis. It was true he had not emptied the grease can full of water; he could go back on that pretext, he knowing and she knowing the reason for his return. His arousal drove him to contemplate what he knew he would not do. Mrs. Crane offered a sexual embrace for which he was not prepared.

Faustino had had his share, more than his share, of whores and clumsy couplings in the back seats of automobiles and in the woods. Mrs. Crane presented him with a kind of sex beyond what he knew. To him sex was as natural as anything a man did. It was understood that a man looked for more than he was apportioned. As times changed, it was not rare for a Chicano to go to bed with a white woman. Some of his nephews who lived in the city had Anglo wives. There, in Buster's kitchen, was something altogether different.

He tried to shape the events into an order which made sense to him. It was not a fear of anything physical which Buster might do. Only his penis made sense. He weighed his erection against the repulsion he felt.

He thought of Mrs. Crane, revolting though she had been. She could after all service him, assuage the incessant pleading of his penis, draw from his body the maddening fluids that made him lose control of himself. To return to the ranch house meant he would walk along the short corridor, follow her into the lair of the bedroom. Once there she would drop upon the bed, poise herself to receive the extension of him, her dark pubic hairs bent in segments like spiderlegs, her vagina stalking his penis, preying, eager and patient to close in around the shaft, her thick arms and legs pinning his body to hers, clutching him, drawing him into her baneful center. No, he could not return to the ranch house.

Faustino gently pulled the gear shift into first and slowly released the clutch. The truck eased evenly forward. As he drove, he tried to roll a cigarette with one hand, as his grandfather had taught him. His hand shook, spilling more tobacco than usual. When the cigarette was finished, it was loosely rolled, lumpy, unfit to smoke. In disgust, he violently tossed it out the window.

The clothesline loomed ahead of him on the horizon as the truck rose up the slope of the land. The breasts with each nipple large and purple, the misty image of the succubus spinning her charm around him, speaking in voices that made his scalp tingle and his cheeks itch, the strange incantations crying out of the quivering flesh. His excitement was again in full force, stronger than before, more demanding; the dull aching pain of his engorged penis radiating outward from the base of the penis into his thighs and lower belly. He massaged his crotch trying to soothe the pain, but the palm of his hand could not penetrate through the denim material, could not ease what he felt inside past all skin, all flesh. The speedometer rose to seventy, eighty. The truck shook. Only his erection mattered.

As he approached the crossroads, Faustino saw the road signs flash by rapidly, bright green sparks in the corner of his eye. The white and black signs identified the road he traveled and arrows pointed ahead to roads yet to come. He slowed the truck as the red stop sign came suddenly upon him.

Across the road, a little beyond the intersection, was the aluminum breadloaf-shaped mailbox with his name crudely painted on the side in large black letters. He waited for a tube-shaped milk truck to go by before he crossed the road. He stopped adjacent to his mailbox. He seldom bothered to check for mail as he seldom received any. Normally, he felt good when he saw the mailbox as it signaled the nearness of María and his children. He could see the rooftop of his house in the distance, seeming to have sank into the drying Johnson grass.

Ahead of him, Buster and Casey waited for the wrench. No doubt Buster would be angry. No matter how long it took him to run an errand, Buster would be angry when he returned.

There was an ominous anticipation in his body as he thought about

María. He imagined she would be inside the house watching those television programs she did not entirely understand. *Mis historias,* she called them. When he came home for lunch, it would be prepared, but she would not take her eyes off the slow-speaking characters on the screen who were seldom photographed below the neck.

Buster would have to wait. Faustino knew he had to see María. He had been gone a long time, but Buster, the wrench, Mrs. Crane, none of that mattered. He had to see her. Only she, María, who sensed things in him even before he knew them himself, only she could help him rid himself of the ache that bulged in his trousers. Only she could be the receptacle for the welling fluids undammed by the incident at the clothesline, now that he was convinced Mrs. Crane had had little to do with it.

Faustino inched the truck forward and carefully turned into his driveway, a winding, rutted pair of clay ribbons worn smooth by his truck tires, separated by intermittent patches of sparse grass down the middle. The weatherbeaten gate lay at a twisted angle, one hinge torn off. He reminded himself to fix it as he would be moving some cattle to graze in the pasture surrounding his house.

Once he turned in, he was sure of what he wanted to do. He accelerated to the top of the hill and killed the engine, gliding down the slope. He aimed the hood of the truck directly at the porch of the house. There, in the house nestled by a clump of mesquite trees, would be María, unaware that he was coming, unaware of his need of her, sure to question why he came.

As the truck gathered speed in the downward roll toward the house, Faustino saw María standing beside the porch, under the muted shade of the large ancient mesquite tree. Years before, he had put a water tap near the tree so she could do the wash. As he approached, she stood in front of her washtub. For him, the scene coming up to him, of his wife performing a similar chore had no suggestion of the previous scene with Mrs. Crane standing and bending over her washtub. María dressed plainly, wore longer skirts, and would have protected her modesty even though there could not be anyone to see her. María would no more expose herself in private than she would in public. It was a habit acquired as a young girl and required no further thought.

María was wringing one of his shirts, twisting and twisting, letting the water drip, drop by drop, back into the tub; some of it, as she shook the shirt turned into a wrinkled rod, fell on her toes. She then walked to the clothesline and pinned it. She took another from the soap tub and sloshed it in the rinse tub before wringing it damp. That batch finished, she dumped another into the soap tub, swirling the clothing in the foamy water. María took another of his shirts out, squeezed it, shook it loose and draped it evenly over the ribbed, brass surface of the scrubboard. She dipped her hand in the water for the scrub brush and applied it vigorously to the shirt. She scrubbed so furiously that she did not hear the approaching truck.

Faustino parked the truck adjacent to the porch, which he did when he would soon be going out again. He jumped out, slammed the door shut. The crash of the door on the truck's body startled María from her work. She straightened up from the scrubboard to look at Faustino, her eyes wide and questioning. María placed her hands on her hips and bent backwards slightly to ease her taut back muscles.

Faustino did not look in her direction, but went straight to the house in long strides which seemed to suppress a run. He threw the screen door open, shaking the hinges, sending the wooden frame crashing against the wall. He went inside, permitting the door to swing shut by itself.

His was a one-room house. In a rear corner, to the left, stood an iron-frame bed, once painted in a dark walnut color. Now, most of the paint was gone, leaving a smoothly worn metal which rusted only in spots. The kitchen corner was immediately to the right as one walked in. A large, two-burner camp stove stood atop a linoleum-covered table. Next to the table, partially shielding a small window, was a fat, bulky refrigerator, its white enamel aged to a yellow, almost brown, tone, dotted with rust pocks like flyspecks.

Just off the center of the room was the only furniture Faustino had bought during the time of his marriage. It was a dinette set. The tabletop was made of a scratchproof surface which had many scratches on it and the chairs were constructed of a thin, fragile, tubular metal and upholstered with a synthetic material. He had bought the set in nearby Nixon, on credit; the store owner unsure Faustino could pay for it, finally agreeing only if Buster co-signed the credit slip and guaranteed the payment of ten dollars a month for two years.

In the corner to the right of the entrance a television set was lodged precariously upon a wooden crate. The channel selector nob had long ago disappeared. In its place, wedged into the metal slit, was a nail, its center filed flat to fit. The picture tube was old, oval; the transmitted images appearing as swiftly moving clouds. The set had belonged to María's mother and she had made a present of it when María's father died. Her mother did not want it to remind her of the deceased. Whenever she came to visit, María made sure to drape a cloth over it.

The house, the room, gave a cluttered appearance because everything seemed so close together, but María had arranged all of the items neatly, each carefully located in its special corner, its proper place, as if separated by walls only María could see. Once, long ago, soon after their marriage, when Faustino had brought her to her new home for the first time, María had shaken her head in dismay. She was not one to be defeated without a struggle. Soon enough, she nailed two criss-crossing wires to the walls just below the ceiling, and then threaded long cloth panels in an effort to create four rooms out of the space. The first morning, Faustino rolled over on the hem of the wall, pulling all four nails from the walls. The cloth walls came tumbling down, the heavy wire landing on Faustino, startling him awake. María cried and he cursed under his breath. He put the wires back up, tighter this time, and María was pleased. Then, his cousins came for a visit. They were their first guests. María worked long and hard scrubbing the floor, arranging some old chairs he had, even finding some flowers to put in a bowl of water. His cousins had made the trip to *La Tacuachera* before coming over. They had a few beers and a guitar with them. Upon entering and seeing the arrangement, they began to laugh. Faustino had been embarrassed and furious. After the cousins had gone, he sat in a chair drinking the last of his beer. In his silence, he was seething, letting it build up until he could stand it no longer. Then, Faustino erupted. He yanked the wires from the walls, gouging bits of wood as he jerked. Afterward, he went outside to smoke a cigarette, calm himself, before coming to bed. María had been awake when he returned, afraid of him. He undressed, got in beside her and took her hand in his. Neither of them said anything.

Over the years, María had become accustomed to the one room. When the two children arrived, she had kept them in a crib near the bed. As they grew older, she prepared a pallet for them each night next to the corner table. The lack of privacy, particularly when she and Faustino made love, bothered her. The first child had ended their nights of carefree, giggling intimacy. When they made love now, which became more and more infrequent, they did it softly and gently so as not to wake the children.

It was hot inside the house. Faustino paced around the dining table. He took three steps to the refrigerator, threw open the door, shaking the rust-eaten appliance along with the floor under it. María had left her wash after seeing him slam the door. She had followed him onto the porch and stood in the doorway watching him. Her features and the outline of her body were hazy through the rusting, dark brown screen. She was somewhat angered by his strange behavior and bewildered that he would be absent from the fields so early in the afternoon.

Faustino did not turn to see María at the door. He searched inside the refrigerator, moving his head from side to side, craning his neck to look over jars and left-over food wrapped in wax paper. His anger rose as he could not find what he looked for. He kicked the door shut. He slapped his thigh and brought his hand up, making a fist which he shook in the air.

He turned to call María and saw her standing on the porch.

"¿Quién chingaos," he yelled, "se tomó mi vironga?"

María shook her head. "Pos' tú, ¿quién más?" she said.

She raised her hand to the red bandana which contained her hair, pulled on the knot, and drew it downward. Her hair fell in black glistening cascades, bouncing on her shoulders. She opened the screen door quietly and stepped inside.

"¡Chingadamadre!" said Faustino.

He collapsed a haunch on top of the table, keeping one foot firmly on the floor. The other, he let swing nervously. He had the appearance of a caged animal. The veins of his neck bulged in thick ridges, his lips were compressed tightly leaving only a thin line for a mouth.

"¿Qué andas haciendo? ¿No tienes trabajo?" she asked.

44

"Cómo chingaos que no tengo trabajo, pendeja?" said Faustino, his teeth packed together.

"¿A poco viniste a comer?"

"¿Quién chingaos te dijo que vine a comer?"

"Oyes, andas bravo, ¿no?"

"Oyes, andas bravo, ¿no?" he mimicked her voice unpleasantly, turning the sweet musical sound of it into a harsh, biting, imitation.

"Bueno, así no vamos pa' ningún lado," she said. "Entonces, ¿qué quieres? ¿A qué viniste?"

"Quién chingaos te dio permiso pa' hablar?" He took the blue bag of tobacco from his jacket pocket. He was unable to smooth the cigarette paper, wadded it and the bag, and threw it against the refrigerator.

María remained where she was, looking straight at him, her eyes never leaving his face. She was concerned, worried, about the strange man in front of her who did not seem to be her husband.

"Yo no necesito permiso para hablar en mi casa, ¿oíste?" she said.

"No me salgas con tu pinche pedo, ¿oítes?" Faustino was ugly, his face covered in sweat, his desire for sex surging as he felt an overpowering need for violence. The two desires rose together, mingled, became inseparable.

"Pero, ¿qué te pasa?" she said, taking a step toward him.

"Nadien te dijo que me preguntes nada," he said.

"Debes de andar en la labor, trabajando. ¿Te dio el día el Buster? O ¿no más te fuiste como baboso?" She ended sarcastically, changing the dark, delicate, pretty face into a grimace which betrayed an inability for cruelty.

Faustino became furious.

"Oyes, tú de veras quieres que te dé un chingazo, ¿no?" He jumped from the table, landing solidly on his feet, clenching his fists, shaking the both of them at her. He took a tentative step toward her.

María ignored his threat. She moved around him and went to sit on the bed.

"Estás bien loco tú. Eso es lo que tienes. A ver cuando aprendes a meterte del sol. Parece que andas asoleado," she said.

Faustino went to the foot of the bed. He began to unbutton his shirt, noticing for the first time that he had not finished buttoning it after being with Mrs. Crane. He yanked the shirt tail out of his trousers, pulled it off his shoulders, threw it across the table, sending a salt shaker crashing to the floor. His hands went to his belt buckle, but before unclasping the leather, he lifted his head toward her.

"Andale, pronto," he said.

María left the bed, went over between the dining table and the refrigerator to pick up the salt shaker and his shirt. She draped his shirt over a chair. Faustino had his back to her.

"Pos', ¿qué traes tú?" she asked.

"¿Qué crees? Te digo que te quites la ropa," he said.

Faustino unbuckled the belt, undid the metal button of the jeans, slid the zipper down, jerked his trousers over his legs, all in one motion. The stove-pipe trouser legs bunched at the knees, held there by his boots. He hopped around the bed, leaning toward it in case he lost his balance, and sat. He had some difficulty, but grunting and jerking, he managed to yank trouser leg and boot off at the same time. He took a couple of deep breaths before doing the other leg.

"Tú andas bien loco, oyes," said María.

Faustino lifted up to slide his underwear into a pile on top of his jeans. He lay on the bed. His penis flopped limply to one side, draping itself over his thigh. He grabbed with his right hand, flicking the ridge of the glans with his thumb, and then he pulled the foreskin all the way down, aiming the dark purple knob at María.

"Andale, pronto," he said, "me tengo que ir."

"Oye, no," said María. "Eso no. Por ahí vienen los muchachos de la escuela. Todas las puertas y las ventanas están abiertas. ¿Qué pendejada es eso? ¿No te da vergüenza? ¿No te puedes esperar hasta la noche? Mira . . . come eres . . ."

"Cállate y hazte pa'ca," he said.

He leaped off the bed in a single bound, landing on his feet. He stared at María, fully naked in front of her, something rare in their reserved intimacy. María averted her eyes, a little embarrassed by his brazen display, unaccustomed to her husband's nakedness. There was confusion and irritability on her face. He spoke to her in a cold voice, exaggerating the control of his rage.

"Te digo que vengas pa'ca," he said. The command had a finality to it, he would not ask her again.

Faustino lay again on the bed, reclining on his side, his torso supported on one elbow. His testicles rolled over on his thigh. His penis was semi-hard. He pulled on it with a half dozen frenzied jerks and brought it to its full extension. The penis twitched spasmodically in anticipation, as if knowing María could not refuse, could not deny an obligation she had accepted as part of her life with him.

María stood where she was, making no move to go to him.

"¡Chingao!" yelled Faustino, flying from the bed, running to where she stood, grabbing her arm. "¿Estás sorda?" he screamed.

Faustino half-pulled her, half-dragged her to the bed and threw her on it. She landed on a hand and an elbow, bruising her ankle on the bed frame. The bed squeaked from the impact of her weight. María crawled over the bed, bouncing to the other side. She brushed the hair from her face, leaned her shoulder against the wall. She cried noiselessly.

With three long strides, Faustino rounded the corner of the bed and was next to her. He twisted María and struck her with the back of his hand, landing the full force of his knuckles on her ear. He tipped her without much effort onto the bed. She started to cry audibly as she made a move to get up again. She stopped her crying and lay still when she saw Faustino, his arms outstretched, poised, anticipating her move, waiting, inviting her to do something, ready to strike at her again. She lay back on her pillow, no longer wishing to resist. Her hair became a black halo around her head. She closed her eyes and crossed her arms corpse-like over her bosom.

Faustino walked slowly around the bed to the other side and sat on the corner of it, María's head at the opposite end. Her feet were pressed together, her toes pointing directly to the ceiling. He looked at her bare ankles. He unclasped the buckles on her sandles, tossing them at his feet, patting a few grains of dirt off the coverlet. He rubbed her ankle up and down with his left hand. His eyes were intent on the hidden juncture of her legs which was covered by a faded green cotton skirt. He rubbed her ankle higher, slipping the tips of his fingers under the hem of the skirt.

His body trembled, his shoulders shook; small beads of perspiration formed above his eyebrows and on the bridge of his nose. He squeezed her kneecap and ran his open hand up María's smooth, brown thigh, feeling the soft, feather-like fuzz burn his palm. His hand continued upward, meeting a slight resistance in the material of the skirt. María rolled over so he could overcome it. He pushed upward and upward until the skirt bunched over her belly.

María's loose-fitting, blindingly white panties shone before him, their waistband high over her belly button, under her skirt. Faustino noted thread-bare patches from repeated launderings. The leg elastic was warped and tattered. They had a round hole to one side of the curved crotch panel, through which poked a shock of wavy pubic hair.

In a rough, hungry manner, Faustino forced her thighs apart with the scoop he made out of his hand. As he reached the point where her legs joined, he swiveled his wrist, snaked out his fingers, slid his hand over the flat of her stomach, and made an arc in the air to the bodice of her dress. He pinched the covered breasts repeatedly trying to find her nipples. It was one of the few things María enjoyed in sex. He could not find them.

Clumsily, breathing heavily, he could not manage to unbutton the top part of her dress. The more difficult it seemed, the more enraged he became. María placed her hand over his. Faustino whimpered.

"Espera," she said, quietly, caressing his arm down to his side.

She sat up, her face level with his, and began to unbutton her dress. Faustino rubbed his thigh nervously, impatiently. When it appeared to him that María was taking more time then necessary to unbutton her dress, in a rage, he leaned forward and with both hands, he ripped open the bodice, popping off the buttons as he pulled. He grabbed her brassiere in the middle and yanked. He shook María, but the garment remained in place. He took a handful of dress at the top of each of her shoulders and tore the back down the middle.

María, seeing the fury in Faustino's face, reached behind her to unhook the bra, letting the straps float uneasily down her arms. Instinctively, as though she were in the presence of a stranger, she crossed her arms to shield her breasts. Faustino moved closer to her. He lifted her arms, tossed them away and began to kiss and slobber on her chest. María's breasts were small and firm, perfectly round and proportioned to her body; with small, sloping nipples which, when touched, became flat, mesa-like eruptions on her soft mounds. She had breast-fed the children but her breasts did not sag. They remained as round and as firm as the virginal pair she had offered to Faustino on their wedding night. He bit into her nipple which became distended from irritation and pain and not from passion. As his teeth sank into the brown nipple, she took a quick breath but did not cry out, choosing to endure the hurt and humiliation lest Faustino become angrier.

Faustino crawled on the bed. He hovered over her body on his hands and knees. He hunched back, placing all of his weight on his knees, his body arched, kneeling in obscene piety. His wet hands rested on his thighs. He took the waistband of her cotton panties in both of his hands and pulled them down over her hips and buttocks. María lay still. He got them past her thighs, over her knees and down to her ankles. He slipped one foot through the leg opening and simply turned them aside, leaving them to bunch around her ankle. He grabbed her heels and lifted, throwing her legs in opposite directions. María remained limp, moving only when what he did jolted her.

María looked into Faustino's face. It was hard, animal-like, his lips tightly sealed, lines of anger streaked across his forehead in jagged irregularity. His lower jaw kept twitching, causing abrupt movements of his head to one side. Each twitch made his jugular burst forth, distorting the lean smoothness of his neck.

He crossed over one of her legs. Straddling it, he lowered himself to her kneecap, positioned the intersection of his testicles and the base of his penis and humped, dropping his face into her stomach, his mouth coming to rest on top of her belly button. He sucked, swallowing it and the flesh around it. The bunched-up dress at her midsection hid the top of his head from María. All she could see were his brown buttocks, rising and falling, appearing and disappearing, and she felt the on and off pressure on her kneecap.

Faustino's mind was not on María's body. Her tense, dusky body, with the skirt in a pile at the center of it, did not interest him any more than a surrogate. María was nothing more to him than a lump of indistinct, shapeless meat. María had a reasonably snug opening to receive the fluids that boiled within him and that was all he needed. Faustino recalled the image of the clothesline, remembering an earlier, distant excitement. His memory of what happened was all the more exciting because of the danger it had presented, the peril it had posed for him. The subsequent repulsion he had felt at Buster's house did not quell the tumult which Mrs. Crane had aroused in him.

María would receive him, not with passion or desire or encouragement. She would submit and accept his penetration of her. She would quiet the storm that seemed at every moment about to unleash its fury. María would draw from him the poisons that made him delirious. Inside her body, the familiar flesh would engulf him and bathe him with secretions that would be an antidote. She would drain the wellspring that his fear and his limited knowledge had uncapped.

The hard, erect penis nudged his belly, as if to remind him to continue with what he set out to do. He positioned himself between her legs. Supporting himself on one arm, he brought the other up to the hair-covered juncture of her legs. He touched the soft flesh. It was dry. Faustino poked his forefinger, deeper and deeper until it slid in all the way, taking one or two pubic hairs with it. It hurt but María made no sound. He jerked the finger in and out, up and down, violently, demanding the mucous response. Faustino was aware that María was not helping at all. He paid no thought to that. Just as Mrs. Crane had been able to get his penis hard even though he had not been interested, Faustino was sure he could prepare her against her wishes.

"Pareces un animal," María said softly, describing what he did in a matter-of-fact voice.

"Cállate el hocico, pendeja," he hissed.

Faustino slumped upon the length of her body, burying his face between her neck and shoulder; the stubble of the day-long beard rasped her skin. He thrust his pelvis at her blindly seeking the entrance. With a harsh, brutal shove, he slid down her silky pubic hair and poked the mattress.

"Chingao," he said huskily, arching on his elbows and knees. "Abrela."

His hair was wet and stringy, cold, as it fell into her face. His thighs were touching hers and the contact was clammy and slimy. María reluctantly, slowly, brought her hands around her hips. She chastely, careful not to touch him, pulled the labia of her vagina aside. Faustino lowered himself. When his penis was in the chute made by her fingers, he intruded her body. He did not put it in a little at a time as he usually did. He rammed it in as far as it could go, his pelvic bone smashing cruelly into hers.

He shoved and withdrew in rapid-fire fashion, feeling the muscles of his groin tense as he was so close to an orgasm. He changed his rhythm into long, deep strokes to make it last a little. His muscles relaxed and he heard María crying in his ear.

With each slithering lunge, his excitement subsided. He was pounding away what was left of his erection. He could feel it going limp inside his wife.

Faustino became frightened for his maleness. He started to hump with renewed vigor, increasing the frequency of his strokes. It did not help. It was becoming more and more difficult to shove it in once he drew it out. The muscles of María's vagina reflexively tried to grip the penis, contract to increase the friction; however, Faustino's penis was becoming so flaccid that the constricted muscles were an impediment. Faustino raised up on an elbow. With his free hand, he slapped María's face. "No hagas eso, cabrona," he said. He was determined to orgasm inside for now it had become a point of honor with him.

His final lunge resulted in his penis becoming a useless wad of human flesh pressed against her body, unable to go in again. Faustino expelled a long sorrowful sigh. He was suddenly tired, his entire body blanketed by a musky sweat. He lost all of his energy and slumped over María, breathing heavily. María opened her eyes which were red and swollen. The sun coming in through the window glistened on Faustino's back. She embraced him with one arm, wiping her wet cheek with the other. The two of them lay quietly on the bed.

After what seemed a long time, Faustino raised his hips. He looked at his limp penis, which had shrivelled to the size of a small cork. It dangled in the air as a useless, impotent appendage. A drop of sweat fell from his face onto María's breast. His face contorted into a fierce, wild mask of anger and frustration. Had she only helped him . . .

"¡Haz algo!" he shouted at her in a shrill, frenzied scream as if fearful he might not be able to have another erection. María's tears flowed like a continuous crystal down her temples, seeking refuge in the lustre of her long, black hair.

She did not know what to do as Faustino had never had any trouble with his erections. She grabbed his penis and tossed it up and down in her hand. He brushed her hand away. "¡Así!" he said and showed her how to masturbate him. She tried to do as he showed her but it had no effect. The penis was stubbornly limp. It remained a tiny extension from his body, a wrinkled, defeated protuberance dwarfed by his fat testicles.

Faustino looked about the room as if searching for something to revive the erection. He masturbated himself furiously until her body juices became gummy in his hand. His own, more experienced, ministrations did not help.

Everything seemed wrong to him now. He realized the brutality of his actions. Out of pity for her and anger toward himself, he began to curse her, to beat her, slapping her face with his open hand and striking her body with his fist. He screamed at her not to shield her face from the wide, swinging slaps. He wanted to hit her face. He cursed her and beat her with renewed force each time he struck the back of her hands. It was not until he saw blood splatter upon the white pillow that he stopped. María's teeth, nose, cheeks and hands were covered with blood. He looked at his hands, saw the blood on them and let them drop limply and impotently down his naked hips.

All expression left his face. He stepped off the bed quietly as if she were asleep and he was afraid to wake her. He dressed noiselessly after he wiped his hands with his underwear. The only sound in the room was his labored breathing and María's whispered sobs.

Without saying a word, without turning to look at his wife, Faustino went outside to sit on the porch. He wanted to be away from her crying. He opened a new bag of Bugler for a smoke. He did not care whether it was well-rolled or not, and he was oblivious to the ochre fingerprint he left on the cigarette paper.

He sat on the porch, elbows on his knees, smoking. He wanted to blot out the memory of everything that had happened to him. The events of the afternoon flashed before him in an image that took in everything. He dropped the cigarette and poked his eyes with his knuckles trying to blank out what he saw with his mind. He clasped his hands together. The blood under his fingernails was already dry. He tried to roll another cigarette but he trembled too much. Finally, he let go and watched the tobacco and paper float away.

He felt he should go inside to see María, to say something to her. Maybe to just sit next to her and touch her gently without saying anything. He felt he should explain to her that he himself did not understand what he did, that there was something driving him that he could not resist. To explain meant that he would have to start with Mrs. Crane. In the end, it would only make things worse. No, he could not go inside to her. He could not face her with any part of the truth. Of the little he understood, he knew she would forgive him and things would return to normal. Everything would be back the way it was. There was too much of importance between them and what he had done would not destroy it. Things are only the same if a man knows how to wait.

He stood up. All of him ached. He walked slowly, deliberately, to the truck, as if measuring or counting his steps. The spring in his step was gone, his head inclined forward.

The truck roared to a sputtering clatter quickly. As he swung the truck around his front yard, he looked out of the cab window and saw María standing in the doorway behind the screendoor. He started to wave to her out of habit but checked himself. She would not want him to just yet. He eased the truck away, afraid to give it more gas, something which María might misinterpret. He felt drained and confused but he was not angry with her.

Instead of driving up to the highway, which was faster, Faustino turned into a dirt road. It was a short-cut to the fields where Buster and Casey waited for him. He had been gone more than two hours. The wrench he had been sent for was not in his back pocket and neither was it on the seat. He could not remember leaving it in Buster's kitchen, although he might have. Or, it might have dropped out of his pants at home. In either case, he could not go back to either place.

The sloping land near his place gave way to flat black dirt. He followed the tractor road. On his left was a field of sorghum which appeared as a copper-colored sea as far as his eyes could see. He was reminded that they would begin cutting in a few weeks. He had seen the advance man for the harvesters already contracting with Buster. He was glad he no longer had to drive the combine.

To his left was Scudder Robertson's pasture. As a younger man, Robertson raised and pitted fighting cocks. As he refused to farm his land, the birds supplemented the income from his cattle ranching. Then, he struck oil. His only son married another man, his English teacher in college, and the both of them moved to New York where they wrote poetry. Each month, an account-ant in a bank in Chicago sent the boy a check. The checks would continue so long as the boy stayed away. Each month, the same accountant sent Scudder a check for a lot less. With it, he fed himself and his four hundred fighting cocks. He no longer pitted them and he raised them because they were more of a nuisance than cattle. He had sold all of his cattle as soon as he received his first royalty check. He sold all of his horses, too, keeping only one, a one-eyed sorrel who, according to Scudder, he would shoot one day when he had enough of him.

At the end of the sorghum field, Faustino slipped the truck into neutral and coasted to a stop in front of a gate. He would cross this pasture, which belonged to Buster, to get to a brown gravel farm road that would take him back to work.

He drove into the pasture. The spindly branches of the mesquite brushed lightly over the cab of the truck. There was only the suggestion of a road left, but he knew it well, maneuvering around the trees, heading in the direction of the farm road. About midway there, he came to the water well with its abandoned cistern. Buster kept the well in repair for the cattle and the trough was always full of water. Faustino pulled over to have a drink.

He opened the spigot and bent down, turning sideways, to drink the fresh, cold water. After he finished his drink, he took his handkerchief, soaked it, and draped it over his face. With one hand, he gathered it off his face and ran it along the back of his neck. He returned to the truck and leaned against a fender, intending to roll a smoke.

Faustino threw his head back, closed his eyes. As soon as he shut out the sunlight, the clothesline appeared along with the apparition who pinned underpants to the wire. At first it seemed a mere wisp of an image floating in the vast blackness of his mind. Gradually the image became larger until he could distinguish the sliver of white panties tucked in between the ghost-like thighs. As Faustino leaned further back to rest his head on the hood of the truck, he saw one mammoth breast, its nipple coming straight at him.

His previous unresponsive, dead body began to revive. He felt his blood begin to flow, rushing through his veins. His mind pursued the image of Mrs. Crane stooped over, willed it back into focus. He held the picture, so clear he could almost reach out and touch the plump body. His penis was beginning to strain against his jeans.

He moved away from the truck, walked around it and across the rutted road to a clearing surrounded by cactus. He avoided going near the red ant hill in the center. He stopped beside an enormous cactus pad which jutted well into the clearing, its needles long and sturdy.

Faustino unzipped his trousers and released the flushed and throbbing penis. He encircled it with the fingers of his right hand. He stretched his uncircumcised skin forward over the glans, releasing it finger by finger, twisting his hand so his palm rubbed the underside of it. He then pulled back on the skin until the organ arched, enjoying the sensation. He saw the fat, erratic veins pop out, coursing their way along the shaft-like elongated warts.

Faustino spread his legs, planting his boots firmly on the drying grass, assuring his balance. He found a pumping rhythm with which to begin, varying it by rolling and twisting the loose skin of his penis on the forward and backward motions. He loosened and tightened his grip, maintaining the slow, predictable, expected stroke. He tightened and loosened his sphincter, tensing and relaxing all the muscles in his groin area, rechanneling the flow of his blood, concentrating all of his energy at the base of his penis, gathering if from all points of his body, storing it. The stroking of his penis cleared his blocked passages, rearranged his blood vessels; soon all that he was pulsed in anticipation at the base of his organ.

He leaned back slightly, rolled his head backwards, closed his eyes to get a better view of the clothesline. One by one, the panties appeared before him, fluttering, the crotch dangling below his nose unclean, female musk wafting into him. A woman stooped over a washtub. She had Mrs. Crane's body, plump and thick, white and pink; and María's angular, coffee-colored face. He squeezed his eyes together to dismiss the image. Instantly, round, ample buttocks inserted in a pair of bikini panties appeared. That was better. He held on to what he saw, increasing the pumping rhythm.

Faustino now quickened the jerking movements of his hand. He shook his wrist furiously as one after another he saw breasts, thighs, buttocks, bikinis, housecoats. He would catch a wave of orgasmic flush flow into the shaft and he would pump faster as if to evacuate right away; and just as flow reached the brink of orgasm, he would stop, squeeze tightly, relax his sphincter, open his eyes, enjoying the sensation of the ebbing orgasm. Before it withdrew too far, he started again; gently at first, coaxing it around, massaging the kinks caused by the abrupt reversal, drawing it forward, gathering speed, building momentum, pumping faster and faster, doubling over his body, his chin against his chest, his eyes pressed tightly shut.

He repeated the process several times until his testicles ached, vibrating with the beginnings of a dull pain. On the next surge, the sperm welled again, the pressure behind it built up. This time the flicking wrist did not stop. This time he humped his pelvis forward, thrusting into a phantom vagina in the air. His body jerked uncontrollably, ejaculating massive gobs of milk-white viscous semen. The first drop shot far into the air. Its arc splattered it against the cactus pad, into a tuft of yellow needles. The excess became a rivulet winding its way down the faded green of the cactus, forming into smaller drops at the bottom before dripping desultorily to the earth where they flattened on contact with the dirt, became a part of the dirt, dried and disappeared.

Spent, Faustino milked the last, residual drops of fluid from his penis. As he did so, the penis became flaccid, as soft and as pliable as his skin. He shook it a little more before stuffing it into his pants. He walked back to the truck, enjoying the hot rays of the sun on his face. He was relaxed now, peaceful, with a calmness he had not known before in his life.

He closed the door of the truck without slamming it for once. Faustino smiled all the way to the field where Buster and Casey waited.

Casey lay under the shade of the elongated tractor body. Buster sat with his back against the giant tractor tire. He was fuming. As soon as he heard the clatter of Faustino's truck entering the field, Buster stood up and adjusted his hat. In as long a stride as his short legs would permit, he went forward to meet Faustino. His ruddy face twitched, spittle foamed at the corners of his mouth and streamed down his chin.

Before Faustino could light down from the truck, Buster yelled at him.

"Where in the goddamned fuck have you been?"

Faustino thought it best to put his smile away for later. By the time he was on the ground, his face was serious.

"I had some trouble looking for that wrench, Mr. Buster. The tool shed is a mess. There is no light in there."

"I just bet the fucking tool shed is a fucking mess," said Buster. "I just fucking bet it is. Why the goddamned hell didn't you go in and ask my wife for a lightbulb, or a flashlight, or something, huh?"

Faustino knew he was not expected to answer. He inspected the top of his boot. Buster turned to Casey.

"Did you hear that, Casey? The fucking tool shed is a fucking mess. That's what it fucking is. This fucking Mexican says my fucking tool shed is a fucking mess. He has been *in* the fucking mess. I'll be fucking damned. He takes three fucking hours to come back with his dick in his hand. I don't fucking see a fucking wrench in your fucking hand, Faustino."

Buster walked back to the tractor. He stretched an arm to lean against the tire and made a fist of the other hand to place on his hip. Faustino followed him, but stopped a short distance away.

Casey lay on the ground using a piece of deadwood for a pillow. His hat was draped over his face.

"You know how they are, Buster," said Casey.

"This fucker is going to say he fucking looked for the fucking wrench and couldn't fucking find it. I bet that's what he's going to fucking say. I just know it. What do you say to that, Casey?"

"I say, ask him," groaned Casey. He recognized Buster's temper.

"Where is the fucking wrench, bastard?"

"I couldn't find it, Mr. Buster."

"I knew he was going to say that, Casey. I knew he was going to fucking say that."

Buster opened the toolbox under the driver's seat on the tractor. He pulled out a long rusting wrench.

"What the fuck does this fucking look like to you, Faustino?"

"The wrench. It was there all the time?"

"Goddamned right it's the fucking wrench. It wasn't in the fucking toolbox. I had to go for it myself. Can't send a goddamned Mexican for nothing."

Buster threw the wrench back in the box and slapped the lid shut.

"While you were fucking off in the tool shed, my wife had it in the kitchen. She was trying to fix the goddamned water fucking pipes with it. It was lying right on the fucking kitchen floor by the door where she fucking threw it. You wouldn't fucking think to ask her for it, would you?"

"No, sir."

While Buster fulminated, Casey sat up and dusted his back. Lazily, he got on his feet and slapped the seat of his pants. He came up to Buster, placed his arm around Buster's shoulder in a fatherly way.

"He probably stopped to knock off a little from his señorita, Buster. What're you gettin' so riled for? You know how they are."

"If he wants to fucking fuck, let him do it on his own goddamn time, not mine." Buster's anger was easing. His voice was not as high-pitched as before.

"Can't fault a man for wanting to get laid. That's what I say." Casey strolled around to the sun side of the tractor to the water cooler. He took the tin cup from its hook and filled it with water. He poured a deep draught into his mouth, swilled it around and spit it out before drinking. Casey replaced the tin cup on its hook. He turned away from Buster and Faustino and looked toward the east, over the horizon into the past.

"You know, Buster," he said, "when your daddy and me came out to this part of the country, one of the first things we learned about was these Mexicans. They like their fucking. Can't do without it. Now, yore daddy was a lot smarter than me and he figured it out first. He figured there ain't a damn thing a Mexican likes to do better than fuck, except maybe drink and fight."

"You and daddy figured that out, huh?" Buster was beginning to smile.

"Shore. Your daddy was always saying the best lay he ever had was a mamacita in Gonzales. Wanted to set her up on the place here."

"Daddy used to fuck Mexicans?"

"Everybody does, Buster. You can do things to Mexicans that you can't do to your own."

"I'll be damned," said Buster.

"He shore liked that mamacita in Gonzales, your paw did. Fucked her off and on most of his life out here. Never knew what happened to her. Man gets hard up, he'll fuck just about anything. Now, me, I can take 'em or leave 'em, you know. At my age, it don't much matter anyhow. Not your paw, though. Not your paw."

"Aw, hell," said Buster. He took his hat off his head and wiped his brow. He struck his thigh with it several times. "I bet that's what this son of a mamacita bitch went and did. Jesus! I got me all this work to do and this fucking Mexican has to go home and get laid."

"Wouldn't you?" said Casey, and he started to laugh in a loud, wheezy sound. Buster, all of his anger gone, joined in, blended his squeaky laughter with Casey's. Faustino, infected by the laughter, not fully understanding its cause, but certain he was out of trouble, joined in. The three of them stood in a triangle, with the tractor inside it, laughing.

When the laughter finally died, Buster took Faustino aside. He placed his hand on Faustino's shoulder.

"Casey and me are going to town. Got some business. Probably have a few beers after. I want you to go to my house. There's a grease can full of water under the sink. I ain't had time to empty it. My wife will show you what to do."

Doctor Castillo

I

The secretary was nervous when she entered Doctor Castillo's office. The hurricane which had dominated the weather news for more than a week had finally come ashore just south of Galveston and was traveling north toward Houston. There would be high winds and heavy rains in the area. The secretary asked if she and the receptionist might go home early to avoid the traffic snarls and the sure-to-be-flooded expressways. Two of his afternoon appointments had already canceled out of concern for the weather. She added that the remainder of his appointments could be rescheduled without too much difficulty. Doctor Castillo concealed his annoyance, consenting with a nod of his head.

Doctor Castillo's house was on the northern edge of Houston, in a subdivision far away from the threat of natural mishap. The expressways north did not congest in terror as did those in the low-lying areas to the south whenever there was the menace of a storm. Once the two women left, Castillo was alone in the office. He thought of going home, ahead of the traffic, but decided against it. The heavy early evening traffic did not bother him. He had become accustomed to it. He decided to stay in the office and work on the correspondence he normally answered on Mondays.

At five-thirty, the traffic was lighter than usual, many commuters having left the downtown area early. The falling rain was a soft mist that rinsed the windshield of his grey Cadillac. Driving home, Doctor Castillo only half listened to the news and weather reports. It was windy but not alarmingly so. The gusting winds, which neared one hundred miles an hour, were still south of the city. He drove steadily, enjoying the brisk pace of the traffic. The storm was nothing of concern to him. He had bought a new home far enough to the north that the winds would surely dissipate by the time the storm passed through his subdivision. Doctor Castillo felt he and his family were immune to any disaster.

Once at home, reading a new journal, with a drink in his lap, he watched the annoyance of the persistent rain on the large living room window. The house trembled in its resistance to the winds, there was a creaking of the crossbeams, the roof seemed uncertain. Doctor Castillo was unconcerned, relying entirely upon the control of the sturdy builders who had wished each buyer good fortune, eternal happiness, and had left the subdivision a few months before. They had assured everyone there was nothing to worry about in case of a hurricane.

When Castillo finished his studies for the evening, as usual, he made a glass of warm milk for his wife. His readings were limited to journals and newsletters which apprised him of the latest research in his field of practice. He walked slowly, soundlessly, on the carpet. He measured the last energy of the day as he went up the stairs to the bedroom. Susan, his wife, was already in bed reading a magazine, waiting for him. Doctor Castillo hoped she was not in the mood for making love. He had not had a particularly enjoyable or successful day and it would be difficult for him to relax in order to provide the kind of response his wife expected. She had been reading entirely too many grocery store magazines which contained the latest information on sexual responses and techniques. Susan would be disappointed if he did not respond according to the latest study on her lap.

Castillo placed the glass of warm milk on the bedstead. Without a word to Susan, he went into the bathroom. He bathed quickly under a hotter than usual shower, rinsing away the corruption of the city and the unproductiveness of the day. The pajamas, woven out of some man-made chemical in the fashion, look and feel of silk, soaked into his still damp skin. Returning to the bedroom, he slid in bed next to his wife.

"There is an interesting sex survey here," said Susan.

"Oh? What are we like, then?" he asked.

"I don't think it's about us, dear," she said with the voice of a teacher who's never been in the classroom. "It concerns young people. Not all of these surveys are even remotely connected to us. I only thought it was interesting that these young people will one day be like us. That's all."

"I see. Well, what is this generation before us like? Do they take more or less pleasure in their bodies.?"

"Oh, more. Defintely, more. Don't you remember me reading to you about that some time ago?" she asked.

"Of course, dear, I must have forgotten."

Doctor Castillo's wife placed her hand upon his chest, rubbing circles on it with her palm. It was one of their signals, developed over the course of the twelve years of their marriage, that if he wanted to, they could make love. Susan had worried about having satisfying sex in her marriage. Over the years, she had read, studied, fantasized and practiced until she was expert in satisfying him. The fact that the wonderful sex she read about occurred over longer intervals seemed normal to her. She was more interested in sex than he but she balanced her desires according to his needs.

Doctor Castillo was tired and the thought of sex seemed dishonest to

58

him. He placed his hand over hers, covering its smallness. Susan rolled over on her side, raising herself on an elbow, bringing her face up to his. They kissed. Castillo brought her hand, still inside his own, up to his face, kissing her fingertips.

"Tell me," he said, "is it true you get horny reading those sex surveys and that instructional crap in your magazines?" He smiled at his wife.

"Not especially. Well, sometimes. I just think it is important to understand that sex is necessary in a marriage. Besides, I saw Ben Robinson mowing his lawn today in his cut-offs. That made me horny."

"Then, why not have an affair with him," he said, irritably.

"Oh, silly, I was just teasing you," she said. Susan brushed Castillo's hair back with her fingers. She looked into his eyes, her face gentle and loving.

"I'm sorry," said Doctor Castillo. "I had a terrible day today. Nothing seemed to go very well."

Susan Castillo placed her face on his chest, kissing, nibbling on one of his nipples. She pulled on the hairs sprouting there with her teeth.

"No need to apologize, doctor," she said. "It happens. Sorry is for other people, not us. I will always be here for you."

Susan Castillo moved closer to her husband and began to rub her pelvis against his kneecap. Her movements became rough and pleading, more urgent, her nails digging into his shoulder flesh. Her mouth moved upward from his nipples, her lips swallowing his neck flesh, her tongue drawing insistent designs on the wetness she left.

Susan's hand slid up the inside of Castillo's thigh, pinching the softness of it, coming to rest on the underside of his testicles. With the other hand, as she arched her back, she lifted her nightgown. Her belly touched his ribcage and he felt her warm breasts on his chest, the hardness of her nipples. A low, urgent groan escaped her throat as her mouth covered his, tongue slithering past his own tongue, sliding in and out. She pulled on his testicles., mashing them roughly against his pelvis, before sliding her palm over his penis. Susan pressed the limp penis against Castillo's belly, rolling it to and fro. She then brought her fingers around it, gripping the penis tightly, sliding the slackened flesh up and down. Her pelvis pressed and relaxed against his kneecap, keeping time with the movements of her hand.

Doctor Castillo, gently, with a sad, pained, expression on his face, pushed his wife away.

"It's no good right now, dear," he said.

"I've looked forward to this all day, darling," she said.

"I'm sorry, I can't. I wouldn't be any good. Here," he said, turning on his side, "lie on your back."

Susan Castillo lay on her side, lifting her knees a few inches above the bed. Quickly, she bunched the nightgown around her neck and lowered her hands to her breasts. She squeezed them, pinching the nipples as though she were picking up butterflies by the wings. She spread her hands, pressing them against her chest, swirling the breasts round and round as though she were kneading bread. Castillo, resting on his elbow, placed a flat hand on her stomach, his fingers spread wide apart. Susan moaned with her mouth closed and made a twisting motion with her entire body. Castillo moved his hand down her waist, past her belly button, stopping at the lacy rim of her bikini underwear where her pubic hair started to sprout through the spiderweb of the lace. He kept his hand there, rubbing in a circular motion, now on the material, now sliding underneath it. Susan's knees rose higher, spreading wider apart as they came up.

The movement of Susan's hands on her breasts was harsher now, rough, almost violent. Her moans became more chaotic, as if coming from far away, deep within, and bottling up at the top of her lungs, unable to escape all at once. Doctor Castillo's hand moved along the smooth, silken material of her underwear. His fingers made a slow, upward, spider-like movement before coming together in a scoop which drew up from his wrist and pressed tightly against the moist softness of the silk. Susan arched her back upwards as if trying to bend her body in two, her knees drawing up higher and wider apart, until her heels left the bed altogether. She moaned again, a long painful sound followed by short, successive ones. He slid two fingers underneath the crotch of the panties. He felt them slide effortlessly into the silky wet, his forefinger plunging, being swallowed.

"Oh, yes, yes!" said Susan.

Castillo made in and out, penis-like, movements with his forefinger. He imitated his own sexual movements, sliding in slowly, drawing out quickly, then pumping with quick, short, strokes. He stopped momentarily, withdrawing his finger. Susan trembled and shook as he did so. He took his hand away from the crotch of her underwear, bringing it around and then sliding it down past the waistband, his first three fingers forking their way down the pubic hair, the middle one shoving deep into her, the fingers on either side of it pressing, pushing, sliding, shoving, rubbing, until the juncture of her legs was soft and silky in the foam of the lather he worked up from her insides.

Susan Castillo's hands suddenly sprang from her breasts straight up into the air. She uttered a quick, feverish, ooh-ooh, shoving a thumb into her mouth. She grabbed Castillo's now erect penis with her other hand. She squeezed it to the point where it hurt, but he did nothing to let her know. The small of her back curved and went into the air, relaxed, collapsed, fell back on the mattress, and then shot up again. Each time, her knees came up almost to her chest and the grip of her hand on his penis became tighter.

With the cry of someone wounded, followed by a long sigh expelling slowly the compressed air of release, Susan Castillo orgasmed. Her body tensed, stiffened, she became small in size, the insides of her body gripping Castillo's forefinger as if to drain from it juices it did not have. As Castillo withdrew his finger, she shook a few more times. She took his wrist and pressed the palm of his hand against her pelvis bone.

Doctor Castillo relaxed, lying on his back once again. She turned over, draping the length of her body over his, kissing his face, finally resting with it against his neck, her cheek against his shoulder. He kissed her forehead, tossing her hair. Neither of them said anything for a long moment.

Susan, as if waking from a long night of dreamless, satisfying sleep, lowered her torso down Castillo's body. She moved away from him, coming to rest on the toes of her feet and on her knees. Castillo remained motionless, his eyes closed, his breathing deep and regular. Susan untied the string to his pajamas, pulling them down over his thighs. Castillo rolled from side to side to help her. She twirled her thumb over the glans of his penis, spreading a crystal drop of fluid over the thick tip as though it were a coat of paint. She changed position so that her face came to rest over his belly button. She lifted a leg, straddling it over his. Her face was above his stomach, her tongue darted in and out of his belly button; her breasts swung gently, brushing the down on his legs. All the while, she kept lowering the pajama bottoms along his legs. Castillo kicked one pajama leg away from his foot when Susan could not do so without stopping the licking of his belly.

The erection Castillo had managed during the excitement of his wife's orgasm was gone. Susan's manipulations could do nothing. When she took the limp penis into her mouth, her tongue flicking at a furious pace, nothing happened. Castillo tried. He flexed his sphincter, he clenched his fists, he conjured up every erotic thought involving both his wife and other women. He desperately wanted to orgasm in her mouth because he knew it would please her. Yet, he could do nothing about it. After she tried for some minutes, Castillo sat up on the bed. The suddenness of his movement pushed Susan's face between his testicles and the mattress, his limp penis coming to rest on its side across her nose.

"I'm sorry, dear, I can't. Not tonight." He said.

"I was doing it for you," she said, "you didn't have to do anything."

"I know," said Doctor Castillo. "Good night."

With his free foot he lowered the remainder of the pajama bottom until he could kick it away. Castillo covered his nakedness up to the middle of his pajama top with the blanket of flower designs. Susan smoothed her nightgown so it covered her upper thighs. Both of them rolled over, facing opposite sides, and began the pretense of sleep. Susan was tense, worried; she dug her fingernails into her palms. Doctor Castillo lay still, listening to the wind and the rain outside.

Doctor Castillo was just entering that thin layer of sleep where he thought he was still awake. The wind, the pale-green light of the streetlamps coming in through the window, the sudden flashes of lightning, all appeared to him as through a grey veil.

Then it happened.

There was a loud crack of thunder and the bedroom filled up with lightning as though a flash fire had mushroomed in the street. The hundred-year-old oak tree, which the builder had spared as a way to get a higher price for the house, came crashing through the roof. First there was a loud, painful, wrenching sound as the upper part of the tree tore from the trunk. The tear and the sound of it were slow, hesitant. Then, louder, higher-pitched, as the thick upper branch became free. A sharp, pointed elbow, which started its growth in another century, came crashing through the roof. As it did so, the ceiling buckled and the Spanish-style beams cracked and fell, coming to rest at an angle against the wall. The rupture in the roof widened. The weight of the branch forced its way through the roof and the ceiling, its spindly, spider-leg limbs crashing on the bed.

Susan Castillo awoke at the first sound of the tree crashing against the roof. In their unsteady and nervous sleep, the bedclothes had been kicked aside and finally off the bed by both Castillo and his wife. Susan screamed. They were showered by chunks of plaster, chalk dust and beam splinters. Castillo was awake now. Before the two of them could get out of bed and run to safety, another beam broke loose, groaning for a moment, then falling parallel to the bed, smashing the bedtable at Susan's side. The remainder of the branch edged through the ruptured space, pinning Susan to the mattress. Doctor Castillo rolled over the side of the bed, crawling along the carpeted floor until he cringed safely in a far corner of the room. Susan lay still, unable to move without scratching more of legs and face.

Then it was quiet. The gusting of the wind was far away. Castillo could see only black through the hole in the roof. There was no other sound to be heard, except for Susan's soft crying. She inched slowly and painfully to Castillo's side of the bed. Scratched and bloody, she slid into a lump on the floor. All around them were bits and dust of plaster, sheetrock, asbestos shingles, splinters from the ruptured beams and the grotesque branch. The window glass had not cracked or exploded under the pressure. It had simply crumbled, falling outside the house.

Doctor Castillo, after what seemed a long time, moved away from the corner to help his wife. As he moved, spindly branches tickled and crawled over his face. On his hands and knees, he made his way to where Susan lay on his side of the floor. In the darkness, he felt the wet of blood from a deep scratch just above her hairline and another on her shoulder. He touched her, feeling for something broken. She whimpered and he could not bring himself to ask how badly she was hurt. The gouging branch had ripped the strap of her nightgown, leaving her right breast exposed, moist with her blood. As he ran his hand over it, Doctor Castillo became aroused. For a moment he wished he were not as frightened as he was. He wished he could move her to the safe corner where he had been and there make love to her. He touched her cheek.

"I think it's over. Come on," he said.

Susan Castillo continued crying in a barely audible way. Castillo pulled a blanket from the rubble in front of the bed, shaking it as best he could. He placed it around Susan's shoulders.

"Let's go downstairs," he said. "We both need a drink."

Castillo helped her up. He began to move with her, clearing or brushing aside the branches in front of them, cautioning her to be careful where she stepped. At the door of the bedroom, as he opened it, he relaxed a little, a feeling of relief easing the tension. He tightened his arm around her, bringing her closer to him in a protective gesture. They made their way cautiously down the stairs in the darkness. Castillo left Susan at the foot of the stairs and asked her not to move. He hurried to the children's bedroom behind the stairs, to the side of the living room. Both girls, one six and the other eight, were sound asleep in their twin beds. The rupture upstairs had not disturbed them. They slept soundly. He closed the door quietly.

He made his way in the dark to the picture window and pulled the drapes. By the light of the streetlamp he made drinks, Wild Turkey for her, scotch for himself. Susan Castillo remained at the foot of the stairs where he left her.

"Here," he said, "drink this. It'll make you feel better."

"We could have died up there," she said without emotion.

"We didn't. That's the important thing."

They stood in the gray dark, watching each other as shadows in the distance. They sipped their drinks in silence for a few minutes.

"Let's go outside. See how everybody else made out. We'll clean you up later. Come, the cold air will do you good."

Outside, there was a chill, funeral quiet along the curving ribbon of street. Doctor Castillo and Susan stood on the tile entrance to their home. Susan's bare feet were cold, but she felt warm with the whiskey. As they stood there, a yellow patch of light came on in a house far away from them. Nothing stirred. Everything was quiet and the subdivision, after the storm, was normal.

"I guess we can sleep in the guest bedroom," said Doctor Castillo.

"I don't think I can sleep right now, dear," said Susan.

"The danger is over," he said, trying to sound reassuring. "The wind is gone, the worst of it was our house from the look of things. There is no need to stay awake."

"I can't get over being so scared. I've never been so terrified of anything in all my life. We could have been killed. For a moment there I thought we would."

"That's absurd!" he said, a little angered. "Let's go back inside. I'll clean up your scratches, you can take a shower, and it'll be all over. The worst of it is a hole in our roof."

"I don't want to go inside. I don't believe you," she said in a desperate voice. "There are a lot of things which, if only slightly different, just that much, could have resulted in either or both of us dying. Don't you see? Just inches! That is what scares me."

Doctor Castillo adopted a smug tone. "You're over-reacting, of course."

"Am I? I only wish I were. Doesn't what happened tonight make you think about things?" she asked. "Don't you realize how close it came to it being all over for us? What about the children?"

"It doesn't do any good to talk like this, Susan. To what purpose? We escaped disaster. We were fortunate. Why place such a dire character on it? Tomorrow will be a new day and we will soon forget it. We have to go on living, we can't dwell on this."

"I don't know. I feel I have to think about it. It won't go away by simply willing it away. It isn't that easy. There are things we can't ignore no matter how hard we try. I have this feeling that I have to know a few things first."

"Thinking about it too much will only make it worse, Susan. We shouldn't think too much about things. It's not good. Makes us paranoid or something, it seems to me."

"Maybe at this stage of my life I could use a little paranoia, Doctor. I've always been so stable. You've always provided everything. I've needed nothing. Maybe you're right. Maybe I shouldn't think about things. I should just accept them as they are. I should be grateful and appreciate what I have, what you've given me."

Castillo came closer to his wife. He placed his arm around her shoulders, patting her head. Tears mixed with the blood on her cheek, staining his pajama top. He turned her toward the door.

"Come on," he said gently, "let's go inside now. I'll clean you up."

Inside the bathroom, Doctor Castillo cleaned and dressed Susan's scratches. he placed a bandage on her shoulder scratch. He then had her remove the soiled and ripped nightgown, stooping at her side to gather the underwear which crumbled on the floor. He tossed it in the wastebasket. Taking her by the arm, he led her into the shower, starting the water for her before closing the sliding glass door. Castillo remained in the bathroom until he saw Susan begin to move her arms under the shower. He left the bathroom door open as he went into the kitchen to put on a pot of coffee. He sat at the breakfast nook, finishing his drink, deciding against having another. It was not long before Susan came in wearing one of his old robes which they kept in the downstairs bathroom closet for guests. Susan poured a cup of coffee for herself and sat across from him. Castillo reached over and patted her hand.

"There, there," he said softly, "don't worry too much about it. Of course, it was a shock, but we were lucky. Think about that, how lucky we are. We should stress the luck of it and nothing more."

Susan was not convinced. There was a pained expression on her face.

"There must be more to this than luck," she said. "If it is only luck and nothing more, then there is something desperately wrong with all of this."

"What do you mean by that?" said Castillo in a tone he usually reserved for his patients.

"I mean, we have planned for our lives so fucking carefully. From the time you were in school until the children were born, we have planned. The children were planned down to the month they were to be born. We have prepared for every possibility, every accident, every eventuality. Everything

64

has gone according to plan for us."

"You're exaggerating, Susan."

"Am I? Things like this are not supposed to happen. Not to us they're not supposed to happen. We even bought the house in this area precisely because something like tonight is not supposed to happen. Now it has happened and there must be something wrong with our planning. That is what we have to think about."

"Now, now. What's all this about planning? You're just upset. Are there any of those valiums left from the time I sprained my ankle? Maybe you ought to take one. Make you feel better."

"Stop talking down to me," she said angrily.

"All right. I'm sorry. But, remember, you're just upset. I can understand that. I think you need to be alone just now. Obviously, whatever I say will only serve to upset you all the more. I am going to the guest bedroom. You can join me there if you wish. If not, just in case, I'll put some blankets by the sofa for you."

Doctor Castillo stood up, looked at Susan, trying to maintain a loving face. She stared into her coffee cup, her wet blonde hair pressed against her scalp. He brushed her shoulder with his fingertips as he walked by. Susan Castillo lifted her head to stare at the giraffe growth charts for the girls tacked side by side on the wall.

II

When Doctor Castillo awoke the following morning, his wife had gone. He awoke at his usual time as though nothing had happened the night before. When he came out of the guest bedroom, he expected to see Susan asleep on the sofa, but she was not there. Rubbing the sleep from his eyes, he quietly opened the door to the children's bedroom, hoping to find her there. She was not. Dorothy, the eldest, opened her eyes as she heard him at the door. "Daddy," she said, and fell asleep again. The girls would not have to be up for yet another hour.

In the kitchen he found the remains of the pot of coffee he had made. Beside the half-empty pot, he found the bottle of Wild Turkey from which she apparently had one more drink. Her coffee cup had been emptied and rinsed and lay in the sink. Castillo made a fresh pot of coffee. As usual, without thinking, he made enough for the two of them. Dragging his feet in his morning stiffness, he took the bottle of whiskey and replaced it on the neat row of bottles over the bar. As was his custom, he went upstairs to bathe. All of his toilet articles were carefully arranged on the right side of the sink, his wife's on the left. The bedroom, he noticed in a quick glimpse, was a mess, but the bathroom had been spared. He showered quickly, not unduly worried about his wife's disappearance. He dressed in his suit and draped his necktie over his shoulder, and returned to the kitchen.

With his coffee steaming under his face, he sat at the breakfast table. He began to dial the telephone numbers of neighbors friendly with Susan. He could not remember all of their names, so he dialed every number with the same three-digit prefix as theirs which he found in her address book. As it was almost time for the children to be up and getting ready for the school bus, Doctor Castillo began to worry about her absence. He reasoned she had been too upset to sleep in the house and had probably gone down the street to stay with a neighbor for the night. He realized it was a perfectly normal reaction to such an accident. He continued dialing the telephone numbers, confident of finding her. However, the answer was the same at each place he called. They had not seen her.

Although the upstairs of his house now had a hole in it from which he could stare straight into the heavens, Doctor Castillo did not feel it was sufficient to interfere with his daily routine. Susan's disappearance similarly was not a matter of great concern. Surely, he thought, she had overslept some place, perhaps she'd gone to a motel nearby. Or, maybe she was out for a long drive to clear her mind. He would go to work where certainly she would call him by mid-morning, as she had never been one to sleep late or to be out of touch with him for too long. He made breakfast for the children, helped them dress and had them ready to put on the school bus when it came. He gathered his papers from the night before that were still lying on the coffee table. Doctor Castillo stuffed them into his briefcase and left for work.

Driving in the heavy stop-and-go traffic toward the center of Houston, Castillo planned his day. He would have his receptionist cancel at least one appointment to permit him to call his insurance adjuster. The adjuster would put him in touch with a reputable contractor who would make his home whole again. The storm damage was really a minor annoyance, he thought to himself, but he was secure in the knowledge that he was well insured. In the matter of Susan, there was not much to worry about. Susan was a serene, intelligent, level-headed woman, who would ordinarily not be disturbed by the aberration of the previous night. It had all been so sudden and he too admitted to himself that he had been more than a little afraid in the situation. He would forgive her for leaving, after all, she needed to be away from the scene of her fright just to clear her mind. In any case, he was sure she would be home when he returned that afternoon. He smiled and was glad he was going to be able to reassure her that the damage to their home would soon be repaired and of course everything would be back in fine order once again.

Doctor Castillo's day went according to his impromptu plan, with the exception that when he returned home, his wife was not there. He found the children home from school. They had attempted to prepare their own after-school snack and had made a mess in the kitchen which they made only worse by trying to clean it up. They were watching television, something his Susan would not ordinarily permit. Castillo felt that under the circumstances maybe it was necessary for an exception to be made in the daily routine followed by the girls. He made himself a glass of iced tea and joined them in the living room. The girls lay on the carpet watching Popeye. He called his brother-in-law and asked if they had seen Susan. Her sister answered and said they had not. She added that she had been trying to reach her all day. Susan's parents were flying in from St. Louis and they had to plan something for them. She was supposed to meet Susan that day at the mall. It was not like Susan to completely ignore or forget an appointment.

Castillo's brother-in-law came on the line to catalogue the expenses for the forthcoming visit. He listened for as long as he could and then interrupted him. They had not been particularly close and no doubt her sister and he would suspect Susan had left him. He assured them he would remind Susan and thanked them. Castillo knew they had always disliked him. He slumped on the sofa, sipping his tea. He was beginning to worry. This was not at all like

Susan. His body shook as he made his decision.

Castillo called the police to inform them his wife was missing. While the voice to whom he spoke at the police station sounded sympathetic, there was something of a smirk in the way certain formulaic questions were asked. It was as if they knew she was probably shacked up somewhere and Castillo was simply going through the motion of a missing person's report to further compound her guilt when she returned. Castillo felt like telling the voice that Susan was not like that at all. He could not interrupt, though, because in front of the smirk there was the efficient roll of questions.

After filing the report with the police, he started calling the hospitals in the area. They were of no help, refusing to give him any information, even after he informed them he was a doctor. He called the police again to ask if they might clear a way for him to conduct his own investigation of the hospitals. He was told not to worry as calling the hospitals was one of their first steps in attempting to locate a missing person.

Susan still did not come home. No trace of her could be found. A policeman went to Castillo's office and asked the same questions the voice on the telephone had asked. Castillo objected. The procedure seemed demeaning to him. The policeman told him that sometimes by asking the same questions over and over again, a person remembers things he could not say the first time around. Castillo nodded, but remained irritated at the measured, complacent attitude of the police. Their assurances that she would turn up sounded hollow and just a little bit lascivious. They might be humoring him.

The days following Susan's disappearance became weeks. It was not long before there returned to the Castillo household the dull similarity of each day. Castillo got into the habit of calling the police each Friday afternoon, just before leaving work, to ask for news of his wife and to receive the same update on the investigation into her disappearance. He knew it was unlikely that they were vigorously searching for her. Still, he called and each time the report was the same, nothing new on the case. He would politely thank whomever he talked to and prepared as usual to end the week at his office.

Doctor Castillo had arranged for his neighbors to take care of his children during the week, as he felt they needed adult supervision. He stopped going for drinks after work with his colleagues to hurry home in the traffic to be with the girls. He became accustomed to caring for them, attempting to do so in the same way he had seen Susan do. He wanted more than anything to have everything as normal as possible for them. He fed them at the same time each day, bathed them at the same time and put them to bed at the same time.

During the first few days following Susan's absence, the girls had cried and over and over asked for their mother. He patiently assured them Susan had gone on a trip and would soon be back. Angered, more at her than at him, they told him she could not have gone without saying goodbye to them. He lied and said she left on a sudden emergency and had not wanted to wake them. The girls did not try to understand more than the fact of her absence.

After the first month or so, they did not ask as often for her or about her.

Castillo was dressed for work except that he wore an apron. He finished with the last pancake and put the stack on the table. He removed the apron. He sat with the girls at the table.

"How many pancakes do you want?" he asked the eldest.

"I'm not hungry," she answered sadly.

There was a brief silence before the youngest spoke.

"She was crying in her bed last night."

"You said you wouldn't tell."

"Are you going to tell him?"

"Tell me what."

"Mommy is dead."

"How do you know."

"I know. She's not coming back."

"And that means she's dead?"

"Yes."

Castillo felt his wife's absence only a little longer than did the children. His notice of her absence had more to do with rearranging his habits and the routine of each of his days. Emotionally, he felt little. There had not been, certainly beyond the first few years of their marriage, a passionate love between them. It was more of a matter-of-fact relationship, each bound to the other in a way that neither of them questioned. If he missed her it was only when one of the children upset a bowl of something or other and he had to clean it up. His sex drive had not been particularly active for many years and he seldom thought about their sex.

He learned to be a good father and mother to the girls. At first, it was new, pleasing and interesting for him. He had never been close to the girls before. Later, when it became habitual, he took no further notice of it, falling gracefully into the routine of it, accepting everything as an unavoidable duty, much the same as going to work. His initial doubts and fears about his ability to care for the children dissipated when he saw that they were not behaving noticeably different than when Susan assumed most of the responsibility for them. Doctor Castillo settled into the comfortable, secure life of a widower or divorcee, a single parent.

His neighbors, whom he had previously seen as caricatures across the driveway, were kind and charitable. He came to know them better and to like them because of it. They acted as though they understood what he was going through and took every opportunity to help him with a meal or an evening away from home or they offered to take the children to give him a weekend away. Castillo was grateful to them and he never missed a chance to indicate he had accepted the new realities of his situation, giving them to understand as well as he could that he was quite accustomed to his life and felt comfortable. Castillo assured them and himself that his life was once again complete. He did not lack for anything.

The months passed and without too much further trouble they became years. Doctor Castillo aged somewhat, going into his forties placidly, his hair turning the color of lead. His medical practice flourished and he became wealthier with each day, from the fees he charged his patients and from the investments his lawyer made for him.

The girls grew despite his efforts to keep them as children forever. He arbitrated their squabbles and they seemed to respect his judgments. Almost too quickly they were at an age where they insisted upon private rooms. He realized the house was too small and thought it was time to move to a larger one in a better section of the city. He discussed the matter with his lawyer and his accountant and, between the three of them, decided it would be best all around to move. It would be very good for the girls, of course, but, also, his tax situation would improve. He sold the house, with the roof long since repaired, and bought another one in a more fashionable neighborhood, nearer to downtown and to his office. He enrolled the girls, over their protestations, in a convent school where the discipline was strict and where they could meet and make friends with young ladies as wealthy as they.

The girls brought their problems to him. He had worried about them growing to adulthood without a mother, but thus far they were not troublesome. The problems they brought to him were trivial, he knew, but he acted as though everything important to them was important to him. He wanted them to confide in him and to know he would always help. He took them on trips, indulged most of their whims, became stern infrequently and then made sure they understood his reasons. As the girls grew and could be left alone without a sitter, he renewed his social life, a better and more active one than before when it was limited by the hours he had to spend establishing his practice.

His sex drive returned and he gave it free rein for a certain period. There was plenty of opportunity for affairs in his new neighborhood so long as he was discreet about it. Among his new friends and acquaintances, there was even more. He was pleased that women found him attractive and sexually desirable. He was pleased as well that the women he met were more relaxed and less demanding in their relationships. He entered into a number of liaisons of brief duration, more to buttress his self-image than to satisfy any essential need. After a year or two of the casual affairs he half-heartedly had, he settled upon a relationship with his secretary. She was nearly his age, divorced, with one child. For her, it was the need for male adult companionship. For him, it was a desperate need for some degree of permanence. The casual affairs he had had distorted his image of female companionship. The affair he began with his secretary promised to bring him something he had not known he needed. Not long after their affair started, Castillo realized she was not the woman to share the remainder of his life. Susan remained his standard for comparison, as she was the only woman he had ever really known. The image of her kept interfering in the way he saw his secretary. The secretary, for her part, accepted their relationship as an affair and did not choose to expect more than that.

Doctor Castillo and his secretary took Thursday afternoons off, going either to a motel nearby or to Galveston for a walk on the beach and an afternoon of lovemaking. She could not bring herself to go to bed with him in her home and neither could he make love to her in his. She worried what her son would think and he knew the girls were at an age where an open affair might make them question his morality.

When he discovered his secretary had her mother in a nursing home an hour's drive southwest of Houston, he insisted she take Friday afternoons off to go see her. He made sure he gave her flowers at least once each month and presented her with a generous gift on her birthday and at Christmas, all this in addition to her bonus. He felt the latter was a professional obligation and not a personal one. They had agreed, one afternoon as they lay in bed, that marriage was out of the question for them, but that the relationship ought to continue so long as it satisfied both of them. It was he who insisted upon it more than she. Nevertheless, she accepted what he considered a condition without resistance. He was bothered by it somewhat, afraid he took advantage of her. These doubts soon disappeared and the relationship continued without further mention of it. He became habituated to it and as far as he could see into his future, everything was perfectly arranged.

Doctor Castillo felt he could not ask for more than he had himself established. In a sense, after suffering the dislocation of losing his wife, Castillo had restored the essential elements to his life, things to which Susan had been only an ornament. He had rearranged everything and now there was nothing out of place. The new order in his life could not include Susan. He found he would think of Susan for several days at a stretch and then he would go months without giving her a thought. There was no longer any room for her in his life or in the lives of his children.

On a Thursday morning, almost ten years to the day that Susan left, Doctor Castillo received his mail from the secretary. Her make-up was more carefully applied and her clothing more cheerful in anticipation of their afternoon together. As was routine, the personal mail was on top. Castillo read his personal mail first as it usually involved correspondence from colleagues in other parts of the country. Occasionally, there was something concerning his investments. The business letters were already opened by his secretary. Between them, they had devised a code by which he could tell which of them he needed to read right away and which were the inevitable flotsam of the professional community.

He picked up an envelope whose address was obviously scrawled in the stereotypical doctor's hand. It was illegible to the point where he wondered how it had reached him at all. He opened it, unhurriedly, between sips of his coffee. Inside was a note scribbled on note paper from a hotel in Detroit. It read:

> Dr. Castillo, I met you and your wife a long time ago. I've heard she disappeared and you were looking for her. I saw her yesterday. She said her

name is Dorothy Cummings. There is a Dr. Cummings who lives at 411 West Drew Drive, in Memphis, Tenn. Don't know if you're still looking, but I thought you might want to know.

Absent-mindedly, Doctor Castillo went through the remainder of his mail. He chose to set aside the note and not think about it until he could be sure of his response. For the rest of the morning, he saw his patients and conducted his usual office routine. At noon, he pushed the button on the intercom to tell the receptionist he was leaving. He met his secretary, who arrived separately, at Harrigan's for lunch. From there, they went to a motel on the Southwest Freeway. Once inside the room, Castillo kicked his shoes away and lay on the bed fully-clothed. The secretary undressed to her underwear. Before she joined him on the bed, she noticed him staring into the mirror hanging on the wall opposite the bed. There was a strange look on his face.

"Is anything wrong?" she asked.

Castillo started to say something, thought better of it and left his mouth open. He turned from the mirror to look at her, closing his mouth after some moments. He seemed unable to look at her, as if it pained him.

"Put your clothes on," he ordered.

The secretary picked her clothes up, holding the bundle against her chest. She would not take her eyes off him. She advanced hesitatingly to the bed, kneeling on it. She touched his shoulder.

"There is something wrong, isn't there?"

Castillo, with a look of disgust, handed her the note. She read it, finishing with a blank look on her face. She put it on the bed between them.

"What are you going to do?" she asked.

"I don't know yet," he said almost too somberly.

"You don't have to worry about me," she said. "We agreed neither of us would stand in the other's way."

"I'm not worried and that's not what I'm thinking about."

"If you're not worried, you have a funny way of showing it."

"I want to go to a movie. What do you say?"

After the movie, he drove back to the motel so she could pick up her car. She reminded him that they still had the use of the room, but Castillo gently begged off. He wanted to go home right away. Once home, he looked in on the girls. The younger was doing her homework and the eldest was reading. They asked if anything was the matter since he seldom came home so early on Thursday evenings. They knew what he did on these evenings but thought it better not to let him know.

Doctor Castillo made himself a drink and went upstairs to his bedroom. He lay on top of the bedspread, fully-clothed, determined to watch and enjoy early evening television. After several drinks, he admitted defeat. He put Vivaldi on the stereo and took out the note. He read it over and over again. He knew what he was going to do, but tried to resist. He was unwilling to admit his curiosity, that despite the years during which he had set aside all thoughts of his wife, there was still one thing he wanted to know. He finished an entire bottle of scotch that evening and did not come in for work the next day.

III

On Friday morning, Doctor Castillo's head ached and his body was numb. He awoke atop his bedspread wearing the same suit he wore the day before. The bottle of scotch whiskey was on the floor beside the bed. As he moved painfully, he heard the noise of the note paper. He picked it up to read again the name and address written upon it. The name was strange, someone he did not know. Only the address mattered to him. The numbers and words on the address possessed all the reality he wanted to care about. The name, Dorothy Cummings, had nothing to do with his wife. Only the address promised to deliver what, in his drunken condition, he had decided he needed to know. Maybe there was a Dorothy Cummings now, but she knew Susan Castillo, and that mattered. He would go to her.

Doctor Castillo finally appeared at his office during the early afternoon. When he entered, freshly showered and shaved, he told the receptionist to cancel the remainder of his appointments. She told him she already had. He was irritated that she could anticipate him so well but he controlled himself enough to tell her to cancel his appointments for Monday and Tuesday. He knew she needed an explanation and he told her before she asked that he had to go out of town unexpectedly and would be back to work on Wednesday. The receptionist, without looking up at him, jotted all of it down on her note pad.

Castillo went into his office and dropped listlessly into the chair behind his desk. He picked up the day's mail, shuffled it like a deck of cards, finally shoving all of it into his 'in' basket. His secretary had watched him come in but as he took no notice of her, she did not bother him. She waited a decent interval before coming in to see him. He had not planned to see her, having come to the office without purpose and without any sense of what he was doing. After she had been standing wordlessly in front of his desk for some time, quietly he told her to go home right away and take all of the following week off. She made a gesture as if to take a step forward. Thinking better of it, she turned and left the office without saying anything.

He was alone as he had never felt before in his office. He thought of calling Dorothy Cummings long distance. He was about to dial but he decided against it as he knew he could only resolve his doubts in a face-to-face meeting. He remained sitting behind the desk for a long while. He took a sip of the coffee the receptionist brought him but it had little taste and he let it get cold in front of him. He drummed his finger on the desktop, anxious to be elsewhere. Castillo stood up, jamming his hands into his pockets; he turned from side to side, unsure of which way to go, and finally he began to pace in circles around the desk.

Castillo, finding there was little he wanted to do, went home after having spent less than an hour at work. The eldest girl was home from her university classes. She was in the dining room, drinking a glass of milk, reading a thick book on economics. She looked up from her reading to say hello to him. When the youngest came home, she was surprised to find his car in the driveway. Before changing from her school uniform, she came into his bedroom to say hello to him. He beckoned her to come to him. He hugged her tightly. She smiled at him and left as quickly as she came in.

Doctor Castillo lay in bed staring at the ceiling, wondering how he would pass the hours until he could get a flight to Memphis on Monday morning, or Sunday night. He had decided shortly after reading the note to keep it from the children. The girls nevertheless discerned something was troubling him. After the youngest had changed from her uniform, and after the both of them had eaten a mid-afternoon sandwich, they came to him as in a delegation. They appeared worried about him and asked if something was wrong. They assumed something went wrong with his investments and that they were not as wealthy now as before. He rose to a sitting position on the edge of the bed, gathered both of them in his arms and thanked them for their concern. He assured them he was just overworked and tired and urged them to find something pleasant to do. As the girls were leaving the bedroom, he told them he would probably have to leave late Sunday or early Monday morning. He told them not to worry as he would be back by Wednesday. They smiled goodbyes at him.

Over the weekend, Doctor Castillo watched the endless succession of football games which he detested. On Saturday night, in a drunken stupor, he packed his bag. The girls, noting he had hardly been out of his room all weekend, brought him a sandwich on Sunday afternoon. He ate carelessly, not tasting whatever it was. The only time he dressed and came out of the bedroom had been to buy more whiskey on Saturday.

He was packed and ready to go on Monday. He awoke an hour before flight time, realizing as he did so that he was hungover and late. He showered quickly and dressed, grabbing his bag as he ran down the stairs. He heard the shower running in one of the girls' rooms upstairs, but decided against taking the time to say goodbye. The non-stop flight to Memphis left Intercontinental Airport at 8:30. He made it with not much time to spare.

When the plane arrived at the Memphis airport, the stewardess announced that the flight would continue on to New York. He wondered whether he ought not to crumble up the note he received and continue on to spend the week there, visiting friends, seeing shows, relaxing, trying to set aside feelings which he thought he could properly manage. Almost automatically, he de-planed with the rest of the Memphis passengers, unable to change the plans he had already made.

Outside the airport, there was a sudden chill to break the warmth inside the terminal. The sun was bright, but cold. He hailed a cab, taking the note out of his pocket to read the address to the driver as if embarrassed to let him know he had it memorized. It was late morning, nearly 11:30, when the cab stopped in front of the ranch-style house in a neatly-drawn subdivision not too different from the one he and Susan had once lived in. There was one large tree near the corner of the house, obviously left there by the contractor to raise the price of the house. Castillo was unsure of what he was to find, unable to imagine the sort of situation to which he would have to respond.

Doctor Castillo figured it would take some time for another cab to come out to pick him up. He gave the driver a twenty, more than twice the fare so far, and asked him to wait and to keep the meter running. No matter what, he told the driver emphatically, keep the meter running and wait. He felt he needed the security of being able to leave immediately if it became necessary.

He walked up the curving walkway to the door, partially obscured by some scrawny hedges. He rang the doorbell. Inside, very weakly, he heard the chimes of Big Ben. He waited for a long moment, anticipating everything, sure of nothing. Just as he was about to be convinced no one was at home, Susan Castillo opened the door.

"Mrs. Cummings?" he said, trying to sound sincere.

"I saw you through the peep hole. I didn't know whether to open it or not," she said.

"I wasn't sure I wanted you to open it," he said. "Maybe I would have preferred Mrs. Cummings to live here."

"I am Mrs. Cummings," she said. "How did you find me?"

"One of our former friends saw you at a convention in Detroit. He wrote to me."

"After all this time," she said. "Do you want to come in?"

"Yes. I want to know some things."

"We have neighbors, anyway. Howard and I have never had a bit of scandal."

"Howard. You're married again, is that it?"

"Yes. About seven years ago. Aren't you?"

"Yes. I'm still married. To you."

"Why? It would have been easy to divorce me."

"I didn't think I could do that to you."

"To me? What are you talking about? To me!"

"There has always been too much I've needed to know."

"I left. That's all."

"Our marriage was perfect until you left."

76

"I hope you weren't waiting for me to return. When I left, I knew there was no turning back. I made the one decision of my life, maybe the only one I could not turn back on."

Susan pointed to the couch for Castillo to sit. As he sat, she walked to an easy chair as far away from him as the arrangement of the furniture permitted. She stayed on her feet. He kept his silence. She began to speak awkwardly but her words were finally firm and sure.

"I have an entirely new life here. Very different from before. I have my children, my home, my husband. Everything is very different."

"You have children?" he asked, surprised.

"Yes, two. A boy and a girl."

"What about the children we had? Ever think about them?"

"Yes, I do. More than I like to admit. I'm sure they think I'm dead by now, or something. No doubt they have forgotten me; in any case, they don't need me. It's best this way. I now have children that I am raising differently. They are happy with me and I am happy with them. Their father is nothing like you."

"What does he do?"

"He's a doctor."

Castillo leaned forward on the couch. "From everything I see here and from everything you tell me, there doesn't seem to be much difference from the life you were leading with me. You say it is very different, but there are more similarities than differences. Tell me what is different. Tell me why it is so important for you to continue this while not admitting that what we had was exactly the same."

"You could never understand any of this. That's a difference. This is not the same in any way. This is nothing like anything we had. I only came to know the emptiness of what we had when the tree fell through our bedroom. I wanted desperately to talk to you about it. You kept patting me on the head as though I was your pet dog or something. You went to bed in the guest bedroom if I recall correctly. With no one else there, I sat for a long time, talking it over with myself. It was something new for me and I liked it. I drank more coffee and made my decision. Simple as that. I got in the car and drove away."

"Just like that, you decided to leave your home and family."

"No, it didn't happen that way at all. I needed to be out of that house, that's all. For a time. I intended to drive to New York to visit some friends. Just for a few days, maybe weeks, however long I felt I needed. Then, I was planning to come back. I thought some time away would make me stronger."

"You never came back."

"On the way, my car broke down here in Memphis. I had no money, except for a charge card. My first thought was to call you immediately. But that was exactly what I was expected to do. Somehow, for once, I did not want to be obligated to you. I had to do this for myself. The trip was entirely for me. I didn't even bring my checkbook . . ."

"How did you expect to get along?"

"I don't know. To have gotten you involved in my trip meant that you approved of it. Had I asked you, you would have said yes. I didn't want that."

"It seems foolish to me, nonetheless."

"Of course, it does. There was more going on than I realized at the time. It was a kind of omen here in Memphis. At least, I think so. By the time the car was fixed, two days later, I had rented an apartment and taken a job. I couldn't have planned it that way. It just happened and it was fine with me. I could have gone back then. I felt I had proved my point. I could do something on my own."

"In coming back you didn't think I would appreciate the point you made."

"No. I was not thinking of you at all. My landlady was so trusting—she trusted *mè*. She said I was sweet and she would let me have the apartment even though I had no money. The garage was the same way. I had to stay and work so I could pay them. After a couple of months, I made enough money for the car repairs and to catch up on the rent for the apartment. It felt marvelous. Not once in my life had I felt so free and independent. I did not have to rely on anyone for my keep."

"That's not what marriage is all about."

"I know it isn't. Memphis, my Memphis, is not like marriage either. I decided to stay here as long as I needed to feel myself again. Before too long, I began to meet different people, quite different from those in our neighborhood and all those pasty wives of your associates. All the people I met here were so very different from those I knew when I was married to you. For me, they were very exciting. I was glad to be with them. I saw more clearly than ever in my life that I had led the wrong life all along. To me, it was your life I led, not mine. I needed my own life and this was the life I was meant to lead. My own."

"It seems to me that this is nothing more than the wish fulfillment of the sexual fantasies you developed from reading all those women's magazines."

"Maybe so, Doctor Castillo, maybe so."

"You sound so formal."

"When you try to be professional you only succeed in being patronizing."

"Still, what you've told me so far sounds very adolescent."

"I don't think so. Just the opposite, in fact. Adolescence was marriage to you. I had no need to grow up. Here in Memphis, I am away from the dull sameness I knew with you. Even our children, God bless them, were ordinary to me. So well-behaved, their lives so planned. Poor kids, they have no life except what we planned for them. Let me guess, one of them is now a student at Rice. My children now do not have their futures as well-planned. I have made sure that there is something there for them to take advantage of. Howard is putting money away for them to go to college, an insurance policy. You're so successful you wouldn't know about that. These kids don't have to go to college, though."

"I never believed our girls would have to go to college."

"I knew you would say you didn't believe that. But there was never any other way for them to go. There was never an alternative."

"What's the alternative now?"

"None. That's the point of it. They can go or not, as they choose. That has given new meaning to my life. That's why I know I have found freedom here. I am not what I was. I don't feel confined or constrained in anything. Here, with Howard and my children, I can still do as I wish. It's all so different. I'm sure you'll never understand. That's the pity of it. That's the difference of it."

"I thnk I made a mistake in coming here," said Doctor Castillo.

"You seem to have grown a little. I can see that. I think it's a good sign. I never expected you to understand any of it, which is why I've kept my silence. It was better for you to not know. I wanted to be free. I took nothing but a car and the little cash in my purse. I've never asked for more than that. If my freedom was to be my own, I had to do it myself. Even a divorce would have left me feeling still obligated to you. I am and have been free. I hope you can understand that. If you've come here with the intention of understanding, then you've changed a little. I hope you won't be a bastard and you won't interfere with what I have here. I want to continue it."

"What about our children, the children you had with me. What shall I tell them about their mother?"

"Tell them anything you like," she said, turning her face away from his. After a moment, she turned to look at him again. Her voice quivered some. "No, don't do that. I think they will understand, in time. I don't think this is the time to tell them anything. Tell them nothing. I'm sure you invented something that places me between the living and the dead for them. What's wrong with continuing the pretense until they can understand the truth?

"I'm not sure I will ever understand the truth of all of this."

"The truth of it all is for them to decide. The time is past when you can decide it for them. Or me. I realized it when the tree fell on the house. I found I needed more of the truth than what you gave me. It has to be that way for our daughters. They are teenagers now, barely flirting with what can be true. Eventually they will be able to decide, if you leave them alone. Whether you want to or not, it's a choice for them to make. I'm sure when you tell them everything, and I know you will, you will try to sway them toward something you feel out of your bitterness to be the truth."

"I don't feel bitter toward you, I don't."

"You're here, aren't you? Why did you come? Anyway. The girls will listen to you out of respect and love because you raised them as mother and father. Only, they won't believe you altogether. It will not be disrespectful of them when they reject your version of the truth. They will side with me even though they no longer know me or love me. They will be women then and there is a bond between women that goes beyond that of mother and daughter.

It is at this level that they will understand me. They may hate me as a parent and that too is understandable. The important thing is that they understand me as a woman. That is all I ask."

"I have never heard so much garbage in all my life. The fact you refuse to recognize is that you turned your back on a perfectly satisfactory and successful marriage. You cannot pretend otherwise, you cannot evade that truth. I cannot forgive you for destroying that and I don't know if I'm willing to let you forget it."

"It is neither for you to forgive nor forget. I want nothing, I expect nothing. I left your life, my living through you, and now I have remade myself according to what I feel I must be. You cannot forgive me because there is nothing for you to forgive. You did not lose anything, I did not take anything from you. It was always your life. I was nothing more than an appendage to it. I doubt if you ever noticed me beyond being someone who was always there. When I left, you lost nothing essential to your life. As far as the forgetting goes, what's to forget? I was just there whenever you took the time to notice. If I'm not there, there is nothing for you to notice. All you need is a small adjustment to your memory."

"I should have known all along that there was something wrong between us. I thought you really needed the things I was getting for you. I was always so god damned busy. Just one more year, I kept saying. It's always one more year. Maybe I should have seen things differently."

"You couldn't have seen anything differently. You are as you brought yourself up to be. You can't change any of that. I managed to change myself but that was because I was always as others wanted me to be. I was committed to what you wanted me to be but not to what we had. Don't misunderstand me. I did not doubt or question any of it. I accepted it as I accepted everything else. That is what saved me. I could leave you and the life you created for us because when I scratched the surface I found nothing underneath. Another man, in time, and another life, were not at all difficult for me."

"You think another man is all you needed to be yourself?"

"No. It's never that easy. Only, with Howard I was able to know a man truly and forthrightly. I know him as I never knew you. He is not as handsome as you, he is not as good a lover as you, he is not as intelligent as you. Ours is not a story-book romance. And that's why I'm as happy as I think I've ever been. There were no applauding parents and relatives when I married him, there were no approving smiles from friends I later came to detest. There was only fat, bald-headed Howard, working more than is good for him because he wants to give me and the children things. He is sincere and he knows his limitations. Unlike you, he has limits."

"Didn't I do the same thing for you?"

"No, you did not. You've not had to work or fight for a single thing in all of your life. There were never any limitations on what you could do. Everything has been so god damned easy for you because your mind could always overcome whatever obstacles appeared before you. You may have been born poor but you were never destined to be poor. People like you never stay poor. It's gentle people like Howard who sometimes lose even what they were born with. Howard tries, he works twice as hard as you do to keep us far below what you provided. With him it means something. With Howard, Doctor Castillo, I am rid of your arrogance."

"Obviously, there is nothing more for us to talk about."

"Yes, there is. With you, all I had was security. Security is the fundamental mistake men make about women. You assume the burden of security for us. All of your actions come from the desire to provide that security. You never think that there has to be more. And that is what, above all other men, Doctor Castillo, you do not understand."

"Whatever you say. I don't know what to think about this illicit relationship you are in now. Certainly, the law ought to be concerned about it. Maybe I could take you back, but I doubt it."

"Fuck you! There is no going back anywhere. This is where I belong. I made this. It's mine. It was not made for me, nor did it just happen to me. I made it what it is. I was in control of myself every step of the way. That's what makes it so different and meaningful for me. I don't suppose you could ever understand that. One thing I will tell you, you will not screw it up for me!"

"There doesn't seem to be much point in me trying to understand any of this."

"That's very smug of you, Doctor Castillo. You are so dead set on your version of how I ought to be that you cannot have an alternative to it."

"I think I have always been open-minded about things. Willing to consider all sorts of ideas."

"This is not an idea at all. This is my life. It is not called 'life.' It is life. That's the crucial difference."

"Perhaps you're right."

"Take your subjunctive and shove it up your ass! Now, get out!"

"This is it, then?"

"I am not what I was. I've said that over and over again. You've brought reminders out of a past that I do not want to interfere with my present. That past with you is no longer a part of me. I shut the door on it. When I walked out of your home, that was the end of it. I am what you see. Happily married, a mother, with a husband and children and a home of my own to care for. I have what I want."

"I would have been prepared for anything but not this. This is exactly what it was before."

"Not exactly, but I never completely rejected what we had. I chose to augment it. You chose for yourself and you assumed your choices were perfect for me as well. For a time, it worked. Then I realized that I could and ought to make my own choices. You don't have to accept the way things are. All you have to do is leave me alone. Burn up the address and the name on that piece of paper in your hand. You don't know me. I don't know you. We are strangers who were husband and wife at one time. My life is normal and I have to get back to it. Go away. Go back to your life, go back to the children we once had. I feel for them as sisters. They are your daughters only for a short time. They will become what you refuse to let them be."

"I'll be going now," said Doctor Castillo.

Portal

Jerónimo Portal wore his usual black suit. He walked slowly, patiently, with the stability of habit, along the uneven sidewalk toward the plaza. The suit was well-worn, shimmering in a few places as it reflected light from the white-hot sun of summer. His walk was measured, almost cautious; but firm and still strong despite his eighty-two years. His eyesight was still very good. He avoided the drooping branches of the trees without having to bend over, dodging them as if they were a leafy obstacle course. Another much younger man would have made the walk to the plaza in thirty minutes or less. Jerónimo Portal needed just a few more minutes than that, but since he was in no hurry, he took nearer to an hour to make the walk. A younger man would have been going some place, would have been impatient to be at his destination. For Jerónimo Portal, the walk was as important as arriving at the plaza.

In the twenty years since his retirement, the plaza had become the center of his day. He calculated well the time it took him to walk there so that he could arrive a few minutes before noon. He timed his arrival to coincide with that of the workers from the surrounding buildings who would come to spend the last minutes of their lunch hour in the plaza. The plaza had become an important part of his daily life. Although he knew no one there and seldom spoke to anyone, he felt something sinister and disconcerting about finding it empty of people. Jerónimo Portal felt the same about entering a dark empty house late at night.

The buildings surrounding the plaza were tall, hiding the sun late in the morning and early in the afternoon. Jerónimo Portal remembered the not too distant past when the buildings were squat and broad, solid testaments to the self-assurance of the business expansion at the turn of the century. They were buildings made of wood, bricks and marble, with ornate façades and opulent lobbies. They were leisurely buildings blending in artificial symmetry with the square of reconstructed nature in the plaza. Now, as he sat there, the buildings were of a different order. These new buildings on three sides of the plaza were made with strange materials not in use or even invented when he worked with construction gangs. Only the glass seemed familiar to him. These were tall spires, trying to pierce the sky, tapered and lean, covered with mirror-like glass which reflected only the nearby buildings. These were also symbols of business; now narrow, specialized, temporary. They would not last beyond the children of the generation which built them.

Still, the trees remained in the plaza, undisturbed by the hurried activity around them. The white bandstand gleamed warmly in the spring. The granite statue commemorating a hero of Texas history whom he never bothered to learn about and who he finally decided was not very herioc at all was still there looking vacantly toward the subdued west. And the pigeons. Above all, there were the pigeons, still coming to feed from the food he carried for them in a little brown paper sack with grease stains. It was the pigeons he loved. He came to think they could not survive without the crumbs he brought them each day. In a way, the pigeons provided Jerónimo Portal with the only urgency of his day.

During the time it took to destroy the fine old buildings and for the new sleek ones to go up, Jerónimo Portal thought of going elsewhere, to another plaza or park in the city, some place where he could rest and enjoy the quiet he came to feel he had earned with his life. He mused about the odd way of the society into which he had grown old. The strong, robust buildings were giving way to lean, anemic-looking ones. Human beings, he thought, cannot ignore, even in their artificial works, the rhythms of nature. They made time so that the old could make way for the new. But, search as he might for peace and quiet, things were not much different at other parks and plazas. There was only noise. If at one park there was too much traffic rumbling by, at another a band would play with amplifiers larger in size than some of the musicians. At still another place, there was the inescapable demolition and construction. He knew there were not many places for him to go and he preferred to keep to the routine to which he had accustomed himself. He reasoned, now with my wife gone, it is better to do the few things left to me to do and not change anything. Change is, of course, inevitable, but it can sometimes be avoided. Not forever, but long enough.

So, he endured the noise of the demolition crews and later of the construction crews. He was careful to move quickly when coming to the plaza, lest some debris fall on him. The old buildings were quickly gutted, leaving them like toothless, empty carcasses of once-fierce lions. Then, in a single afternoon, the shells of the old buildings cracked and crumbled in a swirling cloud of dust. In one swift, effortless motion, the buildings collapsed into a neat pile to the amusement and cheers of a gathered crowd. One by one the buildings went, until the plaza reminded him of the devastated cities he had seen during the Mexican Revolution.

The sleek buildings took so long to build that he became a familiar figure for the work crews putting them up. Eventually, he was a signal to them as they came to know his punctuality. His slow but steady walk, head held up high, became a signal to the workmen to put their tools away, shut down equipment, and prepare for lunch. The workmen often sat near him. He had appropriated a bench for himself which they respected by leaving it to him. The workers seldom spoke to him, except to nod or grunt an off-hand sort of greeting. Despite more than sixty years of living in the United States, he had not learned English well enough to feel comfortable using it. He understood it much better than he let on. Gringos had always made him nervous and no matter how friendly they were or how long he came to know them, he could not be at ease with them. The few Mexicans on the construction projects only stared sullenly at him and seemed to refuse any acknowledgement of their common origins. He'd known that kind of Mexican already, he'd known far too many of them, and he sometimes wondered if they truly shared the bond of work with the gringos to the exclusion of any outsider such as himself or if they simply wanted to avoid the fact that they were Mexican.

Soon after the reconstruction of the plaza area began, he had to be absent for nearly a month. He had had a minor illness, nothing serious he told himself. The doctor felt he should stay in the hospital, fearing complications common to people of his age. After a few days in the hospital, his daughter, Marta, spoke with the doctor and arranged for him to come stay with her. She told the doctor she could take care of him and he would get well much sooner if he had his grandchildren near by. Jerónimo Portal agreed to the transfer, even though he was not delighted by it, because a hospital was not a fit place for a man to die. He thought his Marta might want an adult to talk to. Eduardo Macías, his son-in-law, had been dead for seven years. She must miss adult talk. Marta was a strong woman, past forty, who terrified her children and who had few friends. When he visited or she came to his home, with the children outside playing and laughing, she sometimes would speak suddenly. The sound of her voice would startle him, she sounded so much like his deceased wife. This troubled him. Marta became more and more like his wife each time he saw her.

Jerónimo Portal loved his wife in the way people unaccustomed to displays of affection do. He seldom told her of his feelings and almost never showed her he cared. When it was important that he demonstrate his love for her, both of them had been too busy trying to prove to the other who was the stronger. Later, much later, when which of the two was the stronger did not matter at all, they had fallen into those silences which say what words make redundant. It was then that he realized he had no life apart from her. He suspected his wife of continuing the struggle right up to the day of her death, but he never acknowledged nor accepted any of what he presumed to be challenges for fear they were not challenges at all. Women, he often mused, do not really want to understand men; or themselves, for that matter. They are as self-centered as men are. The kind of world we have created demands only strength. The weak are soon brushed aside, made to serve the strong, or destroyed altogether. The buildings surrounding the plaza are like that, thought Jerónimo Portal. Age, or design, give them the appearance of weakness and so they are razed. New, taller buildings appearing strong and lean take their place. So it is with people. Jerónimo Portal shook his head in a bemused way. Men had so little imagination they could not create a world better than what they found around them. All of man's creations are an imitation of what they think they see. Hence, the strong must forever be posed against the weak. In each case, it is only the appearance of strength or weakness that finally matters.

Lately, Jerónimo Portal's daughter had taken to shouting at him. His hearing was as good as ever, but she naturally assumed that at his age it was necessary for her to speak in a loud voice to him. Marta, in imitation of her mother, perceived a situation at first glance, and then without unduly thinking about it acted resolutely on that initial perception. It was completely alien to her to have second thoughts. He had tried to explain to her, on a number of occasions, that it was quite unnecessary for her to scream at him or anyone when she wanted attention, that it was impolite and that well-brought-up people spoke in level and civil voices to each other. His even and patient words fell upon her deaf, uncomprehending ears as though he were trying to recite the poem of the Cid which he had memorized as a child. Just like her mother, he would say wistfully under his breath to himself and perhaps to his deceased wife.

Jerónimo Portal lived near the center of the city in an old neighborhood. The homes were sturdy frame and brick houses, surrounded by spacious yards. There were plenty of trees to absorb the heat of summer and to pose bleakly in winter. Marta lived further out, near the outer limits of the city where the buses did not go. He no longer drove his car, but he kept it nonetheless. It was necessary for Marta to come in her station wagon to pick him up if he was to visit her. For this reason, his trips to see her and the grandchildren lasted several days, even though the drive took less than half an hour. Marta worried about him living in what she called 'that neighborhood.' She was convinced he would be killed by a punk burglar some night. She had seen the television news reports aimed chiefly at people who lived far away from the inner city, depicting the viciousness of the poor people who lived around him. She implored him to sell the house and buy one in her neighborhood, where it would be safer and where she and Eduardo could be closer to him. She reminded him, what with his pension and the price he could get for his house, he could well afford it. He had explained to her that the economics of such a move were insane. He would be selling a perfectly good house made of perfectly good materials for a much lower price than the house he would be buying in the suburbs. Exasperated, Marta explained to him that it was much nicer where they lived and that was why the prices were higher. Patiently, he informed her that even at his age he could put his fist through the sheetrock wall of her home. In mock anger, he asked if she would like him to show her. Marta threw her hands up in the air and went to another room, leaving him smiling in the kitchen.

The last time he had visited Marta, he left her home sooner than planned. Over the years since Graciela, his wife, died, and especially since Eduardo died, she had taken to treating him as one of the children. The first morning of his visit, she had bustled—not just walked—into the spare bedroom, drawing the curtains with a flourish, permitting an immense gulf of sunlight to sweep over him. He considered himself an early riser, but five-thirty was too early. Marta, who had started working again, was up at five every day, not wanting to break with her weekly rhythms. At five-thirty, she was humming some tune that if pressed even she could not identify. Humming as though she were an alarm clock, she spread his clothes across his ankles. The night before, she had given him one of Eduardo's old robes and had made him take off his clothes. As the last act of the day, she put the clothes in the washing machine in the garage. In the morning, as the first act of the day, she transferred them to the clothes dryer where they would toss as the machine rumbled while she bathed. She draped his clothes, freshly ironed, across his ankles. While he was opening his eyes, she continued to hum—he imagined it to be a sound similar to a hen. He imagined she would stay in the room until he opened his eyes and would continue checking in on him until he was on his feet.

It was then she cooingly asked if grandpa would like to get up and have some nice nourishing breakfast. In a sing-song voice she gave him the menu, nice oatmeal with cinnamon sticks, orange juice and toast. And if he was real good and got up right away, he could have instant coffee, but not too much because we know very well what the doctor says. Jerónimo Portal, in the most formal Spanish he knew, firmly informed her that he, Jerónimo Portal, presently prone on the bed, was in fact her father, as far as he knew, and to his knowledge not at all her grandfather. To which she responded in English, grumpy this morning, aren't we. Jerónimo Portal did not know what 'grumpy' meant, but he knew enough English to realize it was useless. He finally asked her in Spanish to permit him to dress in private. Later in the day, over lunch, he told his daughter he was worried about a cat he did not have and had her drive him home.

That incident had occurred more than a year before. He was back to himself and glad to have his solitude. He had made his peace with society, and more importantly, with himself. In the years since his retirement, and in those following the death of his wife, he had become accustomed to himself as though he were encountering an old friend after many years of separation. The face was there, the gestures, the mannerisms, the voice. The face he saw was his, the voice he heard was his, but this person he was discovering seemed strange, though vaguely familiar to him. It was as if this lost friend, himself, had been with him all along, alongside in fact, and knew of everything in his life, but there had never been any closeness or intimacy. In the solitude of retirement he had come to know and understand himself a little better—at least to the point where he enjoyed being with himself. He did not regret for one moment having to wait so long for the discoveries he was making. I have

87

nothing to apologize for in my life to anyone, he thought. I have lived as I intended to live, as it was meant for me to live. This thinking about himself was new, of course. It meant he had to recover fragments of his past and he would think about them. But he did not think about his past in order to change things in his mind, in order to know the better way to have done something. Nor did he think of his past to make himself appear better in his memory than he had ever been in fact. What was done was done. Rather, he thought about his past because it was all he had, really, and he did not want to lose any of it. In the meantime, he had his repetitive house chores, his modest food which he learned to cook by campfire as a young boy during the Revolution, and he had the plaza.

The plaza, changed though it was by its new surroundings, soon returned to the way it was: a tranquil and quiet respite from the city expanding and rising on all four sides. Gradually, almost imperceptibly, the new buildings were becoming a natural part of the plaza landscape. Soon his mind no longer registered the time when they were not there. The new businesses that were coming into the new buildings were employing many young people. Life changed through them, he knew. The young were the true barometers of age and change. It would be interesting, he thought, to talk to them, to discover how life is changing through them, to know first hand the link which existed between the young and the old.

Occasionally, one or two of them would sit on his bench—despite the new people who now came to the plaza, it was still *his* bench. His attempts at conversation were invariably met with silence. Whenever he began by noting how nice a day it was, his listener would quickly assent and return to the private eating of a lunch or to the reading of a magazine. They were not interested in conversation nor did they seem to want to make new friends. None of them seemed to know one another, although many of them worked in the same buildings. He would see two or three of them walk together into the dark interiors of the buildings. It appeared to Jerónimo Portal that only inside the buildings did they know each other and once outside they became strangers.

He reasoned at first that it must be the age-old animosity of gringos toward Mexicans that prevented the young people from speaking to him. He had only recently been retired from the railroad when he noticed the situation. He had then only a tentative, wary, vague relationship with his solitude. He was not yet at the point where he reflected much. He needed to talk to human beings, to hear human voices. His silent communication with his wife was not enough. He simply accepted the reticence on the part of the young gringos as something he had been familiar with since coming over from Mexico. He knew gringos gave orders to Mexicans or exchanged work talk. Some spoke in friendlier voices than others. But there was never the true bond of intimacy between the two. Even on those occasions when the work boss treated the gang to beer alongside the railroad tracks, there was little affection between gringos and Mexicans. The more they drank the more hostility surfaced, forcing the work boss to send the Mexicans away while the gringos drank the remainder of the beer.

In the years that followed, more and more Mexicans became part of the lunchtime crowd in the plaza. He noticed the faces and gestures of these young Mexicans. They were no different from their gringo counterparts. They were equally reticent. It was then that he began to think about the situation. His wife was gone and he was at a point where he took care of himself automatically, doing everything he had to do without thinking about it. He was aware of a new, aggressive generation of Mexicans. These were unlike the young men he grew up with or those of the following generation who left the farms and the barrios to fight the Germans and the Japanese for the Americans. The dazed expressions on their faces were similar to those of the pachucos of an earlier day. Gone was the overt, seething menace that leapt at the world from the faces of the pachucos. Among this generation of Mexicans, there was an air of wanting success, almost craving it. They had clean, scrubbed faces, exuding confidence, intelligence. Their only imperfection was a tentative determination that made them seem like convalescents taking their first unsure steps.

The people all around the plaza shared the shade of the trees, the grass, the benches. They tossed the leftovers of their lunches into the white trash barrels. They looked at one another with the stern faces of statues, softer than granite perhaps, but hard nonetheless. During a brief period the plaza had been invaded—he thought about the word 'invaded' and decided he liked it even though it was not the right one—by unkempt, raggedly dressed young people. They gave him flowers and smiled a lot. The young girls with long, straight, blonde hair were especially friendly. There was something about the vacant, repetitive smiles that never left their faces which bothered him. He could notice their facial muscles tremble from maintaining the forced smiles so long. To them, he was not Jerónimo Portal, veteran of the Mexican Revolution, retired from the Missouri-Pacific Railroad Company, father of Marta, husband of Graciela—a man who had seen and done many things during his long life. He was instead a relic to them, someone who had survived far longer than they could imagine. He was a curiosity to them. They called him 'man,' which seemed to him disrespectful. They paid little attention—in fact, they became impatient with him—when he tried to explain about his life. For reasons which escaped him then, he felt it important to try to explain to them. His efforts to give them the details necessary to make of him someone besides an old man in the park made them nervous, angered them. It soon became clear to him that they took him to be a gentle, maybe foolish old man, who could share with them a rejection of society.

If they could only know, if only they could be genuinely interested, he thought. The opposite was true. They did make him discover that he had never thought very much about his life, had never tried to analyze the sort of life he had led for more than seventy years. When he considered everything, the major and the minor details, he judged his life to have been a good one. It had been good enough for him and now that he was quite well adjusted to his solitude, he expected the years remaining to him to be also good ones. He found pleasure in this discovery. The best life is the one not judged until it is nearly over. It is best to live as well as one can and not judge until there is sufficient evidence. He knew that there comes a time when one is compelled to make such judgments. His time came during his old age. It was not true for everyone.

Jerónimo Portal sat on the park bench, a mottled sun soothing his face. This time of year, the trees were beginning to bloom, casting a soft, bright green glow over the plaza. Even the pigeons seemed to have fresh, fluffy feather-coats. Jerónimo Portal took the paper sack out of his pocket. He reached inside for a handful of dried bread crumbs and tossed them in a wide arc on the sidewalk. Within moments, the pigeons came. They flew from the trees to light down in a flurry of feathers on the concrete. Others on the ground, walked in a cumbersome pigeon-way toward the bread crumbs, swaying heavily from side to side, unaccustomed to walking. Still others, almost as if on signal, swooped noisily from their perches on the roof of the bandstand. Once on the sidewalk, they began to peck at the crumbs in an orderly way.

Jerónimo Portal sprinkled more crumbs on another part of the concrete so as not to frighten the pigeons. As soon as the first portion was picked clean, in an almost military fashion, they marched to the new location. Without waiting for them to finish, he tossed the remainder of the contents of the sack back on the first location. There the bread crumbs lay until the second spot was picked clean. Only then did the pigeons move.

When the food brought to them by Jerónimo Portal was all gone, the pigeons moved about the sidewalk, pecking at small craters in the concrete. They continued for a few minutes in this way before instinct told them the crumbs were gone. Then the pigeons began to fly to their perches in the trees or on the roof of the bandstand. Others, their hunger not satisfied, sauntered away to peck for food in the grass. One pigeon remained near Jerónimo Portal's foot. It was a curious gray-brown bird, speckled with white feathers on its neck and the upper part of its body. The white feathers stuck out in tufts, like a cowlick on a teenager. The bird reminded Jerónimo Portal of his son-in-law, Eduardo Macías. It had been seven years since Eduardo Macías had taken his own life.

Eduardo had been a lawyer working with a legal-aid clinic. His clients consisted mainly of poor and recently poor Mexicans. Away from the office, away from the clients who knew little of and sometimes refused to care about their rights, Eduardo Macías worried about his work, his life and the system which made it next to impossible to know the simplicity and peace he yearned for. Jerónimo Portal's daughter, Marta, complained because Eduardo made so little money. She constantly badgered Eduardo into applying for a job with a successful law firm, one where he could earn a decent living. Whenever she read about a case in the paper, featuring a prominent lawyer, she would insist he go the next day and apply for a job with the firm. She reasoned that legal aid clinics were staffed by lawyers unable to get employment anywhere else. Marta insisted shrilly to Eduardo that he was much better than the lawyers he worked with and she warned him about wasting his time with clients who did not and would never be able to pay him.

Trying another line of argument, Marta made it clear to Eduardo that the legal aid clinic was a public service. She said one should always do something for the poor. But he had already done more than enough, more than his share, and it was time that he started thinking about the children. She realized that he did not like her very much anymore, that she was getting fatter and older and bitched too much, but there were the children. After all, the children were innocents and should not bear the brunt of anything between them. He should leave her out of it entirely and think only of the children and their future. Eduardo Macías would listen to her intently, but with a passive look on his face, a look of resignation and withdrawal. There was nothing he could do to change his life, but he could not find a way to tell her, to make her understand.

When Eduardo, year after year, continued with the clinic, Marta started complaining to her father. Her complaints began as disjunctive bits of conversation, asides to an audience Jerónimo Portal was not a part of. Soon enough her complaints became more direct, planned and measured speeches. On a weekend visit, when Eduardo had gone to spend Saturday morning finishing some work at the office, Marta sat at the kitchen table with her father. She told Jerónimo Portal that her husband respected him very much. There was an earnest, almost suppliant tone in her voice. There was a look of panic on her face. Her fingers trembled as she began to recite her carefully prepared and rehearsed words, words which Jerónimo Portal noticed must have taken her a great deal of time to prepare and much self-doubt before finally delivering. As she began her peroration, Marta began to tear a paper napkin into jagged, irregular squares. As she spoke, Jerónimo Portal realized he understood his son-in-law. He had met others like Eduardo during his life. In this respect, Eduardo was not unusual. The only difference Jerónimo Portal could detect was in Eduardo's inability to settle with what life had apportioned to him. Eduardo had no clear notion of what it was that he wanted, hence nothing was satisfactory to him. Marta, of course, did not help, but there was more to it than just Marta.

After that first nervous time in the kitchen, Marta continued to beg him to do something with Eduardo. At times she spoke to him in a plaintive tone, at others she seemed to accuse him of taking sides with Eduardo. Marta began to tell him things that he knew she would not tell her husband. She hoped he would take his son-in-law aside and explain to him how she felt in a way that only a man who was not her husband could know. She was afraid to tell her husband that she feared for him, that all the years of defending the poor had made him less capable of defending himself and moving to a more successful practice. She wanted her father to mention it to Eduardo in a way that Eduardo would not know she had put him up to it. She was afraid for her future and for the future of her children. Marta complained to her father in the hope that he as a concerned father-in-law could shame his son-in-law into finding a way of bettering all their lives. Jerónimo Portal then knew Marta was thinking of finding a lover, she wished for one, but she could not bring herself to do it and this failure, too, she transferred to her husband. Eduardo was, for her, the symbol of all the failures in her life.

Jerónimo Portal and Eduardo Macías had never been particularly close. Graciela had been appalled by the young man, many years before, who had come to ask for permission to court their daughter. He was too skinny—a sign to Graciela of someone who did not take good care of himself and consequently would only want a caretaker and not a wife. Jerónimo Portal in a rare instance of sarcasm asked why else does a man seek a wife. Eduardo had been a nervous wreck that first evening. When he picked up the saucer and cup of coffee, they rattled so much he had to place them on the end table and would not touch them again. Marta had orchestrated the entire evening. She cooked and served the meal all by herself, refusing to allow anyone, especially Graciela Portal, to help her. She spent most of the evening in the kitchen, permitting the prospective in-laws to become acquainted with one another. Graciela softened a bit when Eduardo said he planned to enter law school, but beyond that, she thought him unfit for her daughter. Jerónimo Portal remained neutral toward everything.

Jerónimo Portal began to understand Eduardo Macías from that first evening. Though they were never to become close, Jerónimo Portal grew genuinely interested in his son-in-law. He never came to feel sorry for him, but he came to have a sense of foreboding whenever he would think about him. If he thought too much about Eduardo, Jerónimo Portal would be overcome with a sense of desperation, wanting somehow to intervene, to stop something on the verge of occurring, but something the nature of which he did not know. Now, so many years later, Jerónimo Portal realized Eduardo's suicide was not the something that triggered his sense of foreboding, that something had not yet come to pass. The suicide could not have been prevented. Nothing can intervene when a man truly wants to take his life. The foreboding was about something else. Even after Eduardo had gone hunting into the woods, the foreboding persisted. He knew than it had nothing to do with Eduardo.

Over the years of his daughter's marriage, Jerónimo Portal kept up his surveillance of Eduardo. Another man might have kept a journal to record his varied speculations concerning Eduardo Macías. He was a good man, a good husband, a good father. Jerónimo Portal gradually arrived at the truth, but he could not tell his daughter. He could not even tell his son-in-law. Eduardo's goodness was a disease with him. The years struggling to spark life into his clients so they might help in their own defense had only sapped him of the juices which served to spark his own life. Eduardo had become diseased with the goodness that remains after there is a loss of will; so diseased in fact that the life left to him was little by little eaten away to a point where he was nothing more than walking flesh and bone. There was nothing left of him, only the rootless, drifting shell that once housed his humanity.

All that Eduardo Macías had been able to keep at a distance began to converge. He had somehow managed to keep his family, his clients, the legal system, his doubts, all separate from each other. He understood Marta's anger, her despair, her frustration. Eduardo Macías understood that the wives of his law school classmates dressed better than Marta and that they chatted endlessly about vacations and trips and so many other things Marta wanted but had no prospect of getting. The money he was making was all he was ever going to make. His clients seldom paid their bills. He came to a point where he felt he was not serving them well. As a result, he felt uncomfortable sending notices to their parents and wives. He refused to collect money from the relatives of sons, husbands, and brothers he had helped send to prison. Eduardo Macías knew he was finished when he realized he had helped send his clients to prison.

It had started innocently enough for Eduardo. More clients than he could decently and effectively represent. All of them sullen, with the furtive look of guilt about them; and yet, beneath the veneer of toughness, a resignation and an innocence about what went on around them. Eduardo, at the beginning, had been too naive to see it for what it was. The people coming to him were resigned to the fact of prison, too innocent or powerless to be able to manipulate the system to their benefit. They came to him because they knew they were already going to prison, Eduardo being nothing more than a part of a process they knew full well to be inevitable. It took Eduardo Macías twelve years to discover the part he played. He had been too insulated in his youth to discover what his clients knew before their first communion.

When starting his law practice, his clients had been different for him. Eduardo, too, was different. He was enthusiastic, almost joyful at the thought of defending them, of bringing the truth of justice to them. In fact, he often felt glad they had committed the crimes which brought them to him because he would be able to demonstrate to them the rationality and mercy of the court. The courts worked for everyone if only there was sincerity on the part of counsel. He lingered at length over minor details in conversations with his clients, looking for the off-hand remark which would serve as the basis for a dazzling performance in the courtroom. In moments of playfulness, he wanted the perpetrator to be in court so he could turn around and say to the world, not my client but him! That is the man!

The constant setbacks in the courtroom made him defensive and unable to cope with the complexity of the court system. The abstract description of it from law school had concealed the fact of it being weighted heavily on the side of wealth and resources. It was nothing like what he had imagined. Try as he might, he could not adequately come to terms with it. He came to believe the arguments made by the District Attorney's office: these people are guilty anyway, maybe not of this crime but of some other, so why not send them away for a few years; otherwise, they will continue to commit crimes. By bargaining for a pre-trial sentence, the client would not receive the far longer term the prosecutor would demand. At first, he could not believe it was the powerful arm of public justice exacting vengeance for the sake of vengeance. He could understand, however, the frustration of the police and the district attorneys wanting desperately to protect the public as was their sworn duty. His clients were citizens too, he insisted, and deserved some degree of protection. However, there was so much crime and the criminals appeared to be so much smarter than those chasing them. The ones who committed the most exasperating crimes in society were seldom if ever caught, he reasoned. It was only the poor bastards, caught stealing hubcaps or breaking into liquor stores who got caught. Just as the rich could be guaranteed their innocence in court by virtue of the lawyer's fees they could afford, so too those who stole large sums could be guaranteed their freedom by virtue of their cunning and the fact that those from whom they stole were well-insured and not particularly interested in seeing the culprits caught. They got theirs. In fact, they often claimed more than was actually stolen.

What the District Attorney proposed seemed logical enough to him. Not fair, perhaps, but logical. The rationality of it, the logic, was based entirely on the force and power of the state. Eduardo Macías knew their resources far exceeded his, and hence they could easily win their cases. In fact, it was not a trial system of justice at all. It was simply a matter of sending an appropriate number of people to prison. He marvelled at how little the guilt or innocence of the poor souls he escorted to the courtroom mattered. They who were accused of everything from murder in the heat of anger to negligence in the payment of child support were pawns in a game of chess. Hence, since the District Attorney's people did not want to exert themselves too much, Eduardo was offered the only sensible solution to an exasperating problem for everyone. They reasoned for him that by accepting their propositions, he could draw nice fees for doing very little. He would not have to bother with courtroom preparation. Though he he was not interested in the money, he saw in what they proposed a way for him to be of genuine service to his clients. What hurt from the beginning was having to conceal the utter deviousness of it all from them. Within a short space, he could no longer accept the relationship he willingly established with the District Attorney. He could not any longer deceive his clients. And in knowing he could no longer deceive them, he realized he had only deceived himself. He then knew more than he wanted to know about what he was doing. There was no way he could no longer know; there were no further possibilities for him to remain safe and comfortable in the ignorance he wanted so to cultivate.

It pained Jerónimo Portal to see the sadness in his daughter's marriage. A few months before Eduardo's suicide, he sensed the pall that had fallen over the small house on the outskirts of the city. Eduardo was a good man. He did his best, but he was not aggressive and it worried Jerónimo Portal. A more aggressive man would have taken home what there was to take, left what was necessary to leave at the office and would have aggressively enjoyed the family he helped to create and would have gone on with the business of living. But not Eduardo Macías. He became so much a part of everything he did that when he came to realize his part in the suffering of others—a distant, intangible, indirect suffering, to be sure—he could not bear it. He could not remain separate from it. He brought it to his family, brought it into the house with him as if it were some medieval plague.

One Sunday afternoon, Jerónimo Portal and his son-in-law, Eduardo Macías, were in the backyard of the latter's home. They sat in aluminum chairs with green and white nylon strips for webbing, waiting for hamburgers to broil on the barbecue grill. Jerónimo Portal took patient, almost delicate, swigs from his bottle of Pearl beer. Marta seldom permitted him to have beer, but she had bought some for him in the hope that he would speak to Eduardo. Eduardo sat in his lawn chair, looking intently into the distance, as if he saw something there that he had been looking for. The two men were supposed to be watching the hamburgers. It was Marta who was actually doing the cooking and the two men simply sat in the sun near the grill. Neither of them noticed the meat burning. Marta noticed the smoke, ran past them, grabbing the long spatula. There was no saving them. She scolded Eduardo for a long moment. It was clear to Jerónimo Portal that she wanted to slap her husband. After a long moment of angrily glaring at her husband, Marta took her apron off and left for the store to buy more meat.

The two men stared at one another. Jerónimo Portal had been spared her wrath. Not because he was her father or because he was old or because it had been Eduardo's responsibility to watch the hamburgers. Marta spared him because she needed to vent her anger and hatred at Eduardo. It had little or nothing to do with the hamburgers burning. The casualness with which Eduardo took it indicated to Jerónimo Portal that it was not the first time such an incident had occurred. It had happened before and he also knew that the frequency of it was increasing. Eduardo's pained, liquid eyes were almost begging her to slap him, to hit him, to punish him. He was telling her that whatever punishment she inflicted on him was nothing compared to what he deserved. Jerónimo Portal broke his trance with a swig of beer.

The old man and the younger man sat again in the lawn chairs. This time, Jerónimo Portal moved his chair a little closer to Eduardo's so they would not have to speak in too loud a voice. It seemed to him that in doing so he was approaching a skittish animal as yet unsure of the intentions of the human being coming near. It's the law, isn't it? asked Jerónimo Portal of his son-in-law. When Eduardo continued to stare into the distance with the vacant look of a wounded animal, Jerónimo Portal asked why he bothered with a legal career since it did not appear to please him and especially since it seemed the cause of so much pain for him. Eduardo began to speak in the even, measured voice he had acquired in law school—a voice that did not belong to him at all.

I did not want to become a lawyer. Marta decided that for me. I know, I know, we were married after I started law school. You see, that was part of the plan, her plan, most of it, anyway. When I finished college, I wanted to be a naval officer. I did not want to be a naval officer, I wanted to get away from here, away from the misery of the barrio. Away from being always the same. I thought that by getting away I could avoid the life my parents had. I did not want to be like them. They were good people and all but I did not want to be like them. Everybody I knew was the same. I did not want to be like that. I wanted to be different, not like everybody else. Maybe I wanted to be better, maybe I thought I *was* better. At any rate, I applied for an officer's program, but I was turned down. I had really planned on leaving right after college. I was disappointed, of course, but I was not bitter about it. I guess I don't have it in me to be bitter, or I did not know enough to be bitter. There weren't many jobs that summer. There never are, you know that. So I moved in with my folks. They were pleased I was a college graduate and didn't mind if I took a few months to relax and enjoy myself. My father joked about it, I remember. He would say, here you are a college graduate and there aren't any jobs worthy of you. He was even more pleased than my mother. She kept saying thinking is a lot of work and you have earned your rest. So, that's what I did for most of the summer. Nothing. My cousin, Francisco, he's the son of my uncle Pascual, I think you've met him, anyway, Francisco invited me to a dance his girl friend was having. My mother and father were listening and they immediately encouraged me to go. I had not been out of the house for days and I think my father was getting nervous. He even offered me twenty dollars as an extra inducement. I was a little embarrassed to take his money. I decided to go with Francisco even though I wasn't all that interested and would have preferred to stay home and do some reading. I read a lot then. Even before college. Sir Walter Scott was my favorite. I went to all the movies made of his novels, but they were never as good as the books. That's when I met Marta. At the party. She was just graduating from business school. She told me she was going to take a job as a bookkeeper in a drugstore. I was very impressed with her. She had found a job right away and she seemed to know exactly what she wanted to do with her life. She was different from all the girls I'd ever met. She was not going to waste any time waiting for someone to come along and marry her and take her out of your house. She was going to rely on herself. She was strong and resolute, so unlike many of the girls my relatives tried to get me interested in. I think I was the project of every aunt, uncle and cousin. My family was going to get me married. Marta and I started seeing each other without you or my deceased mother-in-law knowing anything about it. It wasn't disrespect or anything like that, you know. I was in favor of being proper and coming to your home to ask permission to see her. Marta would not hear of it. She wanted to be sure first. I didn't know what she wanted to be sure of, but I trusted her judgment and went along with it. I told my parents about her. When I told them I had not met you, they scolded me in the quiet and gentle way they had. They said I was brought up better than to be sneaking around. They never had daughters, so I guess that they were concerned about everyone else's. After only a month of seeing each other, we had pretty much decided to get married. Well, I shouldn't say that. We didn't decide. It was Marta who decided for us. Maybe we decided. I don't know anymore. I was confused about a lot of things just then. She seemed so strong and more than willing to take charge of everything. If she wanted to take charge of my life as well, well, I was grateful, really. It made a lot of things easier for me. She made it possible for me to actually have some fun. I spent most of my time worrying. When I was with her, I didn't feel so worried. That was the best time we've ever had. I thought marriage would be better, but it wasn't. That was the best time we ever had. I would go to the drugstore where she worked every afternoon just about the time she took her break from work. The drugstore had one of the few remaining all-marble counters left in the city. It was not far from my parents' house and I could walk there without having to borrow bus fare from my mother. Marta drank cherry cokes which she got free from the soda jerk. Sometimes she paid for mine or we would share hers. Since then I've tried to make cherry cokes at home. I guess I've wanted to recapture those times, but they haven't been the same. One afternoon, she suggested I go to law school. Out of nowhere. She just told me it would be better if I went to school and became a lawyer. I think I laughed at the idea because I hadn't really thought about a career. I certainly had not thought about going back to school. She was so sure of everything. It never occurred to me to think like that. Four years of college was about all I could handle. Still, I was charmed by her ambition, and pleased, too, that her ambition included me. Anyway, I laughed and told her my grades were not good enough to get into any law school and I didn't have the money it would cost to apply and take the exams and so forth and I didn't want to burden my family anymore with my education. And that was only the beginning because were I accepted, there were living expenses, tuition, books and so on. It wasn't easy and it wasn't cheap. I could only think of my parents having to borrow even more money for me. I couldn't do that to them, they had sacrificed enough already. Well, about the middle of August—we'd been going together for just over a month—I went to see her as usual at the drugstore. The way she smiled then would drive me crazy. As she came out from the back of the store where she had a little office, she was smiling. And she kept smiling. I knew she was up to something. Something playful, like the time she gave me a present all wrapped up with yellow paper and a blue ribbon. I was about to tell her not to spend money on me, but I opened the little package and discovered a piece of candy in the shape of Texas. Anyway, I asked her what little trick she was planning, but she just kept smiling. Finally, she handed me a large manila envelope. She said it was a present. I opened it expecting another of her little practical jokes. I found a ticket to take the entrance examination for law school and all the forms necessary to apply. Clipped to the application forms was a money order to pay the application fee at the law school. Now, you're all set, she told me. I told her that I could not even think about taking it. Any of it. I said I would try and get a refund on the examination fee. She smiled some more. Each time I said no, she just smiled, as if she was patiently abiding my protests as part of some ritual. She expected me to say no and she knew I would end up doing what she planned. Before I left the drugstore that afternoon, she had convinced me that since we were getting married in a year, it was my money too and her future as well. It was all for our future together she said. To sort of seal the pact, that night I came to your house for the first time to ask permission to see Marta. There was so much going on for me on that one day, I was nervous and excited at the same time. Looking back on that afternoon, everything was so detailed, so well-planned. She knew exactly what she wanted. What troubles me most of all, father-in-law, is the not knowing. I'm never sure of anything. Marta knows damn well what she wants and she eventually gets it. It's not that there is anything wrong with that. In fact, she's always been very good about convincing me that what she wants is what I want and for the most part I really have wanted the same things as she. I have to be fair, at least about that. I really have wanted the same things. But now, after twelve years, I'm not so sure. I'm not sure of what I want now. It troubles me to think that. Maybe I have not wanted any of it at all. That everything in my life has been a mistake. It's like canceling our twelve years together. For a long time, I refused to think she had made a mistake about me. We were happy, I don't think I can deny that. Happier than most, for sure. Some of my lawyer friends have more money, but they worry more than I do about it. By their standard, I'm the one that's been a failure out of our law class. You know, I've had to loan some of them money. They don't make enough to keep up their successful appearances. I sense—no, I know—that Marta wants to have that successful appearance, too. She wants to have the things others have and I can't give to her. She doesn't want to feel out of place when we visit them and she doesn't want to feel ashamed about our home when they come to visit. She doesn't understand how I feel about it. And there's more to it. I sense that my clients want their freedom a lot more than Marta wants things but I can't seem to get it for them and that is what I'm supposed to be trained for. I'm supposed to be able to free them. Right now, I'm at a point where I hate my clients. I hate them so much I want to tell them that I enjoy sending them to jail. I hate them because they don't care whether they go to jail. I worry about them and they don't give a shit about themselves. Sometimes I think I don't know anything about freedom. I think I can get it for them or I should be able to get freedom for them, and it's like they are above it all, that freedom is something else for them, that it is two different things, what I want for them and what they know they already have. When the judge sentences them, when he pronounces upon them what everyone in the courtroom already knows—I think the court stenographer is the only one who isn't included in the negotiations—I become terrified. What have I done, I ask myself. I feel as if the guilty one, me, is going free while they, the innocents, go to prison. Worse yet, I feel I can only be free if they go to prison, as if they must serve my sentence for me. At home, I feel things falling apart. My children laugh at me. They don't know what they are doing, of course. They see Marta laughing at me, ridiculing me every chance she gets. Sometimes we will be sitting in front of the television and she'll say something which starts the kids giggling. She speaks to me as if I were some strange neighborhood kid who just wandered into the house. It's as though it's not my home at all. Lately, I've taken to beating the kids. I would rather have them hating me than laughing at me. They think it's funny when I spank them. They continue to laugh as though it is some sort of game. It just makes me angrier and so I hit them harder. I'm afraid of what I might do to them some day. I can't bear them laughing at me. I accuse Marta of setting them against me. I accuse Marta of everything. I want to hit her. Not as much as she wants to hit me, but I wish I could hit her. I don't hit her. I never provoke her enough so she'll strike me. It would be pointless for me to hit her. And so, I try to convince myself that I am a failure. I think through my life trying to find enough evidence to prove I've failed as a husband. As a lawyer. As a father. But I can't do even that. I can't conduct a review of my life with enough objective passion to judge myself. I can see and understand everything that has happened to me, that I've done. I am not firmly convinced enough to make any sort of judgment. I know precisely my motives in every instance, but even so, knowing everything first hand, I cannot judge. It's easier for me to seek the judgment of others. In that sense, I need Marta to rebuke and reproach me. But, finally, even that is not conclusive enough for me. I don't feel that I have failed at all. I only feel that I've lost control. So much so that I can't abide by the standards of judgment of other men. I only wish I could judge myself a failure. *21 8 4 8 9*

The pigeon, just a few feet away from Jerónimo Portal's feet, pecked at the craters in the concrete walkway. The bird reminded him of his son-in-law. Eduardo's thick, coarse hair, erupting in a cowlick always gave him the appearance of not being properly cared for. Jerónimo Portal gazed sadly at the bird which now looked back at him with a wistful, sidelong stare. The bird too appeared curiously uncared for. Where do you birds find food now that so much of the city is paved over? asked Jerónimo Portal. What happens to the worms under the concrete? You're a survivor, bird, aren't you. You have more than wings to take care of you, even though it doesn't look like it. You're not like my son-in-law at all, are you? You don't want to be an eagle.

Jerónimo Portal recalled painfully the tearful telephone call from his daughter. The ringing awoke him a few minutes before midnight. Seven years had passed since that ringing startled him from his dreamless sleep. My

99

husband is dead, Marta had said. Jerónimo Portal recalled now, on his park bench, how she did not mention the name, how she almost deliberately refused to say it. The man was only a husband to her, an appendage, perhaps. Jerónimo Portal recalled too how at the moment she told him his son-in-law was no more he tried to remember if he had ever heard her say his name. He could not remember a single instance. Even when newly wed, Eduardo was always my husband. Eduardo and he had never been close enough for both of them to use first names. It was always Eduardo and father-in-law. Father-in-law, *mi suegro*, from a tradition few any longer maintained or thought important. Jerónimo Portal imagined the children would now go through life having Eduardo referred to as your deceased father, *tu difunto papá*. In time, even his image for them would fade, ending finally with only a name, strange and alien to them, which would be required on the documents they would have to fill out as adults. Jerónimo Portal similarly had never been anything but grandfather, *güelito*, to the children.

What has happened to Eduardo, he asked of his daughter, enunciating each syllable of the name slowly and clearly. Marta responded, as though preoccupied with something else, he went hunting today and took his life.

Jerónimo Portal was not surprised. Nor was he upset. There was time to help take care of things the following morning. Only a certain compassion for his daughter and the children made him get up and make the drive to be with them. Without being cynical, he was more surprised that Eduardo had not committeed suicide earlier. He had seen it written in Eduardo's demeanor. He had seen death clearly on Eduardo's face. It had not frightened him at all. Eduardo Macías was still at a point where he could not recognize the inevitable signs, but Jerónimo Portal who had had more experience with death, could all but reach out and touch it. It was not the death which he saw enshroud Eduardo that bothered Jerónimo Portal. It was something else that nagged at him. It was something else that troubled him whenever he looked at or thought about Eduardo Macías. Eduardo had been too good a man to commit suicide any earlier. There was a process, almost a ritual of disintegration, necessary before his suicide. He had to observe each step leading to the inevitable conclusion. It was his goodness in a world he did not make and could not have made that killed him, Jerónimo Portal thought. The poor boy should have left my daughter a long time before. He should have gone away as he orginially planned. But, then, there is really no place for him to have gone. Besides, he was too good to leave. He was too good to leave and too good to stay. That was the shit of it.

Eduardo Macías had a presentiment but did not know what it was until too late. Some will say he took the coward's way out, thought Jerónimo Portal, but what does anyone know about it, finally. Maybe it does not matter at all. Jerónimo Portal knew only this: Eduardo Macías did not take his own life. He may have pulled the trigger, but that act only made him a corpse. He was dead a long time before the rifle explosion. It was Marta, who, in supposing to help him, destroyed him. It was the children, too, who are never as innocent as we would wish them to be. It was his clients, his job, the people he dealt with each day. And me, too, he thought. Me, too. All of us killed him.

The final, glorious, painful irony of Eduardo Macías, essentially a good man, was this: we may have killed him, driven him to it, or whatever, but not one of us individually or collectively is guilty of it. There is no law, not even God's, against being insensitive and morally brutal. It had to happen. It was inevitable. It was fated to happen and in matters of fate, there is no turning away and it is not possible to interfere or intervene. The things of this world occur because they are meant to occur and we have little to do with changing them. In this world, with things as they are, there is little need to accept guilt for the things that happen beyond our ability to control them. We are only responsible for those things we can control. But even those things are seldom apparent to us. In the end, there was no saving Eduardo. In the long run, we only think it is in our power to change the course of events. Even then we only wish to change things when they are unpleasant or unfortunate. We only want change when there is less than what we expected.

For some months after the suicide, Jerónimo Portal felt he should have talked more with Eduardo, spoken to him more as the additional father to him he was supposed to be. He felt he ought to have been closer to him, to have made himself available for confidences and advice. He felt he ought to have sat Eduardo down, perhaps over a beer or something stronger, and advised him seriously to go away and discover the life he genuinely wished for. Jerónimo Portal felt he ought to have advised Eduardo to leave Marta and the children for his own good and ultimately for theirs. But the thought of it, even in retrospect, seemed ludicrous. Eduardo would have only ended up suspicous of him too. Just as any advice that he ought to find a mistress or some other diversion would have been suspect. Eduardo, the good husband, the good father, would have found it unmanly and cruel to drink or to see other women. His whole life, however limited it finally was, revolved around and depended upon his wife, his children, his home. These were to be the constants of his life, the anchoring to prevent him from drifting away. It would have been alien to Eduardo to take refuge in the sorts of diversions and evasions other weak men seek. Eduardo had a strong image of how he should be in the world although he may not have had a clear idea of how he should be in relation to everyone else. It was this last which eventually did him in. He could not, was not capable of, living up to his own image of himself because he wanted to be fixed in a world constantly changing. Eduardo chose death as the only way to fix his place in life. He chose the image of what he should be and found its expression only in death.

He, Jerónimo Portal, veteran of the Mexican Revolution, had lived with death daily, hourly, for six years as a conscript. Death became no more extraordinary than any other event in war. He, Jerónimo Portal, could not, would not, have stopped Eduardo from his final act. For Eduardo, it was not a denial of life, a retreating away from it. It was the only way Eduardo could come to know life, not by the living of it but by the taking of it. He chose to take his own because he had already known what it was to have others set the standard by which he had to live. To know life, he had to arrange his own terms, and having set them, fundamental to them was knowing death directly.

Eduardo Macías was a good man and therefore weak. Good men are weak and have little chance in the world because it is never they who make the world. It is never they for whom the world is meant. The world has been made over in the image of dispassionate nature by men who see themselves as the perfection of nature. Instead of an imaginative world, with the delight of the unexpected and the incongruous, man has made reason reign. And reason is finally the refusal to engage the imagination in the aggressor, the predator, the violent, the destroyer. It is the strong who bend the world to reason, thought Jerónimo Portal, not those who imagine. One must remove himself from the world if he is to imagine. It is the men of reason who see submission as the necessary consequence of force. It is they who shape the world into a reasonable place where force and strength prevail. It is they who determine how the rest of us must live. I have known those men, thought Jerónimo Portal, in the Revolution, and I too have been among them. It is against the standard they set that good people like Eduardo must be judged. Since they are the strong, in fact, the standard of judgment, poor Eduardo never had a chance. His suicide was all he could ever have.

Jerónimo Portal had felt death ride along side him on many campaigns during the Revolution. He could feel, so many years later, the cold shroud gathering about his shoulders. It would not be long for him, he knew. He wondered why he had lived so long to see so many things, so many changes. He calculated that he was neither good nor bad. His life was balanced. It was only after having lived his life that he began to contemplate the difference. When earlier he had thought that he'd lived a good life, that judgment was in error. He had only lived. There is no judgment in life. Perhaps there is a judgment after death, by a Creator somewhere, but there cannot be any in life, he thought. People like Eduardo Macías wanted to be good men and in the end they devoted all of their waking days to it. Jerónimo Portal knew that Eduardo Macías, his son-in-law, previously an indifferent, confused and disinterested human being, had willed himself into goodness and having done so could not survive in a world so inimical to it. His goodness unconfirmed and unnoticed in the world, Eduardo came to feel as an abstraction. Suicide offered him the only way to confirm his life. In the taking of it he would at last know for sure what he had doubted all along: that he had lived.

Jerónimo Portal stood up, ready to begin his walk home. In his ruminations, he had lost track of the bird with the cowlick of feathers. He must have flown away, said Jerónimo Portal out loud.

Monologue of the Bolivian Major

Thank you, sergeant. You may wait outside. No, it is not necessary, he is wounded. I'm in no danger. Thank you, go, please.

So, it is you, the great revolutionary. I see you've suffered a fall from Rocinante. Of course, I apologize, it was a bad joke. Are you in pain? May I get you something? No, it does not matter to me whether you are comfortable or not. I can only guarantee your pain will not increase from my doing, you will not be tortured. Yes, it is so. But, you've known that. You will be executed. No, there has been no time posted, it is not definite. It would be cruel to keep you in suspense on that matter, certainly. We may talk for a moment, if you wish. After. . .my men are at your disposal whenever you are ready. You choose the time. It is easier all around if you do that. No, I have no wish to wash my hands of the matter. I'm sure you've known of your fate for some time, and I've known of it too. The matter was settled long ago.

Torture? Again, let me caution you not to mistake my altruism. I can indeed be generous, I suppose, but you will not be tortured because it is not necessary. I have brought none of our specialists in that field with me. All of your compatriots have been captured, and the one or two that escaped will not be troublesome any longer. They were not dangerous men. You are the dangerous man and we've wanted you from the beginning. But, understand, we wanted you on our terms. Now, you are in precisely the proper situation we wanted you in. Last night I interrogated the last of your men. They surrendered yesterday afternoon without much resistance. I gave the order from La Paz, and helicoptered in almost at the moment they laid down their rifles. To a man, they claim you betrayed them. No, we made no attempt to falsify your image to them, we did not try to discredit you in any way. We spoke no ill against you. They were convinced you betrayed them long before they surrendered to us. So, you see, it was not necessary for us to vilify you. Oh, of course, we would have done it had it served some useful purpose. Perhaps you've heard our radio broadcasts. I wrote some of them myself. But, that is political, propaganda. You and I understand action much better. Fabrication can be effective, but it is always much better if the object of our interest performs that function for us.

You are naive if you don't understand. It is very simple. It was always only a matter of hours before we captured you. It served our interests, the interests of my government, to have you begin this insurrection. Our president is not very popular, you know that. The miners posed a far more serious threat. We diverted the attention of the people to you, and in doing so, we deprived the miners of needed support. We are a nation with sacred boundaries, our borders are not to be transgressed by intruders of any sort, for whatever purpose. Our people come together against any foreign intruder.

I respect the success of your comrade and the Granma expedition. But he was returning to his homeland to rid it of an unpopular president. His president was stupid. He waited until the last moment to trust his generals, but then it was too late. It would have been very easy to turn the invasion to an advantage, but the man was stupid. Had he trusted his generals earlier, from the beginning, the calamity could have solidified the government's support. The military always knows better because we understand discipline. The Granma expedition was doomed to failure, there was no organization, no discipline, not enough proper training. I have studied it with great interest. The invasion succeeded because a number of factors came together at the precise moment. Had any of the leaders fallen at a given moment, the outcome would have been different. An undisciplined, fortuitous success cannot easily be duplicated unless ideal conditions exist. The conditions of Bolivia are far different from those of the Caribbean. Our people are of a different temperament. Our peasants are different, not better, different. They love liberty as much as your peasants, or I should say, the peasants of your adopted country. If our government inhibits their liberty, then it is for a Bolivian to rise and lead them. My God, man, only a few of your men spoke Quechua.

You might have been successful. But our president trusts his generals. He fears them, respects them. They keep him in power and he does not interfere with their mission. And, we have the Americans. It would all have been much more difficult without the Americans. You would still fail, but I would have slept less. We use the Americans to our advantage. No, it is not as your rhetoric would have the world believe. I'm sure you don't believe it yourself. We are not puppets of the Americans. The Americans are very immature, easily used, and we use them well. They are like little boys with a lot of money and technology and they eagerly want to see what can be done with it. We take what they have and show them what we can do with it.

We knew of your plans from the American intelligence units long before your departure. We knew of your destination as soon as you began preparations. That is when I was brought into the case. I am not a specialist in counterinsurgency at all. It is an accident that I am here. I did not train to be here. I was an aide to the Chief of Staff. After a general staff meeting, where the subject was you, the general asked me how I would handle the situation. You see, during the meeting, I kept silent, deferring to the counterinsurgency experts. I was bothered by the unimaginative thinking, by the rigidity of their plans. I expressed my doubts to the general. I was not surprised to see he agreed with me. Our experts merely mouthed textbook responses from their American teachers. I suggested the mission required someone with a more Bolivian point of view and not so much an American anti-communist view. That is why the Amercans are doomed to failure in their battle against communism. To them, wherever they can join battle with the communists, they are fulfilling a divine mission. The Americans fight with a rifle in one hand and ideology in the other. The communists fight with a rifle in one hand and a piece of bread in the other. They are more patient. First, win the stomachs, then the hearts, then the minds. The Americans have been confronted with that over and over again, and they continue to lose. The Americans do not know how to struggle, as I do, as you do. They intend to battle communism on the same basis as their Wall Street executives battle world-wide economics— from 9 to 5, and then it is time to relax, to be comfortable, to rest for the next day's activities. And the more intellectual the struggle, the better. It is a sign, is it not, of an intellectual inferiority complex. It's their basic immaturity and insecurity. They wanted to be the ones to execute you, you know. Oh, not some blond, blue-eyed yankee in a starched uniform. They are not so stupid. But, their intelligence agency has operatives within our military, in high positions. We know of them, surely, and they are helpful from time to time. Most are zealots, which is also the sign of a bungler. The plan, I imagine, was to send a counterinsurgency colonel with me who would later insist on pulling the trigger. Then, they could report to Washington that one of their local operatives performed this vital service. Why didn't he come? My general interceded. It would still have been a Bolivian that executed you, but the Americans would have taken some of the credit. Our propaganda machine is not so sophisticated. Besides, there is no need for a formal execution. It will be done quietly. Here, in the jungle, just you and perhaps three soldiers. I will not be present. I will gain no satisfaction from your death.

No, we don't know if your friend betrayed you. The Americans have a very good intelligence network in the Caribbean, but I have nothing definite to tell you. Yes, I know of the speculation, and I'm sure there will be more, but I have no information to give you.

We are on the same side, you and I. You should be aware of that. From the moment you decided to come to our country, we became spiritual brothers, comrades in the same struggle. When I first received your file, the first reports showed me a man not unlike myself. Your file grew thicker each day and with each report, I saw a different facet of your personality. And there were photographs. I have the elaborate physical changes you went through to conceal your travels. I received extended reports on all of your contacts throughout South Amerca. You knew them, you talked to them, and they also became acquaintances of mine. You made love to a woman in Bogotá. I felt better because you had not had sex for some six months—the Americans are particularly scrupulous in collecting this sort of information. When Tanya became your comrade in the field, all of your activities were reported in full. The Americans like to be so thorough. I became embarrassed at some of the details and I stopped reading those reports.

Yes, we were on the same side from the beginning. We could have captured you as soon as you set foot on Bolivian territory. In fact, we argued in a general staff meeting, with our president and his civilian ministers present, until after the sun was up. We, the military, prevailed in the end. You were to be allowed to enter with only token difficulty so as not to arouse your suspicions. We gave assurances that your activities would be closely monitored and that your proposed revolution would be managed out of La Paz as carefully as possible.

Surprised? You are a philosopher, I know, and it should come as no surprise to you that your revolution was as much our doing as yours. In fact, it was entirely our doing since we made sure you went where we wanted you to go and did almost what we had in mind that you should do. Yes, you were simply the instrument of a revolution we needed very badly. Had you not come, the generals would have had to appoint another president. That is always very troublesome. No, you were never troublesome. With your presence, our adequate propaganda machine, the people easily became afraid and that is what we wanted all along. They rallied behind our government. From the very beginning, our work was helped considerably by your activities. The peasants began reporting your activities as soon as you left village after village. They did not like your manner. It is not a Bolivian manner. Your Granma success worked against you. You changed in character. The reports about you from the field showed a different you than the you of the diaries of the earlier revolution. You have grown old. It is not good for revolutionaries to grow old. So, you see, I do not boast when I say I could have captured you at a moment's notice.

No, do not be sad. All is not lost for you. I came to know you through the intelligence reports. The Americans make everything sound so official. It was difficult to know you at first, but, in time, I knew you. I dreaded the day I would have to kill you. I actually believe in what you are doing. You and all the rest. The others have been executed already. No, we will not make a mockery of their deaths. They were buried immediately. They were of no consequence, really. Faceless beings that no one will remember. They were not colorful. There was no Camilo Cienfuegos among them. And Tanya? Yes, Tanya. The Americans almost destroyed the entire operation. They wanted to make her an agent. I personally staked my career against it. It was too much of a risk. She was young, passionate and devoted. The coercive means of the Americans would have been of no use. Fortunately, we quieted the Americans.

We dream as you do, of course. But, we are also practical men. We save our dreams for our private moments. Our dreams are the same as yours. The only difference is you involve others in your dreams. And the involvement of others makes it a collective dream. And the collective wishes to put it into praxis. The will of the collective is to make the dream the dream of others as well. And, when we of the government hear of your dream, we want to be a part of it too. But, we open our eyes, our minds, and know it for what it is: a dream, only.

Government is a practical matter. At best it is designed to be unpopular. The practicality of government must come before all idealism. Revolutionaries never consider that. You see, no government is really any better than another. One merely substitutes tyrants. The sponsors of a government, whether revolutionary or reactionary, as the terminology goes, do not matter ultimately. Governement has a will of its own, a praxis which is not understood except by those in government. Some learn quickly and the government is stable. Those who do not are quickly replaced by counterrevolutions. Those with the highest and most firm ideals tend to lose control of the government sooner.

And yet, revolutionaries are very necessary. You bring a hope to the people. You remind them that things could be better. We remind them that things could be worse. But, the power must rest with people like me. Mankind only wishes something to eat, something to drink, and someone to make love to. More than that complicates life. Mankind desires order and we, the government, can give them that order. The discipline of life can only be maintained if there is hope. The church provides hope in one area, a transcendent hope. We practical men realize that there must be hope on earth as well, and that is where you come in. The revolutionary places before the people an image of paradise on earth—a preposterous image, but a necessary one. Those goverments that do not see the necessity of it are doomed to failure. Those that recognize it, as our government does, will last, at least until we lose sight of it. Though we are practical, we are only human and make mistakes to our detriment as well.

Thus, when you die, your image will be tarnished somewhat. The impracticality of your actions will be seen for what it is. That is our concern. Your death will inspire some of our people, and others throughout the world, no doubt. There will be groups founded in your name, but they will concern themselves mainly with theoretical discussion—no threat at all. Oh, to be sure, from time to time, we will arrest a few of them, perhaps torture them as an example so that the discussions will remain at the theoretical level.

If it is any comfort, you will not die in vain. Your name will become synonymous with guerrilla activity. I will be sure to tell the press of your activity in the Congo and in North Vietnam. That will be helpful. The world needs you, needs your failure. Perhaps in that failure is your greatest success.

Before I go, let me finish with this. We are oppressors, if you will, of people's bodies. We cannot control what they think. It is of interest to us what they think, but of much more immediate concern is what they do—that we can control. Let us then call it a tyranny over the people. What you offer, with your ideals, is a freedom that people do not want, a liberty that ultimately oppresses them far more than we do. You offer them, as you should, the freedom to make choices, to be responsible. That is a far greater tyranny. As it is, the people hate an external oppressor. You wish to take the power for that oppression away from the government and place it within the individual. Man will be master and slave to himself. It is an antagonistic duality that destroys the spirit, that withers the mind. No, it is far better that we be the external oppressors. It is far better for the people. And, if there were no revolutionaries, the military would have to enlist them, to manufacture them as it now trains technicians.

So, I admire you and I thank you for what you have done for the people and for my government. I know you do not believe in God, but I hope He takes you into His care. You were never a bad man to me.

The soldiers will attend to you when you wish.

Do you hear the windmill starting to creak?

Memorias

The dog who slept outside by the door awoke almost at the same instant that the radio automatically clicked on the morning polkas from San Antonio. Don Fulgencio had been awake for nearly an hour. He lay upon the bed, eyes open, staring at the ceiling he could not see in the darkness. A threadbare sheet and an unfinished quilt covered his body from his shoulders down to his upper ankles. The quilt was missing a large diagonal piece from a corner. Were he to cover his feet, his upper torso would be covered only by the sheet. His cold feet were an irritant, but, still, between the quilt and the sheet, he kept warm enough.

The radio announcer exhorted San Antonio and the surrounding countryside to get up as the dawn was beginning to break and the sun should not catch anyone in bed. It was time to go to work, he yelled.

"Despierten, gente!" the announcer screamed out of the radio on the floor by the bed. "¡Ya llegó la hora!"

The buzzer on the alarm radio began its urgent signal for Don Fulgencio to rise. Once the alarm went on, he could not lie there enjoying the faint blue light coming in through the window. It was the best time of the day for him, a quiet, peaceful time. A time between waking and not waking, when the world was never a disturbance for him. The buzzer nagged at him from the floor a small distance away from the bed. He had purposely placed it there to make himself rise and walk over to silence the persistent bleating.

Don Fulgencio turned the sheet and quilt aside. His thin, cadaverous legs were sparsely covered with white hairs against the dark brown skin. The wooden floor was cold under his bare feet. A cold draft of air forced its way through some of the cracks in the floor. Don Fulgencio walked slowly, painfully. The buzzer continued its insistent roar, seeming to become louder, more urgent. He felt he had to urinate. When he neared the radio a few steps away, he knelt on one knee, feeling in the darkness for the vibrating box. The radio was still cold, the heat of the tubes still had not warmed the casing. Don Fulgencio pressed the button which he found by touch and silenced the impertinent buzzer. He stood still for a moment. He now did not need to urinate as urgently as when his warm feet first touched the floor.

Don Fulgencio returned to the bed. The light coming in through the window had turned everything into shadows. He picked up the quilt, shook all the kinks out of it, folded it into a neat square. He draped it over the back of a chair nearby. He next stretched the thin sheet tautly over the bed, tucking it under the pillow. When he was satisfied that he had pulled all of the wrinkles out of the sheet, he placed the quilt on top of the sheet at the foot of the bed, centering it.

He stretched his arms and upper body, squeezing away the last remaining sleep. He dug his knuckles into his eyesockets as if trying to scrape away the film of sleep. Upon the back of the chair, neatly folded, he found his trousers. He could not see them clearly in the dark shadows, but he knew they were there. He shook them vigorously, partly out of habit and partly out of precaution. He had not seen a scorpion nor a spider in the house for many years, but he continued it as a ritual each morning. Don Fulgencio slipped his thin legs into the trousers, after which he clasped a worn leather belt around his emaciated waist.

The grey light brightened as it came in through the window, illuminating the room which was his house. Don Fulgencio pulled on the long string in the center of the room, almost even with a corner of the bed. The room was suddenly dazzling, momentarily blinding him, causing him to shut his eyes as a reflex. He needed the light from the naked bulb to cook his breakfast.

The opening of the door pushed the dog aside as the old man stepped outside on the porch. Don Fulgencio looked at the dog lying at his bare feet. The tenderness and affection which he felt for the animal was not reflected in Don Fugencio's stern morning face. The dog was very still, his only sign of life was the bellows motion of his breathing mid section. The dog's head rested on its paws, its eyes were closed but he was not asleep.

While looking at the dog, Don Fulgencio remembered his shoes. He went back inside the room and momentarily he was again on the porch, feeling the stiff shoes begin to soften under the pressure of his body. Don Fulgencio walked to the edge of the porch, stopping at the top of the three porch steps. He looked far off into the distance where the horizon was beginning to form, his eyes searching beyond the limits of the hazy light of daybreak. Don Fulgencio seemed to be straining to see something, something which beckoned to him. Not being able to distinguish what it was, he stepped off the porch, careful of the rotting porchsteps. He walked a short distance away, along a worn path until he reached the single-seat cubicle which leaned to one side amidst dying brown grass and weeds.

Finishing his morning elimination, Don Fulgencio returned from the outhouse along the wavering path. He did not walk onto the porch again.

Instead, he turned and walked along the grassless front yard to the side of the house. There, on a bench coated with peeling white paint, sat a wash basin. Beside the basin were his soap, toothbrush and toothpaste. He picked up the basin, carried it over to the spigot rising like a metal root out of the ground. He turned the faucet, filling the dark blue, white-dotted, porcelain bottom with water. When the basin was half full, he carried it back to the bench.

Though it hurt his back to stoop over, Don Fulgencio endured the pain, splashing the clear, icy-hard water over his rough brown face, feeling the grogginess of having lain motionless in sleep leave him completely. He was now fully awake. He felt the dull pain in the small of his back, but he would not give in to it. He straightened after cleansing his teeth and stretched his arms once again. As he relaxed, his body trembled and shook all the way down, causing his knees to buckle slightly. He steadied himself and brought his right hand to his face to see if he needed to shave. He shaved more often now that his wife was no longer alive. She had never mentioned his sandpaper whiskers during their life together. He smiled and twisted his head as he remembered his wife. Don Fulgencio slid his hand up from his cheek and ran his fingers through the thick white hair on top of his head.

He had taken a few indecisive steps toward the house when he decided to shave after all. He smiled again as he rubbed his forefinger along his upper lip, remembering the moustache that was no longer there. Though he tried, he could not remember how long he had been clean shaven. He knew with some certainty that while preparing for his wife's burial, he had absent-mindedly shaved part of it off and had to get rid of the rest. He had been sad burying her without the moustache. She loved to place her cheek against the bristles and would giggle like a little girl because she said it tickled her. The smile pulled his lips away from the large square teeth, slightly yellowing from age and tobacco. They were strong, healthy teeth. Don Fulgencio shook his head from side to side, continuing to smile, unwilling to let go of the memory of his wife.

He applied the coarse soap to his lower face and neck, rubbing briskly, applying more soap to build up a sparse lather. The razor was the same one he had bought in Gonzales as a young man. That entire year had been one of coming into manhood for him. He had received advice from his father, from his uncles, from his cousins and neighbors. A man, he was told, ought to have his own razor. He also remembered that he had carried it in his pocket, his hand never letting go of it, on those Saturday afternoons when the whole family went to town during the trouble with the Urrutias. He could not remember what had caused it, nor how it had ended. He only remembered that one Saturday he no longer felt he had to take it with him.

The razor stayed sharp and he needed only to strop it a few times before it glided smoothly over his cheeks, scraping away the white stubble which had sprouted during the night. After he finished shaving, he was done with his morning ritual. He always remained in his undershirt until he finished with his wash. Once that was done, he needed only to return inside the house, put on his blue cotton shirt, and cook his breakfast.

"¿Por qué no tomaste el trabajo que te ofreció don José?"

"Porque no quise."

"Ni que fueras millonario, desgraciado."

"Ya no me estés fregando porque te voy a dar un chingazo."

"No me amenaces, que yo no te tengo miedo, ¡viejo cabrón!"

"Vieja, pata rajada, ¿a quién le dices cabrón?"

"Pos, a ti, desgraciado, bruto, que ¿no ves que eres el único cabrón aquí?"

"Vieja perra. Vale más que te cuides ese hocico porque uno de estos días te lo voy a quebrar."

"A mí no me digas perra, viejo arrastrado. Te viene a ofrecer trabajo y tú, muy ancho, no quieres nada. Debías irte a trabajar en vez de estar aquí amenazando a la gente."

"Arrastrado, dice la bruta. Si no fuera por mí, todavía estuvieras comiendo raíces y piscando algodón con toda la bola de tu familia. Puros rateros chingaos."

"Vale más que te cuides con mi familia, baboso. Con ellos no juegas."

"¿Y quiénes son ellos, esa familia tuya?"

"¿Ya crees que porque yo te aguanto tus pendejadas ellos también son iguales para aguantarte?"

"Aguantan y más, los cabrones. No se atreven toda la bola de animales. Patas rajadas. Mojados. Es lo que son, toda tu pinche familia. Mojada. Tú también."

"Ya lo verás uno de estos días."

"Y crees tú que van a arriesgar que te mande pa' tras con ellos a que te mantengan. Pos' encantados de la vida están porque yo soy el que te da de comer."

"Viejo mañoso. Qué hablar de mojados ni qué hablar de mojados. A tu familia los corrieron de México. Tan apurados andaban que tu madre te parió en el medio del río. Ya mero te ahogabas cuando te cagó."

"Cuidado con mi madrecita. Con ella no chingas."

"Ni ganas tengo."

"Mira, vieja pendeja, mejor dame de comer y cállate el hocico."

"Comer, comer, es todo lo que sabes. Nomás comer y comer, como si fueras un rico de nomás estar aquí comiendo y chingando. ¿Y dónde crees que vamos a comer la semana que entra? No has trabajado esta semana."

"Esta muy mojada la tierra. No hay trabajo. Nadien ha trabajado."

"Mojada la tierra, dice el arrastrado. ¿Y lo de don José? ¿Qué es eso? Trabajo hay para los que quieren. No como tú."

"Ya córtale. Ya no puedo aguantar ese hocico tuyo. Voy pa'l pueblo. Allí como."

"Seguro, cómo no, señor muy rico, ¿cómo no? Vaya usted a comer al pueblo mientras que su vieja pendeja se muere de hambre en la casa."

"Buen favor me hicieras, vieja desgraciada. ¡Muérete! Hazme de malas ese favor."

"¡Salte! ¡Vete! Ya no quiero verte esa pinche cara. ¡Vete!"

Once inside the house, Don Fulgencio stopped briefly to listen to the advertisements on the radio. The one which always caught his attention and was his favorite was for Centeno's supermarket. The announcer prattled on at a furious speed trying to squeeze in as many words as possible during the allotted one minute. Don Fulgencio remembered without emotion that his wife had always insisted on traveling the fifty miles each way to buy their groceries at Centeno's. There, they would buy hundred-pound sacks of potatoes and beans, fifty-pound cans of lard, and several twenty-five-pound sacks of flour.

Don Fulgencio's wife loved to stop by the mechanical horse just inside the store which would begin to shake and vibrate once a nickel was dropped into a coin box on a platform. She would stand there, and would likely have stood there for hours if he would not urge her, sometimes forcefully, further on inside the store. She would watch as the children gleefully held on to the gaudily painted saddle horn as the contraption rattled and swayed to and fro. She would often search in her purse for nickels to give to those children who had strayed from their parents and who stood in front of the metal animal without the money for a ride.

She knew she was getting older, near the time when it would be difficult for her to bear children, and yet she and Don Fulgencio had not had any. She worried that the two of them would grow old alone, without children, without grandchildren. Her family still lived close by, but Don Fulgencio only grudgingly agreed to visit. His brother and sister had both died in a fire, leaving their two children orphaned. His mother and father took the orphans in and raised them. Once grown, they moved away after his parents had died. She knew they lived in San Antonio and it was not a difficult trip to make, but they never visited. When she and Don Fulgencio went to San Antonio to shop, he did not mention them nor did he indicate he cared to visit them. They would shop at Centeno's and return home immediately, the only break in the journey being a restaurant in Lone Oak where they would buy hamburgers.

Don Fulgencio unwrapped the brown purplish butcher paper where he kept a slab of salt pork. He placed the slab with the rind side up on a plate to slice it. He cut three thick slices and set them to one side, wrapping again what was left. He looked around absentmindedly for the box of matches, finding it at last on the crude shelf above the camp stove which sat on a table in the corner opposite the bed. The fat match head flared up in a bright yellow flame when he struck it on the wall. The smell of sulphur briefly permeated the room. When the match settled to a pale yellow flame, he applied it to the left wick of the two-burner camp stove.

She had cooked all their meals on this stove. Don Fulgencio remembered that he had once promised her a new range stove, one with an oven, like the one they had seen inside the Western Auto store. He had never been able to afford it. They had saved for it, but somehow the money always had to go for something else. For a time, though, they had been happy together, dreaming of the day when he would bring home the stove. She had promised to bake him a cherry pie. That would be the first thing to cook on the stove. He scolded her gently for making such a promise. He reminded her that she had no idea of how to bake any pie, much less a cherry pie. She would retort, earnestly, that he need not worry about her not knowing how to bake a cherry pie. All he had to do, she would tell him playfully, ironically, was bring the stove home. She would take care of the rest. He believed her. He knew, somehow, that her pies would have been better than those he bought at Don Pedro's General Store in Smiley. He never bought the stove and she never learned to bake him a pie.

The skillet he had placed on top of the camp stove was beginning to sputter and smoke as the built-up grease which coated its bottom began to burn. In his reverie, he had forgotten all about it. He tossed the bacon slices into the pan, spreading them in an even row. By now he should have had his shirt on, as he prepared to begin his day fully dressed.

As he had thought about his wife, he had remained standing, shirtless, in the middle of the room. He had no idea of how long he had been standing there thinking, remembering. His days and nights were increasingly devoted to thoughts of his wife. The world of his mind, having lapsed long ago, returned from far away where it wandered; his memories so fresh and near he could touch them, would dominate whatever he was doing and he would forget everything else. It bothered him at times that he would lose five minutes here and ten minutes there, returning to the now of his life unable to know for certain how long he had been gone into that other world of memory. He reasoned that it might be because of his age and that it was natural for it to happen to him. Once he convinced himself that he was simply getting old and that there was nothing wrong nor anything to become upset about; it was a comfort to him to know he was not going crazy.

He loved remembering the life he'd had, but by far, the best memories were those in which his wife came to him so real that he could almost reach out to her and run his fingers through her thick black hair. He could almost feel her standing in front of him. In the beginning, soon after her death, he would remember her and pace about the room, unable to be still, yearning for her, cursing her for having left him. As the years passed, his memories were less anxious and gradually became a source of calm for him. He felt peaceful when he thought of her, at ease. Lately, all he could remember of his life were those moments filled by his wife. He seemed not to have any other memories. Although it was disconcerting at first, he did not mind if entire chunks of time disappeared out of his present. He had his life and he enjoyed it.

Don Fulgencio's still nimble fingers worked deftly with the buttons of the faded blue denim work shirt. He loosened the cracked leather belt, allowing his trousers to slide down a little over his shrunken hips. He stuffed the shirt

114

skirt into the gaping trousers, after which he hitched them up in a way he had seen Jimmy Cagney do and he refastened the belt. He made his way over to the small shard of mirror on the wall, held there by some bent nails. He combed the thick white hair, parting it on one side.

By the time he finished combing his hair, the grease was splattering over the sides of the skillet. He rushed to the stove, drawn by the sizzling hiss. He flipped the bacon over. After a few more minutes, during which he tapped a fork in rhythm with an inaudible tune on the rim of the skillet, the bacon was done—brown and coarse. Don Fulgencio pushed it aside with the fork as he cracked an egg with one hand into the pan. He saw a jagged triangle of eggshell in the center of the yolk and plucked it out with his fingers. The egg white bubbled as soon as it slid into the grease. Half turning the upper part of his body, he tossed the eggshell into a greasy paper sack in a corner of the room. With the fork, he flipped the egg over, puncturing an air pocket as the egg bloated.

On another table, a smaller one, next to the one on which he kept the stove, there was a pail of water. He took the tin coffeepot and filled it. He opened the bag of coffee grounds leaning to one side of the water pail. He dipped and dropped three spoonfuls of coffee into the pot. Don Fulgencio came back to the stove, placing the coffeepot in front of it. The egg was done now, the outer edges burnt a dark crinkly brown. He took the only plate he owned and slid the egg onto it, pushing the bacon alongside the egg. He set the pan aside and positioned the pot with its uneven bottom over the fire. He increased the size of the flame by turning up the wick. The fire overflowed the bottom and slithered up the blackened sides. He brought over the chair he kept next to the bed and sat down to eat while the coffee boiled.

Don Fulgencio ate quickly, hardly tasting the food. While his wife was alive he had eaten quickly because there had always been so much to do. There was plenty of work in those days. His strength was good then and he enjoyed an energy that constantly drove him, seldom permitting him to be still for long periods. It became a habit with him. Constantly pacing or going to and fro. His friends and neighbors would mimic him. His wife had scolded him time and again about his movements and his eating so rapidly. He might have even promised to eat slower, to enjoy the flavors of his food, and perhaps to talk with her more as they grew old together. He could not be certain, however. He could not remember when he did not eat fast. Now, his movements were slower but he continued to eat rapidly. And, too, she was gone. He was growing old alone and there was no joy in eating. At times, as he sat there thinking about her, remembering the way she moved around the room preparing food, washing dishes, rearranging them, his food would get cold. His memories robbed him of hot food, but he did not mind. The food kept him from dying, the memories kept him alive.

"¿Por qué lloras?"

"Tú sabes."

"Por eso te pregunto, pendeja."

"Di que no sabes donde pasaste la noche."

"Mira, vieja, te doy de comer, tienes tu casa, ahora, no andes con reproches ni chingaderas. ¿Oíste?"

"Tengo derecho de saber dónde andabas."

"No tienes ningún derecho de nada."

"¿Andabas con otra mujer?"

"No."

"¿Por qué no me miras cuando me contestas?"

"Porque no me dan las ganas. ¿Oíste?"

"¡Desgraciado! ¡Andabas con otra mujer!"

"Si ya sabes, ¿pa' qué chingaos preguntas?"

"Yo soy tu mujer. Aquí tienes a tu mujer."

"Pos, sí, eres mi mujer, pero quiero que sepas que no eres la reina de España. ¡Pinche!"

"No quiero ser reina de nada. Estoy contenta siendo tu mujer. No quiero creer que eres tan desgraciado y malvado para olvidarte de mí."

"Pos, no me olvido, ¿sabes? Y no andaba con otra. ¿Eso es lo que querías saber?"

"Entonces, ¿qué traes con toda la noche?"

"Pos, andaba tomando y cantando, pero no andaba con viejas."

"No andabas borracho cuando llegaste. Andabas bueno y sano."

"Es porque puedo tomar toda la pinche noche como puro hombre y no ando cayéndome como chamaco baboso."

"Mentiroso. Jiedes de vieja en toda tu ropa. Hombre, no seas sinvergüenza. Di la verdad."

"Pos no vayas creyendo que te tengo miedo."

"No quiero que me tengas miedo. Quiero que me digas la verdad. Seré tonta, pero no tan pendeja como crees."

"Mira, manita, no llores. ¿Pa' qué quieres que te diga? ¿No crees que es mejor no saber?"

"Soy tu mujer."

"Yo sé."

"Entonces, ¿pa' qué andas por allá toda la noche?"

"Andaba tomando. Ya te lo dije."

"La próxima vez, me voy. Gracias a Dios que todavía tengo a mi familia. Ahora, lárgate, déjame en paz por un rato."

"Está bien."

Don Fulgencio finished eating. He stood up and stretched his arms. He placed the plate and fork next to the pail of water. Later, he would take them outside to rinse them at the faucet and wipe them clean. By now, the coffee was boiling, foaming and bubbling, spilling over the sides of the pot, causing a crackling-hissing noise on the fire. Without hurrying, in a measured step, he walked over to extinguish the flame. He poured some water on a threadbare dishcloth which he then wrapped around the pot handle, pouring the steaming, bubbling coffee into a cup on the table. He set the coffeepot on the bare wooden table, scarred from years of use. In places the scars were worn smooth, oiled by human sweat and cooking juices. Don Fulgencio sat down again, adjusting his chair at an angle to the table. When he was comfortable, he started to drink his coffee.

He began to think of his wife, relaxing, offering no resistance to the memories he longed for. As his food settled, he felt peaceful and calm. Before the image of her face and the sound of her voice filled the small room, he heard a noise outside the door. He heard footsteps. It seemed strange to Don Fulgencio. If someone approached the house, the dog would surely have barked. There was no warning from the dog. There was a knock on the door. He placed the cup of coffee carefully on the table so as not to spill it. He stood up and went to the door. Through the rusting screen on the door frame he could distinguish a figure.

"¿Quién es?" he asked.

"It's Jack, Fulgencio. I've come to take you to breakfast."

"Oh, Jack, it's you. Breakfast? I don't think I can eat again."

"You've eaten already, Fulgencio?"

"Yes, Jack. I always eat right after sunrise."

"Well, come to the dining room anyway, Fulgencio. You have all your friends there. They want to eat breakfast with you. Who knows, you might be hungry enough to eat again when you get there."

"All right, Jack."

"Here, Fulgencio, let me help you with your robe. It's cold outside."

"Yes, I know. I was just outside shaving."

"Of course. It looks like you missed a few places. We'd better shave you again after breakfast."

"Well, I'm ready, Jack. Just let me turn off the radio."

Don Fulgencio walked over to the empty table to turn off the radio that was not there.

Doña Petra

When Pedro and José brought Jacinto home, Pedro drove the car. The '51 Chevy, green, glistened in the late afternoon sun of South Texas. The car was Jacinto's love. He took very good care of it. It was all shiny new green paint and chrome. Jacinto tried to make it look better than when some gringo first owned it ten years before. He took every cent he could spare to improve the condition and appearance of the car.

Pedro drove it carefully, almost tenderly. He knew very well that Jacinto would not approve of anyone mistreating his car. José sat in the back seat with Jacinto's head resting on his lap. Tears streaked down from José's eyes. Jacinto's eyes were closed. The bump in the road appeared suddenly, too quickly for Pedro to avoid it. As the three passengers jumped up, Jacinto's jacket fell open, exposing a dark red, almost black, splotch of blood covering the two bullet holes in his chest. There was no longer any bleeding.

Pedro braked slowly in front of doña Petra's house. It was a small, wooden house, painted in white, with a sloping tin roof in front covering the porch. On the porch stood two straightback chairs. The street in front of the house was unpaved, formed out of white, dusty gravel. Pedro opened the door, pushing the backrest of the front passenger seat forward so he and José could take out the body.

"Pásamelo," said Pedro.

"Cálmala, ¿no crees que debíamos decirle a la señora primero?" asked José.

"Chingao, bato, no sé. Creo que sería mejor."

"Orale, ponle."

"¿Por qué no vas tú, pinche?"

"Tú la conoces, yo no, ése."

"Orale, 'ta de aquéllas."

"Aquí te calmo, ése."

José stepped out of the car, laying Jacinto's head gently on the backseat. He stood beside the car for some moments, looking alternately at Pedro and at the house. He didn't know what to say to doña Petra, how to begin. He thought of asking Pedro, but decided against it. He remained standing next to

Pedro for a few moments in silence.

Doña Petra, inside the house, heard the noise of the car but did not stop the patter of her hands making tortillas. She felt relieved that Jacinto was home. She did notice, however, that Jacinto had not raced the engine and she had not heard the popping of the muffler pipes. It was always Jacinto's signal to her that he was home.

She did not often make tortillas de maíz anymore because of her age, but today was special. Today, Saturday, was the end of the first week of Jacinto's new job. He had spent almost two months without a steady job. He was not completely idle during those two months. He would go to the town square and take jobs for the day in the neighboring farms and ranches. Don Jacinto, her husband, dead now for so many years and yet so alive to her, had spent his life working from day to day, season to season. But that was before they had moved into town. She hoped Jacinto would not spend his life without the steady income a job in town could afford. The job looked very promising for Jacinto and that made today even more special.

She reasoned that he was paid at noon, as were most of the workers in town, and he must have gone to have a few beers with los muchachos. He had mentioned they were a good friendly bunch to work with. She approved of Jacinto and his friends' beer drinking. They were all good boys, not like some of those cabrones from the neighboring towns who never worked and were always fighting. No. These boys worked hard and they drank a little, but they always brought home money for the family. They knew they had responsibilities to the family and they took care of them first before squandering too much of their money. That was good. She had anticipated Jacinto would be home around two o'clock. It was now one thirty. He was early.

José could not stall his trip to the house any longer. Pedro was no help. He simply stood there looking at the ground. José would have to go. Shrugging his shoulders and shaking his head from side to side in a sad gesture, José hitched up his trousers and began the long walk to the porch of the house. He decided to just tell her straight out. He knew it was terrible news he was bringing and he sensed there was some gentle way of breaking it to doña Petra, but he was not good with words. It was best to just tell her.

Slowly, he drew aside the gate to the peeling white picket fence. He continued up the walkway which was paved with round stones imbedded in the dirt. Once on the porch, he knocked softly on the wooden door frame. The sound was almost inaudible over the patter of doña Petra's hands. She heard the knock, though, and continuing the clap-clap of the dough between her hands, she went to the door. She walked slowly so as not to tear the moist tortilla.

Her eyes were not very good and the figure blurred by the screen was unfamiliar to her. It was not Jacinto. As she neared the screen, she recognized José.

"Ah, eres tú, Joselito. ¿Qué sucede? ¿Dónde está mi hijito? ¿No andabas con él?"

"Señora," José was fighting a losing battle to suppress the tears he had not been able to shed, "lo hirieron los rinches."

"Pero, ¿qué dices, muchacho?" In her sudden fright she did not notice she had let go of the tortilla, which fell flat with a plop on the floor.

"Sí, doña Petra, lo mataron los rinches. Murió en el pueblo. Lo llevamos con el doctor, pero ya era muy tarde. Ya estaba muerto. Ahí está en el carro."

"Malditos rinches," said she, softly, under her breath, controlling the rage which was beginning to swell in her breast. "Bueno, ayúdame a traerlo pa' dentro."

"Pues, Pedro está con él en el carro. El me ayuda."

José hurriedly went back to the car. Pedro formed a question with his face, but José said nothing in response. Together, after some difficulty, they gathered the body and brought it into the house. Doña Petra stood serenely in the middle of the room, unmindful of the drying crusts of masa on her hands. She motioned them to place Jacinto's body on the frayed and tattered sofa. As José and Pedro were adjusting the body full length on the sofa, doña Petra hurried into the bedroom for a pillow. She returned quickly and placed it under Jacinto's head. Pedro and José stepped to one side, observing doña Petra with her son. She knelt beside the body and began stroking the warm hair flowing from the cold scalp. She bowed her head and prayed.

Pedro's eyes were glistening and there was a quaver in his throat as he spoke.

"Pos, Doña Petra, si no nos necesita más . . ."

"Esperen," she commanded in a sharp, clear voice. She sounded strong and resolute.

Doña Petra remained kneeling for a few more minutes before she finally stood up. She went to the kitchen, irritably waving her hand for Pedro and José to follow. She bent slightly over the table and quickly cleared it of the stack of warm tortillas wrapped in a damp towel. There were only a few other items on the table which she also picked up to place on the sink counter. Once cleared, she asked the two young men to take the table into the living room. After they placed it in the center of the small room, she brought a chair and positioned it a small distance from the table. She was in complete control of her emotions.

"Pónganmelo en la mesa," she said.

Pedro and José again lifted Jacinto's body. It was not as awkward lifting him from the couch as it was getting him out of the car. The body was heavy, but they managed to set it on the table carefully. They were even more careful now out of respect for Jacinto's mother. They had managed to place one of the legs on top of the chairback, but the other slipped off and dangled over the edge of the table in a curious contortion. Doña Petra quietly, tenderly, lifted the leg by the calf and placed it next to the other one on the chairback.

"Déjenme," she ordered in almost an angry tone.

120

"¿No podemos ayudarle más?" asked José.

"Vayan con don Rodolfo y le dicen que prepare un cajón para mi hijo."

They told her they would arrange for the coffin and walked backwards toward the door, unwilling, out of respect, to turn their backs on her, her dead son, her grief. They opened the screen door, stepped out, and held on to it for fear it would slam shut.

After the two young men left, doña Petra went to a corner of the house where a small table stood. Over the table, on the left wall, hung a reproduction of Jesus Christ with His heart outside of His clothes. His hands were outstretched. On the adjoining wall, was a reproduction of la Virgen de Guadalupe, wearing a triangular outfit, with her head fixed to the top of it. Four cherubs, pinkly naked, were caught in flight at each corner. On the table was a black and white portrait of her deceased husband which was retouched in color, the cheeks a little rosier than they had been when he lived, his forehead a little whiter. A black ribbon traversed a top corner of the portrait. Doña Petra lit the candle and made a sign of the cross.

She went to her bedroom, to a tall dresser. In one of the middle drawers, she found another votive candle. Once in the living room, she took down Jacinto's picture from the wall adjacent to the television set. It was a picture taken when he was in Junior High School. He had not had a portrait made since then. She brought the picture to the little table, dug out the wedge of cardboard in back of the frame, and stood it, leaning slightly, beside the portrait of her husband. She then placed the candle in front of it and lit it. Her face was wrinkled only a little, shadowed and brown, accentuated by the flickering flames of the candles in the dim room. There was no emotion or grief on her face, only a stern, harsh visage. She picked up a black rosary which lay on the table.

She returned to the large table in the center of the room. She looked steadily at the still features of her son. She knelt on the floor beside Jacinto's head, bowing as she did so. She looked up briefly to see his head and began to say her rosary, silently most of the time, occasionally allowing a hushed murmur to escape her lips.

She finished saying her rosary, lingering over the kiss to the crucifix. She gathered the chained beads in her hand and made another sign of the cross, this time pausing briefly with a kiss to her thumb. Jacinto was her only son. Her face softened somewhat as she gazed tenderly at the body.

After she replaced the rosary on the small table in the corner, she began undressing Jacinto's body. Soon, she had him completely naked except for the underwear. She brought a brown paper bag from the kitchen and stuffed the soiled and bloody clothes into it. She would burn them tomorrow. She shook her head as she glanced at his shoes which she had placed side by side, evenly, next to the chair. They were brand new. He must have bought them right after work.

Doña Petra went into the kitchen. She opened the cupboard where she kept her towels and threw them all into the sink, running water over them until they were soaked. She rinsed them, after which she brought them into the living room, placing the bundle beside Jacinto's naked body. She wiped his face, arms and hands. With another towel, she began rubbing the dried, caked blood around the bullet holes. One of the bullets had entered the body on the right hand side of the chest, just under the collarbone. The other was an inch or two above the belly button, also on the right hand side. The blood, entangled and caked on his body hair, was difficult to scrub off. She rubbed briskly, using two towels, until the area surrounding the holes was clean. No matter how hard she tried, she could do nothing with the innocent looking black holes where the bullets went in.

Jacinto looked eerily asleep as she stepped around the table in a wide arc. There was nothing to mar the body except for the two black dots. Doña Petra used the last towel to scrub his legs. Efficiently, she gathered the used towels, keeping the bloody towels separate. Back in the kitchen, she spread two of the towels on the sink to dry before tossing them into the wash basket. The two bloody ones she stuffed into the brown paper sack along with Jacinto's clothes.

She could not cry.

Doña Petra leaned against the counter in the kitchen to rest for a few moments. She did not think of anything in particular. Her mind was clear of her memories of Jacinto. Nothing flashed through her mind, it was completely blank. She started suddenly, knowing there was much to do. It was best to do it all at once.

From a nail on the wall of the living room, which also served as Jacinto's bedroom, she took down his only suit. He seldom wore it and it was clean and pressed. From his dresser in her bedroom she fetched the least frayed of his shirts. He was supposed to buy shirts with his first paycheck, not shoes. She had some difficulty putting on his shirt and suit jacket, but the trousers were no problem. She got clean socks for him, put them on, along with his new shoes. She was finished now. The only thing missing was the coffin. It was doubtful that don Rodolfo would have one already available. He would have to make one. Nothing to do but say another rosary and wait.

It was five o'clock when she finished her second rosary. She had not eaten since morning. She had delayed her lunch to eat with Jacinto. That morning he told her to make tortillas as he was bringing barbacoa for lunch. She was now hungry. Almost in a daze, she went into the kitchen to prepare something to eat. Saturday evenings, Jacinto drove her to the grocery store for their weekly shopping. There was nothing in the refrigerator except for some eggs and some chorizo. She took a skillet, tossed the chorizo into it, after which, when the chorizo was well cooked, she cracked two eggs into it, scrambling them furiously with a fork. Once finished, she uncovered the tortillas which she had set on the counter. By now, they were cold. She did not bother to reheat them. There was no table in the kitchen now, so she brought the stack of tortillas to the stove. She forked the chorizo con huevo directly from the skillet onto the cupped tortilla, rolling it into a thin taco. There was no taste in her mouth.

She had not finished eating when Jacinto's car drove up again. She heard it, she recognized the distinctive roar of the engine. There was not another car like it in the neighborhood. For a moment, she was startled. She had not realized that Pedro and José had taken it. She heard the car doors slam, the footsteps on the porch, the knock on the door. A timid knock from an embarrassed hand. She went to the door.

"Doña Petra, don Rodolfo dice que el cajón estará listo pa' mañana en la tarde y dijo que él mismo lo trae."

"Gracias."

"También le manda el pésame."

"Agradezco su ayuda, muchachos."

"También fuimos con el padrecito y él dice que tendrá el cementerio preparado pa' mañana en la tarde también."

"Gracias. Les iba a pedir que me hicieran ese favor. Pero se me olvidó."

"Ya comprendemos."

"Acabo de hacer algo de comer. ¿Ya comieron? ¿Gustarían echarse un bocado?"

"No, gracias, doña Petra. Gracias comoquiera."

"Bueno, como gusten. Ahora, si pueden regresar mañana, se lo agradezco."

"Seguro, ¿cómo no?"

"Y se pueden llevar el carro. Al cabo que yo no puedo manejar. También, si pueden, mañana después de sepultar a Jacinto, quiero que me lleven .. un encargo."

"Está bien, cómo no, doña Petra. Seguro."

"Entonces, déjenme. Buenas noches," she said, dismissing them.

She watched them step down from the porch and drive away in her son's car. It was already becoming dark, long dark orange shadows spread over the barrio. By now, everyone would know of her tragedy. She imagined her neighbors preparing themselves to come visit her. She went outside and sat in one of the chairs on the porch, listening to the rumble of cars on the nearby highway as they swooshed by. Soon, the crickets would keep her company in the darkness. The barrio was quieter than usual, there were not as many cars as usual passing by.

Doña Petra continued to sit in her chair until long after the sun set. Shortly after seven, the first of her friends and Jacinto's friends began to arrive. She had not bothered to notify anyone. The news would quickly spread throughout the barrio. She had no surviving relatives, no one to call in other parts of town, in other parts of the state. But, she and Jacinto had many friends. They began arriving, singly, in twos, entire families. They would stop briefly in front of her and stoop a little to give her their condolences. They spoke in hushed, slow voices. The men would murmur their pésames inarticulately. The voices of the women were lower than normal, many of them cried and were confused because Doña Petra was dry-eyed and stern-faced.

Doña Petra remained where she was, sitting on the porch. She would not go inside. When Father Ramiro came to say a rosary, she still would not budge. The women all had rosaries with them. A few of the men did. The priest stood in front of the small table in the corner of the room, framed by the two religious pictures. All of the people inside knelt in front of him. Some of the women were crying softly. The men shifted uncomfortably, placing their weight first on one knee and then on the other. Occasionally, they would cast a glance at the still, rigid body lying on the table. An old fat woman, older than doña Petra, laboriously rose to her feet and went outside to notify doña Petra that the rosary was about to begin. Doña Petra did not answer, continuing to stare in front of her at some distant object. The old woman desisted and returned inside the house. She shook her head at the priest and began the difficult descent to her knees. The priest nodded he understood and, in a deep, loud voice, he began the rosary. Doña Petra remained sitting, saying the rosary silently, without the black beads to count.

Doña Petra was surrounded by people throughout the evening. It was not until midnight that some of the older people began to leave. José and Pedro had returned, wearing white shirts and dark trousers. Soon after they arrived, some other friends of Jacinto arrived. Some from work, some whom he had gone to school with. He had known all of them since childhood. They would arrive, deliver the pésame to doña Petra and step inside the house. Inside, they would stand beside Jacinto's body, glancing at his still features. Some prayed quietly, others did not. They all made a sign of the cross before leaving. Jacinto's young friends could not remain still in the funereal atmosphere. Eventually, they went outside the yard where they leaned against the cars. Some wine and whiskey bottles were passed around. Still others arrived with quart bottles of beer. They could not see doña Petra sitting in the dark on the porch. Some of the more irreverent made jokes and doña Petra could hear their low, hushed laughter.

As soon as the older people started to leave, the signal reached everyone. Within a short time, she was alone. Doña Petra did not feel alone, though. She thought about Jacinto lying inside the house. This would be his last night with her. She knew he was in Heaven even as she thought about him. He had always been a good boy. Sure, he cursed. She knew he cursed. All boys his age cursed. God would still take him, she thought. He was such a good boy. Never any trouble. Even when he was a child, he had never been any trouble to her. Now, he was gone from her forever. Dead. Killed by los rinches.

Then she began to think about los rinches. Jacinto was not the first they had killed. There was not a person in the town who had not had a son, a husband, a father, some relative, killed by los rinches. There was anger among the people where the rinches were concerned. No one ever did anything about it. For la raza of the town, there was no one to turn to. Immediately after a shooting, the rangers would increase their trips through the barrios almost as if daring someone to take revenge. It was a clear challenge to the men of the barrio. But no one ever accepted the challenge. And the rinches continued to shoot from time to time, confident they answered to no law but their own.

Doña Petra, still sitting on her porch in the damp, starless darkness of early morning, recalled her husband, don Jacinto. He, too, had been killed by los rinches. Fifteen years earlier. And, now, they had taken her baby Jacinto from her. After the burial tomorrow afternoon, she would be alone. The rangers were responsible for the loss of her entire family. What she only fleetingly, in anger, was tempted to do when she first saw Jacinto's body, she thought about now, quietly, resolutely, with more determination than anything she had ever decided to do. She knew what had to be done and she was the only one to do it.

As dawn was beginning to break, doña Petra yawned and stretched her arms. Her bones ached from the motionless night she had spent on the chair. Except for the ache in her bones, she was not tired. Her eyes were clear, her mind was alert. The stiffness left her body as soon as she stood up. She went inside the house for the first time since she had dressed Jacinto. Inside it was pitch dark, but she knew exactly where everything was and she easily found her way to the bedroom. She knelt beside the bed, taking an old, battered cigar box from under the bed.

The cigar box was wrapped in old, yellowing newspaper tied with brittle twine. As she tried to undo the knot on the string, it snapped. She sat on the bed, placing the box on her lap. She began to unwrap the newspaper, surprised as it crumbled in a few places. Once all of the paper was off the box, she pushed it away, letting it drop on the linoleum covered floor. Doña Petra opened the box. The first thing she saw was a fading picture of her husband, don Jacinto. In spite of the stern visage and the swooping moustache which flowed in a gentle arc away from his cheeks, his eyes shone. Doña Petra recongized and remembered the mischievous look which time had not obscured. She grew a little lonely for him.

Doña Petra expelled a long, lingering sigh. Gazing nostalgically at her husband's photograph, she remembered that he too had been brought to her dead as she prepared his dinner. The remembrance only cemented her determination. She put the picture aside, on the pillow she would not use that day.

Underneath a red and green scarf, which don Jacinto had bought for her at a traveling carnival, she found his pistol. She placed the carefully folded scarf underneath the picture on the pillow. she turned her attention to the pistol.

It was wrapped in a yellow oiled cloth inside a waxen bag. In the fifteen years since don Jacinto's murder, she never told Jacinto chico about the gun. He was a good boy and she was afraid of what he might do. He was all she had after her husband was taken away from her. Jacinto was seven when his father was murdered. As he grew older, the resentment and bitterness began to change him. He told his mother how he wished to avenge don Jacinto's death. He told her he longed to do it. She would become angry and tell him that he would end up getting himself killed. Each year he grew more and more bitter, visibly changing from a quiet, serene youngster to an often moody and morose young man. Still, she kept the gun and never told anyone about it.

Wrapped in a smaller square of oiled cloth were three bullets. They appeared new and usable. She had never handled a weapon of any kind before and it took her some time before she managed to expose the chamber to insert the shells in the waiting cylinders. That finished, she slid the loaded pistol into the pocket of her skirt underneath the apron that was her trademark in the barrio. Doña Petra was never without her apron. After the funeral, she thought.

She left the empty cigar box on the bed, along with the crumpled pieces of wax paper and oiled cloth. Her eyes were still alert, but she seemed to be in a daze. Doña Petra walked past Jacinto's body in the living room without looking at it. She returned to the porch and sat on the same chair. There she would wait.

The sun emitted an orange glow over the trees of the barrio to the east. In the light of morning, she noticed the large droplets of dew clinging to the uncut blades of grass in her yard. Soon the children would be issuing forth from the houses along the street on their way to school. At other times, she was happy to see the children. Each one would say good morning as they passed the house. The thought of the children did not make her happy this morning.

The sun was bright and hot when she awoke. Her entire body felt stiff and sore. There was an uncomfortable taste in her mouth. The dew had evaporated from the grass. She could not tell the time nor how long she had been asleep. The bulge of the pistol was heavy against her thigh. From the position of the sun, high overhead, she knew it was near noon. It would not be long before don Rodolfo came. Pedro and José, too. Then it would all be over.

She thought of going inside to fix something to eat. She did not feel hungry at all, and decided against it. The thought of Jacinto's death was heavy on her. It flowed from her mind to her stiffened face, making her muscles and bones ache. She felt unable to breathe. The thought of going inside to view Jacinto's body again and say another rosary over him repulsed her. She could not go inside. Without it being a choice she could control, doña Petra remained outside on the porch. A dog in the distance yelped and was answered by a long, mournful wail from another dog far away.

The clattering of don Rodolfo's truck made her turn her head toward the entrance to the barrio. The truck was extremely noisy and seemed on the verge of falling apart. When he stopped the hissing truck in front of her house, her eyes went immediately to the truckbed where the coffin of new wood

126

glared brightly. She felt suddenly weak. The presence of the coffin, which don Rodolfo was now lifting on his back, brought the final certitude of Jacinto's death to doña Petra.

"Buenos días, doña Petra," said don Rodolfo, peering from under the coffin. When he was on the porch, he set the coffin down in an upright position.

"La acompaño en su sentimiento," he said, stooping over to embrace her and to pat her back.

"Gracias, don Rodolfo." The harsh sternness returned to her.

"Me hace el favor de meter el cajón pa' dentro," she said.

"Seguro," he said, a little bewildered that she would think to ask, when it was what he intended to do.

Don Rodolfo edged the coffin near the screen door. He opened the door and held it open with his back while he grabbed the coffin around the wide middle section. Doña Petra made no move to help him with it, or to hold the door open. Clumsily, awkwardly, don Rodolfo dragged the coffin inside the house. The screen door slammed shut, but he did not pay any attention to it. When he had the coffin adjacent to the body on top of the table, he set it down gently, straining not to make any noise, as though he was afraid of waking a sleeping Jacinto. He straightened up slowly and painfully. He looked at the still features of Jacinto and made a hurried sign of the cross. He turned to ask doña Petra if there was something else he could do for her, but she was not in the room. He went outside to the porch.

Doña Petra looked up and said,

"Ahora esperamos que vengan los muchachos, los amigos de Jacinto. Ellos lo echan al cajón. Si quiere, se puede ir, don Rodolfo. Ya está arreglado lo demás. Después me arreglo con usted."

Don Rodolfo was surprised and hurt at the curtness of her voice. It was almost as if she were dismissing a servant. He had never been good friends with her or her husband or the deceased, but don Rodolfo was proud of the good relations he held with everyone in the barrio. Making coffins was a favor to his neighbors who could not afford the expensive coffins sold by the gringo funeral home. It was a simple matter for him to make the cheap coffins. He was a carpenter and not a coffinmaker. He charged people only for the materials and not for his labor. He hated to make the coffins, but someone had to do it. When people could not pay, he never asked for money. He was offended that doña Petra had mentioned a payment. He was about to scold her, but thought better of it.

"Está bien," he said, a little sadly, returning to his truck and driving off.

No sooner had don Rodolfo driven off than the priest arrived. He was to walk with her and the body to the church. The priest wanted to say something to her, he wanted to say some words of condolence, something to ease her grief. But she did not appear to him to be grieving very much. Not only that, but he did not know her well. At least, not as well as some of the other women of the barrio. Doña Petra attended church only once a year: on the anniversary of her husband's death. It was awkward for him to be there with her alone. He sat on the porch step, not looking at her, at pains for something on which to concentrate his gaze. Luckily, Pedro, José and four others arrived.

"Tiendan a mi hijo en su cajón, por favor," she said to them as they entered the yard. Her tone was tense, harsh. The men nodded at the priest and went inside the house without greeting her. Doña Petra continued to stare blankly at something in the distance.

Pedro came to the door shortly and said they were ready. The priest stood up and went to the screen door to hold it open while the six men walked slowly with the coffin on their shoulders. After they had the coffin outside, doña Petra asked them to wait while she went inside to get her black shawl. She did not bother to change her clothing. She was not long inside and the procession began.

The six men walked slowly, in unison, attempting to keep the coffin steady. Behind them, came doña Petra with the black shawl over her head, her hands clasped together, balanced on her stomach. The priest walked beside her. He noticed she was not carrying her rosary. The church was up the street, to the west, then north for one block. They did not have far to go.

Vecinos who knew doña Petra, or Jacinto, joined the procession as it passed their houses. By the time they reached the church, the procession had grown to over a dozen people. More of Jacinto's friends from other parts of town waited at the church steps. Inside the church was empty.

During the Mass, the priest noticed that doña Petra was not joining in the responses. She merely fixed her glance at the communion rail and said nothing. Her lips were firmly set and did not part at all during the service. She did not move.

After the Mass, the coffin was placed in don Rodolfo's truck. Doña Petra would ride with doña Juana to the cemetery which was located a mile or so outside of town. Those vecinos who had walked to the church obtained rides with those that drove. There were ten cars that drove the short distance to the burial place.

There was a barbed wire fence around the perimeter of the cemetary for la raza. White Catholics had their own cemetery beside their new church. At the entrance to the cemetery were two long poles with a cross pole on top. The sign hanging from the cross pole read: Cementerio Méjico-Americano. Don Rodolfo led the procession to a freshly dug grave beside which sat two elderly men who smoked Bull Durham cigarettes.

The gravesite ceremony was short. There was only one chair provided for doña Petra, and don Rodolfo had thought to bring it from his home. The priest was brief. Doña Petra, without emotion, tossed a handful of dirt over the coffin, after which the remainder of the mourners filed by the grave and did the same. When Pedro and José returned to Jacinto's car, doña Petra was waiting for them. She reminded them they were to take her on an errand. José

128

held the door open, pushing the backrest forward as she climbed in the back seat of the car. Before they could drive off, doña Juana came to the car. Pedro idled the car as the two women spoke.

Doña Petra rolled down the window to speak with her friend.

"Mire, doña Petra, el señor y yo sabemos que ya usted está sola y pensamos que, si quiere, puede venir a vivir con nosotros. Por mientras, siquiera."

"Gracias, doña Juana, es usted muy amable, pero no será necesario."

"Bueno, como guste. Pero, recuerde que nuestra casa es suya cuando quiera por tanto tiempo como quiera."

"Gracias, lo recordaré."

Doña Petra turned her face forward, rolling up the window as she did so.

"¿A dónde quiere ir, doña Petra?" asked Pedro over his shoulder.

"A la estación de los rinches."

"Pero ¿qué quiere hacer allí, doña Petra?"

"Quiero que me cuenten por qué y cómo mataron a mi hijo."

"Pero, doña Petra, ¿por qué no nos pregunta? Pedro y yo estuvimos presentes ahí y le podemos contar todo. Y mucho mejor que esos rinches habladores. Usted sabe que le van a decir alguna mentira comoquiera."

"Pos, me dirán una mentira, pero quiero oírla de sus propios labios."

"Bueno, si insiste."

"Sí, mis hijos. Ya saben que no tengo familia. No tienen que entrar ustedes. Les agradezco todo lo que han hecho, pero esto lo tengo que hacer yo sola. Yo bien sé cómo son los rinches. Ustedes me esperan afuera."

Pedro and José were nevertheless afraid for doña Petra.

The Texas Ranger headquarters was in a small building located some five miles outside of town. As they approached the headquarters, they noticed two patrol cars, one of them with a horsetrailer hitched to its bumper. It was empty. Behind the squat building was a corral in which three horses clustered around a circular water trough, drinking water, shaking their heads. There was no one in sight.

Pedro steered the car onto the gravel apron in front of the building, not parking too close to the ranger cars, keeping a discrete distance from them. Doña Petra sat in the back seat with her hands still clasped together, balanced on her stomach. José stepped out of the car quickly, holding the door for doña Petra to get out.

Doña Petra walked painfully, slowly, around the car going directly into the Ranger headquarters without knocking as was usual. Inside the building were two desks, one with a black telephone on top, and three bunks toward the rear of the room. A fat, red-faced Ranger sat behind one of the desks, feet up, reading a magazine. He had seen her as she walked in, but he said nothing and returned to his reading. Doña Petra took a few slow steps inside the room, not making a sound, standing silently between the two desks, waiting to be addressed.

She heard a commode flush, the water rushing in a muffled roar. Abruptly, the bathroom door opened near a far corner of the building. A young man, perhaps 28, with a crew-cut, walked inside, drying his face with a white towel.

"Who she?" he asked.

"How the hell should I know? She's been standing there," the fat man said from behind the desk, irritably tossing the magazine onto a pile of papers on the desk. He took his feet from the desk, leaning forward on it, addressing her in a rough drawl.

"What do you want, Mex?"

Doña Petra knew and understood enough English to get by, but chose to ask in Spanish: "¿Cuál de ustedes mató a mi hijo?"

"Cain't you speak English, woman?" the gruff fat man asked, becoming visibly angry.

"¿Cuál de ustedes mató a mi hijo?" she persisted.

"Well, shit! That's all I need on a Sunday morning! Some dumb Mex woman!" yelled the fat man.

"I'll get Juan," said the young Ranger.

"What for? Just turn her around and shoo her on out of here. We don't need tamales," said the fat man derisively.

"I'll get him anyway. It might be important."

The young Ranger walked to another door, this one leading outside to the back of the building and yelled for Juan.

After a few moments, a small, thin man, with the look of starvation and fear on his face, walked in carrying a broom. There was horse manure on his shoes.

The fat Ranger spoke. "Ask this Mex señora what she wants." When he said "señora," it was vulgar, obscene, as if the word was dirty inside his mouth.

"Dile que quiero saber cuál de ellos mató a mi hijo ayer."

The small man became alarmed, a painful grimace spread over his features.

"¿Pa' qué, señora? Váyase. Usted no tiene negocios aquí."

"Pregúnteles."

"What the hell she saying, Juan?" the fat man asked, without looking up from the magazine he was thumbing through.

"Mister Joe, sir, she want to know who killed her boy yesterday."

"Now, you know Jimmy there got him, but I would've killed the son-of-a-bitch myself, given half a chance. What difference does it make to her anyway."

The young Ranger now realized who doña Petra was and took a few steps forward. During the exchange between doña Petra and Juan, he had put on a khaki shirt and had not yet buttoned it.

"Ma'am, that was your boy? I'm sure sorry about what happened. I thought he had a gun, ma'am, I swear it, else I wouldn't have shot him. I got kinda scared, you know? He didn't do anything real bad. He was just drunk, but I thought he had a gun. I'm sure sorry."

Doña Petra listened to the young man, registering every word, her face betraying nothing. She unclasped her hands, reached into her skirt pocket, pulled out the pistol and shot the young Ranger three times in the stomach. The small man, Juan, with a look of astonishment, dropped the broom, diving to the floor, rapidly scurrying under one of the bunks. After firing the third shot, doña Petra let go of the pistol, not hearing the thud it made on the floor.

The fat Ranger jumped around the desk, his hand on his holstered gun, unable to draw it. When he heard doña Petra's pistol hit the floor, he carefully unsnapped the safety strap across the hammer of the gun, drew it slowly, and taking deliberate aim, shot her in the face as she looked straight at him. There was a slight smile of contentment on her face.

La Tacuachera

I

La Tacuachera stood atop the crest of a small hill five miles outside of Nixon on the road to Karnes City. Behind it and across the road in front of it were sloping terraced fields of rich black farm land. The tavern was situated in a gravel clearing surrounded by tall, ancient mesquite trees whose pale green leaves dulled the stinging heat of summer suns. In the back of the tavern, beyond the trees, the land lay fallow, overgrown with grass and weeds, rats and rattlesnakes. A narrow ribbon of cream-colored gravel extended beyond the half-moon of parking lot, circling around between the building and the trees. Approaching cars, turning off the black-top, produced a crunching rumbling announcement of their arrival.

As Nixon to the north was dry, *La Tacuachera,* located just outside the county line, sold the nearest legal beer. Bootleggers in town sold to teenagers and to those who could not find a ride to the tavern. Over the years, it had become a gathering place for people from Nixon and from a cluster of farm houses and a cotton gin known as Schoolland. The building was constructed out of stone up to waist level, and out of wood for the remainder. The sign above the entrance, supplied by a forgotten Coca-Cola salesman, read *Pleasant Hill Tavern.* Only the Anglos knew it by that name. The Chicanos of the area, mindful of some legendary or mythical occurrence, or perhaps remembering it as a clearing in which to rest after possum hunts, referred to it as *La Tacuachera.* More likely, the hunters never went beyond the tavern to their possum hunts.

No one really remembered when *La Tacuachera* began admitting Chicanos into the bar. It could be that it was always so, but the driveway around back, still used by Black people, served as a reminder. Of course, there were many who knew, but they seldom wanted to talk about it. When they did talk about it, it was with a laugh. When they, for some reason or other, remembered, when they chose to talk about it, it was said that Chicanos were allowed to open the back door, to poke in their heads, but they were not permitted to enter. The Chicano at the door would try to get the attention of the bartender.

Failing to do so, he would have to ask an Anglo seated at a nearby table to please call the bartender. Once the bartender saw the waiting Chicano, the Chicano held up as many fingers as he wanted six-packs. There was no signal for brands and the bartender would bring him whatever kind of beer was handy or the kind he had overstocked. The transaction would be concluded at the back door, the bartender often keeping the Chicano's change as a tip because he would not want to go around the bar again to return it. But, that was a very long time ago for everyone. Black people, although permitted to drink inside, were not particularly welcomed and, after buying their beer and whiskey there, would drink it elsewhere.

It had been an uneasy period for those who remembered it, a period to which all of them resigned themselves. They accepted it without question. The patrons of La Tacuachera, white and brown, were embarrassed to think about it. They could neither defend nor condemn the arrangement. It was a time and an imperative which most—at least those who were old enough to have participated in it—deny having supported, refusing to accept either blame or guilt for an inherited system. They were quick to point out that the conditions of the past no longer prevailed and that it was time to concentrate on the present. Black people were allowed to enter and drink in La Tacuachera, an Anglo or a Chicano would emphatically point out, but they chose not to come in. What more could decent people do?

The man who owned and ran the place was pleasant enough. He was short, stocky, given to wearing bright-colored flannel shirts year around. What distinguished him from his customers was his face and hands which indicated a man who did not work in the fields. His wife helped him on busy evenings, Friday and Saturday nights. She was thin, almost frail-looking, but she had enough energy to evict a recalcitrant drunk and she was diplomatic enough to persuade two contenders to go outside for the fistfight necessary to settle their differences. The atmosphere at La Tacuachera was not belligerent, it did not have the reputation of the rough places that could be found in Gonzales or Karnes City. A man could confidently take his family there, although it was loud and often arguments dangled just below the cloud of cigarette smoke.

Fights, however, were not rare among the Anglos and among the Chicanos. They were seldom if ever mixed. There might have been a push-and-shove incident once in a while between a Chicano and an Anglo in the urinals, but it never developed into a fight. On those occasions when a fight was unavoidable, the participants knew they had to go behind the tavern, beyond the trees, into the darkness of the field. The path behind the trees was well-worn, leading to a rotting barn which was caved in at one corner. There were those who remembered the cock-fights held there on Thursday nights. After the sheriff had stopped them, the barn served as a shelter for those wishing to settle an argument. After a thunderstorm destroyed part of it, the contestants had to battle in the open field, their falls cushioned by the soft earth and grass. No one was ever seriously hurt. A bloody nose was not common, although the would-be pugilists in their uncertain equilibrium, ended up quite sore from falling down so much.

The most serious incident anyone could remember was the time Juan Ríos suffered a bite from a startled rattlesnake. Juan Ríos went outside to watch a fight between his compadre Pablo Ramírez and his other compadre Samuel Gutiérrez. Before the first punch was thrown, as Juan Ríos moved back to give his compadres some room, the snake struck. The two fighters immediately lost interest in their argument. Juan's compadre Pablo, aggravated the snake bite when he tried to bleed the venom by cutting into Juan Ríos' calf. Juan Ríos ended up spending two weeks in the hospital, more as a result of his compadre's good will than the damage caused by the poisonous snake.

All in all, La Tacuachera was rowdy and boisterous, but good-natured. The people who came there were never involved in long-lasting feuds of any kind. In the fights, after a few wildly launched blows toward a blurry and elusive face in the dark, the cause of the fight was quickly forgotten and the antagonists would return inside, arm in arm, laughing, yelling for more beer. Invariably, when they returned to the subject of their recent fight, to the cause of it, the two friends would shed glistening, beer-soaked, male tears for the amusement of those present.

Inside La Tacuachera, next to the entrance on the left, was a long wooden bar. The varnish had been worn away long before. Elbows and sweat from the frosty beer bottles had coated it near the edges. It was lustreless and functional rather than colorful. There were still spots of varnish left and these islands would shine the reflection of the neon beer signs on the wall, bright colors framing lakes, rushing waterfalls, glittering trademarks, neatly dressed cowboys. Below the signs, upon a ledge, was a salty assortment of corn chips, potato chips, dried beef jerky, polish sausage, pickled pig's knuckles and feet, corn nuts, peanuts, cheese crackers and whatever else the salesman brought from San Antonio. The antique cash register would ring loudly, and this was followed by the dull thud of the erupting cash drawer. Under the bar were the beer coolers which contained the "coldest beer in Texas" as the sign outside proclaimed. Beside them, cases of warm bottles and cans were stacked, waiting their turn.

The belly-up bar was integrated. Chicanos and Anglos could lean freely against the bar without breaching an unspoken arrangement carried over from the past. In front of the bar, in an area as wide as the bar was long, were the Chicano tables. At the far end, all the way across, was the jukebox. To the left were two billiard tables, to the right was a clear passageway leading to the urinals outside of the building. Across the narrow walk-space adjacent to the Chicano area was the Anglo section. The tables and chairs were grouped together at one end leaving a glossy square of cement floor for dancing.

In the Chicano area, Spanish was the common language, English used more often than not to punctuate a joke. The jukebox mingled its twangy, mechanical country music dirges with the animated Chicano speech. The conversation of the Chicanos would often be interrupted by a piercing 'hoohuy' or an 'ajúa' from an exuberant celebrant. In later years, the owners of *La Tacuachera* added a few polkas and some corridos to the jukebox in recognition of the Chicanos.

The Anglo customers would bring their wives and children. None of the Chicanos did. For the Anglos, *La Tacuachera* and the weekend evenings they spent there was a family affair. The owners of the place, accustomed to it, began providing one of their bedrooms upstairs for unenduring, sleeping children, that they not be a burden on their drinking parents. The couples would dance to the music from the jukebox, except when a mischievous Chicano would play a firi-fidi-firi-fidi polka that would insinuate itself among the gringo selections. None of the Anglos would dance to the Chicano polkas, although they would dance to German polkas played by Myron Floren. While the Chicano polka played, an adventurous couple might dance to it, but most of the Anglos would return to their tables to wait. As things continued to change, the owners of *La Tacuachera* began booking third-rate country-western bands to play on weekends. They soon discovered that, inexpensive as the bands might be, it was not worth the cost and none of the customers noticed when the bands did not come anymore.

Friday and Saturday nights were the busiest at *La Tacuachera*. The Chicanos would rush home from their tractors, cotton-chopping, fence-mending and chicken-plucking at the packing houses. They would eat slowly but in anticipation of going out. After a bath, wearing freshly starched jeans and white shirts, they would speed toward the tavern. Just after sundown, before the pale blue of starlight begins to cool the night, there would be a crunch of tires on the gravel, sputtering mufflers, squeaky brakes, all signaling the arrival of the early Chicanos.

There was a gay, festive air in the gravel parking lot when several cars arrived simultaneously. The Chicanos would greet one another with hand-shakes as if it had been a long time since they had last seen each other. A small group might congregate beside the hood of a car. One would slip away to bring beers for everyone. After a sort of ritual introduction, someone would invite the rest inside the tavern. Once seated inside, the procession of arrivals would continue until the place overflowed with bodies and laughter, each new arrival greeted heartily by those already there.

The orders for beer kept the bartender busy; he seldom spoke to anyone on these evenings. There never seemed to be a shortage of money. No one who came to *La Tacuachera* and happened to be out of work or short on cash would be without a friend who made sure he had plenty of beer. These stretches of hard luck were brief and rare, the Chicanos knew. When he could, he would return the favor. Even if he didn't, it was always better to have a friend.

The talk was incessant, each member of a table vying for a turn to speak,

135

no one ever satisfied with the little he got to say because someone always managed to interrupt. The conversation at the tables, and sometimes across tables, would include a recount of the activities of the past week, plans successfully concluded, plans gone wrong, jokes, legends, repetitions of past memorable events, gossip and chisme, raunchy sex-talk. It was never a matter of having to say something particularly funny. During the conversation, the crowd seemed attuned to the appropriate pause and then raucous, hearty laughter would erupt.

The Anglos would arrive much later than the Chicanos. They, too, would hurry home from the fields and the packing houses. However, they had to wait for their wives and children to get ready. For them it was a family gathering which had all but replaced the picnic, the reunion, the church social. For them, *The Pleasant Hill Tavern* was a place where they could meet and conduct the necessary social intercourse with friends and neighbors. It was the culmination of a week of hard work and isolation. The children would have other children to play with, the wives would exchange small talk, recipes, gossip, the men would discuss all but a few of the same things as the Chicanos. While the Chicano area was loud and noisy, the Anglo area was subdued but not at all somber.

When the Anglos began to arrive, as the door opened, the Chicanos would lift their eyes toward them. Upon seeing it was not an acquaintance, they would ignore the Anglos who would come into the tavern sternfaced, a condition made to seem all the more ominous and ill-humored by their squinty eyes and thin compressed lips. The Anglos, out of habit and tradition, avoided looking in the direction of the Chicano area. Occasionally, it could not be helped, and there would be a brief exchange which consisted of a nod, sometimes a forefinger salute. At the bar, which was neutral, Anglos and Chicanos could talk together, but never in a relaxed or free way, as they shared very little in common.

One could see two and sometimes three couples at each table in the Anglo area. The children would play in the dark corners, run up and down the staircase, and periodically they would make an appearance at their parents table to cadge small change for soda waters and chips. As the evening progressed, the couples would begin to dance out affection laden with alcohol. They considered it bad manners to ask someone's wife to dance, although it was permissible to swap dancing partners on the floor. Each time after the music, a husband would escort his wife back to the table.

Throughout the evening, noise and fellowship would continue to flow from the Chicano side. On the Anglo side, things were more restrained in keeping with the proper family atmosphere they strove to maintain. The men refrained from exchanging the off-color jokes they had heard in the fields. It was only when they went outside for some fresh air or to urinate that they would have more masculine conversation.

The people, white and brown, who came to *La Tacuachera* were friendly

136

to outsiders, to those who were just passing through and needed to stop for a brief rest. They were friendly up to a point and beyond that, someone passing through would soon realize that he was nothing more than a stranger. They produced a simple, rustic, kind of excitement, peculiar to themselves, quaint perhaps to an outsider, but serious and nurturing to them. It was, finally, a closely guarded membership at La Tacuachera. To be a part of it, all one had to do was live in the area. A stranger could only observe but not share in the fullness of life that was La Tacuachera.

There were two exceptions. Ambrose Tench, who, it was said, would not live to see the age of thirty, lived in the area, in a shack on the outskirts of Nixon. He had such a reputation as a troublemaker that he was a permanent outsider at La Tacuachera. Ambrose Tench would be an outsider wherever he happened to be. The owner of the tavern had discouraged his business and was ill-at-ease when Tench came into the bar. The other exception, was Chango, whose real name was Joaquín, a native who no longer lived in the area. He returned as often as he could weekends and was thus included in La Tacuachera as though he had never moved away. It was assumed Chango lived in San Antonio because of the clothes he wore, but he never verified it, and the Chicanos were too polite to pry. He had friends there, had made new ones, and to many of them he still lived nearby.

II

Ambrose Tench was born four miles from where Chango was born. Both were born several months apart, in the same year in Schoolland, a once prosperous community surrounding a country store and a cotton gin. It was the cotton gin which served as the hub of the area, ginning for farms within a ten-mile radius. When the land started to give out, most of it going into the Soil Bank, the ginning equipment was dismantled and moved further south, near Refugio, where the soil was still producing plenty of cotton.

For many years after, only the dull grey-ribbed aluminum siding remained, slowly peeling away from the telephone-pole frames, exposing a dark, cavernous emptiness that made the children of Schoolland believe it was haunted by the ghost of a man who had been killed there. At one end of the gin, that facing the general store, the concrete loading platform still jutted out, strands of cotton still caught in the iron rims that made it look like a long bale. Not far from the loading platform, a misshapen, forgotten cotton bale lay on its side, the burlap having turned grey over the years, with large chunks of cotton pulled away from a corner. It resembled a mutilated loaf of bread.

The little cotton still grown in Schoolland was ginned either in Nixon or farther away in Gonzales. Only the shell of the building remained, a monument to the town that cotton was to have made. When someone set fire to the building, it was natural that Ambrose Tench was suspected. There was not enough evidence against Tench to charge him with anything and the owners of the gin shell were not overly concerned about it. The sheriff, however, while giving Tench a ride into town one day did ask him some questions about it.

Ambrose Tench had been the bully of Schoolland ever since he discovered he could make a fist and strike someone with it. He was thin, with sharp, angular features that made him seem taller than he actually was. His large, hooked nose had been broken several times, giving a peculiar distortion to his boney face. His eyes were set deep in their sockets, framed by a sharp, protruding forehead. His skin stretched so tautly over his face that one could swear it was not skin at all but waxen bone. Several anonymous people contributed to the further distortion of Ambrose Tench's face. A citizen of Houston had chipped in with a scar which started just below his right ear and

138

extended down the side of his neck and curiously swept up around the hub of his Adam's apple. He had lost his lower teeth from a gum disease combined with the effects of several fistfights. His upper teeth were crooked, chipped, yellowed, with greenish-black half-moons just below the gums. They did not match the perfect evenness and whiteness of the lower plate which he purchased in Gonzales. When he smiled, which was not often, his face took on a perverse, ghoulish aspect.

His lower teeth had been already rotting and slipping away from their mooring in his gums when he had taken a trip to Corpus Christi. Tench had been sitting in Flippo's, drunker than usual, badgering the waitress. When the waitress could stand him no longer, she took a bowl of chicken noodle soup destined for an elderly tourist couple and poured it over Tench's head. As he stood up to attack her, the bartender came over carrying a piece of lead pipe wrapped in electrical tape. He told Tench to behave, pay his bill and leave quietly. The Chicana waitress suggested that he go to Robstown if he wanted to fight. There, the Mexicans loved to fight and they would be more than glad to knock the shit out of him. Upon hearing the suggestion, Ambrose Tench took a step toward the waitress, grabbing a bottle of ketchup from a nearby table. The bartender took a step forward which made Tench stop abruptly and momentarily lose his balance. He quickly stretched himself to his fullest height, which was just a little below the bartender's shoulders.

Tench said, "If there's anything I can't stand, it's uppity Meskins!"

Angrily pointing to the waitress, he fulminated, "I'm going to this Robstown place and every Meskin I see will pay for you, lady. I think I'll go out there and kick ass until I don't see your face anymore."

On his way out of the restaurant, the waitress made a reference to his grandmother. On his return to Schoolland, Ambrose Tench never mentioned anything beyond his encounter with the waitress and how the bartender had not dared to strike him. He was, however, without most of his lower teeth and he had to work steadily for four months to pay the dentist in Gonzales.

Ambrose Tench was a lazy, belligerent, unreliable worker. The landowners and share farmers of Schoolland knew it and would hire him only out of desperation during harvest season when there were not enough hands to go around. He would work for a day or two, draw his pay on some pretext or other, usually an argument or a fistfight, and go on a binge for as long as the money lasted. Hung-over, without having changed his clothing in days, Tench would return to ask his employer for an advance on his pay or for a loan. As no one trusted him, and as most were glad to be rid of him, he would have to look for another job.

Sooner or later, the farmers would regret having sent Ambrose Tench to work in the fields. Tractors would run out of gas in mid field with little or no plowing done. Cultivators would lose their feet. Tench could work, but someone had to watch him constantly. When other workers were in the fields, Ambrose Tench posed a different problem. Most of these workers would be

Chicanos and Tench would intimidate them, demanding they do his share of the work or lie for him when he went into adjoining pastures to sleep. The Chicano workers generally ignored Tench. If, however, the worker was elderly or a youngster, Tench would punch and kick at them, causing more than a few to quit and seek work elsewhere. There had been a reluctance on the part of Chicanos to strike an Anglo, even one who needed it as much as Tench. The Anglos did not like the idea of a Mexican striking a white man, despite Ambrose Tench being embarrassing trash to them.

The landowners and farmers soon realized that Tench was not worth the trouble he caused. They could not depend on him to work alone and many Chicano workers would leave when they saw him appear in the fields. It was not long before they refused to hire him at all. When Tench found it impossible to obtain work in Schoolland, he became furious. He convinced himself that everyone, Anglos and Chicanos, were depriving him of work for no good reason. He decided to leave the area, but not before he had had his revenge. Tench set fire to a barn, killing two milk cows. It belonged to a retired Army officer who had only recently bought the farm and whom Tench did not know at all. The place happened to be close by. Next, he toppled a field gasoline tank and tried unsuccessfully to puncture it with an axe he found nearby. Afterward, on his way out of town, with his bindle dangling over his back, Tench was not entirely satisfied with his farewell to the area. On his way through Smiley at dusk, he saw don Miguel García, an elderly widower whose custom it was to sit in front of the Red and White Grocery Store each evening. As Tench approached, don Miguel moved over to give him some room on the bench in front of the store. Tench grabbed don Miguel, taking him behind the store, broke what remained of the old man's teeth and cracked two of his ribs with a vicious kick. Satisfied that people would talk about him and not soon forget him, he left the area for more than three years.

The Tench family, until Ambrose became the last surviving member, was well liked and respected in Schoolland. The elder Tench drank a little more than the patrons of La Tacuachera thought prudent, but he gave insult to no one, was never a burden to friends, and his excess was a tolerable one. He had owned some watermelon land near Smiley. It was clean, sandy, fertile soil which could have provided a prosperous living for someone willing to work and astute enough for the business aspects of farming. Without anyone taking much notice and because of something no one was ever able to explain, old man Tench drank himself to death before Ambrose reached his twelfth birthday.

A neighboring couple took Ambrose Tench in after his father died. They were childless. The wife saw in him the child she had not been able to bear and the husband saw in Tench an unpaid field hand. The land left to the last Tench, at the petition of the neighbor, was to be held by him as Tench's guardian until Tench was old enough to care for it himself. It was an informal arrangement set up by a magistrate in Nixon.

By the time Ambrose Tench was fifteen years old, the land had been sold without him receiving a penny from the sale. Soon after, the good neighbor ordered him away from his foster home. Ambrose Tench, at fifteen, found himself alone and penniless as a result of two unrelated events. Tench was thin and sickly in appearance, given to preying upon the compassion of his foster mother. He would run to her for protection at the first sign of hard work. He was not producing the kind of work his foster father had envisioned when he agreed to take him in. He felt that he had something coming to him for his generosity and the only asset Tench had was his father's land. The farmer sold it, forging the deceased Tench's signature, and kept the money.

The neighbor was not in the least guilt-ridden over the theft of Tench's land and money. The way he figured it, it took plenty to feed and clothe the boy. Besides that, the boy was so scrawny he couldn't get a decent day's work out of him. It was not that the farmer was reminded of his crime each time he saw Tench and simply wanted to be rid of him who posed as a constant reminder. The neighbor ran Tench off his place for another private, more personal, reason.

The farmer caught Tench behind the outhouse on his hands and knees lifting the trapdoor. The farmer's wife had gone in there a few minutes before and Tench was looking up at her bare buttocks and other virtuous parts framed by the circular aperture of the toilet bench. The neighbor could not understand the combination of innocent curiosity and inchoate manhood that was rapidly transforming Tench. He was ready to shoot him on the spot and would likely have done so had not his wife come out of the coffin-like structure and intervened.

"Now, now, old man," said she, "he's just a boy."

"Boy, hell!" yelled the outraged old man. "He ain't no boy no more, woman. I saw that bulge on him. I tell you, he's dangerous!"

The old woman, who had submitted to sex with her husband only sparingly over the years and then only from a sense of unavoidable duty during their married life, did not completely understand the reason for her husband's anger. Nor did she completely understand what Tench was doing, exactly, although to her he was still a child and as such she was determined to be tolerant of him.

"Now, paw, don't be too harsh on the boy. He's just curious, that's all. I reckon all boys are like that at his age. It's only natural," she said, her toothless pink gums showing under her thin lips as she spoke.

"I'll just bet he's curious," the old man roared. "Get in the house, woman!"

"You watch yourself, old man. And watch that no harm comes to that boy," she said as she started up the path back to the house.

"Get in the god-damned house, I said!" He pointed to the house with an outstretched arm.

The old man turned to Ambrose Tench who cowered behind the

outhouse, terrified of the beating he expected. The old man swung his arm toward the road in front of the house.

"Get off my place. Right now," he said. "And when you get down the road, way off where I can't see you, get on your knees and thank God I didn't shoot you like I should have."

Tench began to run along the ochre-colored gravel road as fast as he could, not bothering to stop to say the prayer his ex-benefactor had suggested. As abruptly as that, Ambrose Tench left his days of carefree, horny youth behind him and entered into a precarious manhood.

When he got to the paved farm-to-market road, he stopped to rest at the cattle pens belonging to the man who had bought his land. He perched himself on the loading end of the chute and started to think about his situation. He had no idea of how to find work. He would have to work, but the thought of it was not pleasing to him. He decided that work and how to support himself was something for another day, something that would probably just happen. Of more immediate concern was where to spend the night. It was already late afternoon. He could not tell how long he had been perched on the chute. As the afternoon turned to gold and the sting of the sun's heat left the air, Lou Horner stopped to ask him if he wanted a ride. Ambrose Tench was nearly in tears from desperation. He told Horner his sad story, wiping his dripping nose as he blurted out the words. Horner spared no affection for the old man because of a horse trade years earlier. He told Tench he could stay with him until he found what he wanted to do.

Lou Horner allowed Tench a few days to get settled. Mrs. Horner rememberd Tench's mother as a kind woman and she took pity on his condition. Each night she would place a pallet on the floor of her son's room for Tench to sleep on. After about a week, sleeping late, saying nothing to the Horners about work or leaving, their son ran crying to them. He said Tench would take all of his clothes off at night, crawl into bed with him and demanded that he do dirty things. He also told them Tench had threatened to kill him if he did not or if he ever told anyone about it. Lou Horner was not a man to become upset or excited to a point where anybody noticed. He had come in for his mid-morning coffee when his son came to him. Tench was still asleep. He went into the bedroom to nudge him awake with his boot. Tench was annoyed to be awakened so early, but he went along with Horner and got into the truck. Horner drove him to the cattle pens where he'd found him and left him there. He told Tench not to come around his place anymore.

At the cattle pens, Tench considered what to do next. To his left, the road snaked along to Gonzales to which he had seldom been and which seemed like a foreign country to him. To the right, the road went to Smiley, about five miles distant. If he wanted work, he would have to go to the cafe or the gas station and make it known he was looking for work. Behind him, the gravel road went through Schoolland and ended in Nixon, some ten miles away. He was too frightened to risk walking toward Nixon which meant going past his ex-benefactor's place. After an hour of sitting with his feet dangling from the cattle chute, he jumped off and began walking toward Smiley. From there he would find a ride to Nixon. Nixon was larger and he felt he would more likely find something there.

He had to walk the five miles to Smiley because only one car passed by. It was full of Chicanos and as they passed they indicated they had no room for him. He cursed them, thinking one of them should have gotten out and waited where he stood while they drove him to town. Tench was raised in an atmosphere where Mexicans and Anglos did not mix very much, where the superiority of the Anglo is assumed if only because he owns the land and distributes the jobs. Tench's father had been particularly bitter about Chicanos and Tench inherited his attitude, focussing some of his own bitterness upon them. The lines between Chicanos and Anglos were clearly if subtlely drawn, but Tench was not content to leave well enough alone.

He reached Nixon that evening, realizing he had not eaten all day. He went into the drive-in, ordered two hamburgers with cheese, french fries and two cokes. After he finished, he told the waitress he did not have money to pay. She told the manager who came out to see him. He recognized him and told him to bring in the money some time. Tench thanked him, not quite understanding the reason. He found a shed behind the movie house and slept for the night. When he went back to the drive-in for breakfast, the owner came over to him and asked him for the money from the night before. Tench blurted out his story. The manager told him he could not afford to feed him. Out of respect for his father, he told Tench to forget what he owed from the night before. He advised that the best thing for him to do would be to go to the packing house and ask for a job. In a soft voice, Tench thanked the man for his kindness and began cursing him as soon as he was outside the drive-in. Before crossing the street, he picked up a rock and debated whether to toss it through the window.

At the packing house, they put him to work right away, moving barrels of chicken guts to a loading platform. It was wet, slippery, smelly work that permeated a man's clothes and was nearly impossible to scrub away. Tench lasted about two hours suppressing a constant urge to puke, before leaving without bothering to ask for his pay. For several days after that, he did yardwork in exchange for food. He continued to sleep in the shed behind the movie house until the city marshal discovered him and suggested he find another place to sleep. He found an abandoned house whose owner never appeared. With his yardwork and the abandoned house which he considered a permanent place to live, Ambrose Tench was settled.

On Saturday, Tench waited at the IGA Grocery parking lot for his former foster parents to come into town. He wanted to speak to the old woman alone. She went into the store alone while her husband walked toward the Pool Parlor to play dominoes and talk. When she came out of the store, her arms full with a box of groceries, Tench ran up to her and fell in step, not offering to help with the box.

He said, "Ma'am, I got to talk to you."

She shook her head in a sad and confused way. She had expected he would approach her before this, and so did her husband. Her motherly feelings had been weighed against her wifely duty. Tench came out the loser.

"Ambrose," she said, "I'm sorry. I promised the mister. You can't come back. There's no more to discuss on the matter. It's already settled."

"That ain't exactly what I want, ma'am," said Tench.

"What is it you want, then? I thought . . ."

"It's my clothes, ma'am. These is all I got and I been wearing them for a long time. I can't take a bath without clean clothes."

The farmer's wife, a little relieved, said, "I see. Of course, you're right. But, you know the mister don't want you near the place. Besides, if he knew, he wouldn't want to give them to you. Out of meanness. He's still mighty upset. I'll see what I can do, though."

"Thanks, ma'am, I appreciate that."

"Yes, dear. Now, let's see. How to get them to you. I have it. My cousin Maude is coming to visit me tomorrow. I'll give them to her and you go to her house and get them."

"Yes, ma'am," said Tench and he took off running. The woman put the groceries on the truck bed and sat inside to wait while the old man finished playing dominoes.

Tench became known in Nixon and at first was offered plenty of work. He went through a succession of jobs, lasting at none for more than a few weeks. He began to develop a hatred of people, Mexicans in particular, reasoning that their intolerance of him was some fault of theirs and had nothing to do with him. After a year or more of living in the abandoned house he came to believe that there were too many people in Nixon. He found an old, abandoned shack with a good water well a mile or so off the road between Nixon and Smiley. There, he lived alone, found it to his liking, went in either direction to find work to supply his simple needs. He liked doing chores when he had to, working long enough to just get by, and he enjoyed not having anyone telling him what to do.

An old mongrel dog appeared on his porch one day. Someone had obviously driven him out of the city and left him. Tench tossed the remains of his supper at the dog. The next day, the dog was asleep on the porch, curled up as if he belonged there. Tench promptly named him "Bastard" and cut off one of his ears to show him who the master was. The dog remained faithful to Tench, silently suffering Tench's abuse, coming to know instinctively when Tench was in an evil mood and to stay away from him until it passed.

When Bastard stayed away longer than usual, Tench went looking for him. He walked to the nearest pasture where the dog went hunting for rabbits and armadilloes. He kept calling the dog's name. Tench feared the dog might have been bitten by a snake. He spent half the day walking the pasture, looking in every clump of cactus, finding no sign of him. He went to Nixon and walked every street in the city fiendishly planning to murder the person who would steal his dog. When someone complained of Tench's quest, the marshal found him and asked what the hell he thought he was doing.

"I'm looking for my god-damned dog, is what I'm doing," Tench said defiantly.

"Well, you're making folks nervous. What's your dog look like, anyway?"

"Kind of sandy-colored. Missing one ear."

"Uh, that one," the marshal said, shaking his head.

"You do something to my dog?" Tench was beginning to let his fury loose.

"Had to, son. That damned animal was foaming at the mouth, shying away from water. Pretty sure it was rabies. Won't know till I get some tests back from San Antonio."

"Where's my god-damned dog?"

"Well, I shot him first off. Then, the Doc said he oughta be burned. Deputy Jeff and me did it last night. I'm real sorry, son. Probably caught it from a skunk somewhere."

Tench fell straight back on his buttocks, landing in an erect, sitting position on the paved street. He cried in an almost animal howl, beating on the pavement until his knuckles bled. The marshal placed his hands under Tench's arms and said, "Come on, son, I'll take you home." He was completely limp as the marshall picked him up, but he stayed on his feet when the marshall let go of him.

As the marshal led him to the waiting patrol car, Tench said, "Marshal?"

"What is it, son," said the marshal softly.

"Marshal, if you ever tell anyone I cried over that god-damned dog, I'll shoot your pecker off!"

The marshal never told anyone that Tench cried over his dead dog. Had he done so, no one would have believed it. In Nixon and Smiley, when people heard that the rabid dog belonged to Tench, some said he probably caught it after Tench bit him.

He saved enough money to buy a .22 caliber rifle at the Western Auto. He hunted rabbits when it rained too much and there was no work or, as time went on, when no one would hire him. Somehow, he managed to talk a used car dealer in Seguin into selling him a dilapidated pickup truck on credit. He calculated he had to work twice as much to keep up the payments on it. He made two payments, driving all the way to Seguin to surrender the money in person, drove it for four months before two burly men found his shack, took the keys from him and repossessed it.

It was natural for Tench to start drinking, as if that too was part of his family inheritance. He began by going to *La Tacuachera*, standing in the rear driveway, near the urinals, waiting for the first person out to buy him a six-pack. More than a few were glad to oblige him on account of his father who had been a good friend at *La Tacuachera*. Tench was not like the other teenagers who had cars and drank beer on the way to dances and parties. Tench had no friends his own age. When the six-pack was delievered to him, he would cross the barbed-wire fence into the pasture and drink all six hurriedly and alone. Afterward, he would weave and wobble along the road to Nixon until someone recognized him and took him home.

The news soon circulated that Tench was a mean drunk. In the few months he had his truck, he would drive slowly from the tavern to Nixon, sometimes stopping at the roadside rest area. By the time he reached the city limits, he would have finished all six beers. He would park his truck on the street in front of the movie theatre, not careful about denting someone's bumper. He stumbled up and down the sidewalks shouting obscenities at the after-movie strollers spending their last moments in town before going home. Tench often tried to goad a startled lover into a fight.

The fathers of the teenagers whom he threatened and intimidated were the ones who bought the beer for him. When they realized this, they stopped doing so. Tench tried to threaten the Chicanos into buying him beer, but the bartender made it clear that anyone buying Tench beer would no longer be welcomed at *La Tacuachera*.

It was customary for *La Tacuachera* to recognize the approaching manhood of certain sons of Anglo patrons by allowing them to buy their own beer before they were of legal age, provided they looked old enough and a parent was always present. Some could start drinking as early as eighteen, three years before their majority. No one would vouch for Tench and the courtesy was not extended to him, in spite of the fact that Tench looked a good ten years older than he was.

During the course of an odd conversation, someone mentioned that Tench had not been seen prowling around the back door of the tavern for some time. A quick survey among the drinkers present revealed that he had not been seen around Schoolland, Smiley nor Nixon. For the following three years, no one heard from or about Ambrose Tench. Some assumed he had gone to San Antonio or Houston and good riddance. Others, for personal reasons, hoped some generous soul had performed a service to the world by killing him. Still others thought the Army might have taken him. A veteran of the First World War dispelled that notion by averring that he would be drafted before the Army was desperate enough to take Tench.

On his twenty-first birthday, Ambrose Tench walked into *La Tacuachera*. He was dressed in a blue-gingham cowboy shirt with diamond-shaped mother-of-pearl buttons, a clean, starched, creased pair of new Levi's and brightly shined boots which squeaked when he walked. He wore a new, grey Stetson, the most expensive of the line, but which was cheapened because he tried to block it himself. He had also contributed a gaudy red silk hatband. He would have presented a neat appearance had he bathed at any time in the preceding few weeks. There was dirt under his raggedly cut fingernails and a black grease spot on his wrist.

Moses Jackson, eyeing him from head to toe, was the first to notice the jingling spurs with rowels two inches in diameter. Moses was about to ask Tench what the hell he was wearing spurs for when Tench noticed him staring and snarled.

"I'll knock your fucking head off!"

The still fresh bright red scar trailed down his ear to be swallowed by the dark blue bandana around his neck. It would be weeks before anyone saw the entire length of it and would see the curious hook it made over his Adam's apple. Remembering how he had been before his disappearance and the recent remark to Moses Jackson, no one was curious enough to ask about the scar.

Tench moved from the door, swaggering further into the tavern, turning left to the bar. He laid a twenty dollar bill on the bar, in a round puddle of water left by a beer bottle. He unsnapped the button of his breastpocket, took out his draft card and tossed it at Jake, the bartender. It flew past Jake and landed on the floor. Jake squatted to pick it up, did not bother to examine it, placed it on the bar for Tench to retrieve.

"What's your name, fella? You're new here." Tench said.

"Jake."

Tench raised a corner of his mouth in a twisted smile. He swivelled his head to look to both sides of the bar.

"This son-of-a-bitch you're looking at, Jake, is twenty-one. I can drink here now. I don't want any shit from you . . . ever."

"Law says I can serve you so long as you don't cause any trouble."

"That's right, Jake. I cause the trouble, get me? Give me a Lone Star and set up beers for everyone except the Meskins. I've come back home and I may stay. Don't know yet."

That was at six o'clock and by ten o'clock he had passed out once and had had his nose broken for the third time in his brief life. It was broken by a husky young husband, who spoke with a Polish accent, and who would not stand for Tench coming over to his table, grabbing his wife's buttocks and saying, "You're cute enough to fuck. How'd you like to have a real man?" The husband did not invite Tench outside as was customary. He simply half-stood from his chair and shot his fist across the table, landing it flat on Tench's beak nose. The blow knocked Tench out.

Tench lay on the polished cement floor for a long interval, preventing anyone from dancing. One of the wives became nauseous listening to the gurgling sounds issuing from Tench's nose and from looking at the blood-soaked shirt. There was a pool of blood welling under his head, matting his hair. Except for the blood and the strange rattling of his nose, Tench looked peaceful, serene and restful.

Moses Jackson called the bartender and asked him to find one of Tench's friends to take care of him. There followed a debate as to whether Tench was seriously hurt and might need a doctor.

Jake scratched his head. "Ain't you folks his friends? I ain't never seen him before."

Receiving no reply, he asked again, bewildered. "None of you?" Again, silence. The men turned their backs or shifted positions in their chairs. Jake shook his head, placing his hands on his hips. "Well, it don't seem to me that none of the Mexicans is any friend to him. Not the way he spoke about them earlier."

Moses Jackson became impatient with the bartender. "Jake, just ask one of the Mexicans going home to take him to the doctor. My wife is gonna puke right here and now if you don't move him."

"I'll try," Jake said. "Can't promise nothing." He started for the Chicano area of the tavern. Before he got too far, Lou Horner, who had just come in to see Tench lying on the floor, called him back.

"Oh, Jake," Lou Horner said, "Can't you take him with you, drag him out somewhere, away from the ladies."

"He might die right in front of us. That would be awful!" Mrs. Horner said.

Mrs. Jackson sneered. "That might be the best thing for him."

The bartender dragged Tench, lifting him by the arms, away from the dance floor. He left him leaning against a stack of empties. Jake then hurried behind the bar for a wet mop to clean the blood from the floor. That done, with the mop still in hand, he walked to the Chicano area of the bar.

"Any of you boys going home want to take that man over there to the doctor?" he said.

No one responded.

"How 'bout you, Chencho? You oughta be ready to go home."

"Uh-uh! When that man wakes up, I think he's going to think the first man he sees killed him. He's going to want to kill me. I'm not that crazy, yet." Chencho laughed and the others at the table joined him.

Don Florencio Ramírez, who came by *La Tacuachera* each Friday and Saturday, drank just three beers and went home, stood up. He had been sitting at an adjacent table. As he stood he hitched up his trousers and adjusted his Stetson.

"I will take him home," he said, "if some of you will put him in my car."

Jake took a wet bar rag and wrapped it around Tench's head so as not to soil Don Florencio's car. Tench was breathing easier, though heavy with drunkeness. Jake beckoned a couple of Chicanos to help him carry Tench outside to the car. When nearing Nixon, Don Florencio tried to wake Tench to ask him where he was staying. Not being able to do so, he remembered where Tench had been living before his disappearance, took him there, deposited him on the porch and went home. Thus ended Tench's twenty-first birthday celebration.

From that time, Tench remained around the area, never leaving for very long. He bragged that he couldn't stand living out in the country by himself, saying that he had gotten used to city ways. He rented a two-room house sitting on a large lot separating the Black and Brown sections of Nixon. None of the Anglo property owners would rent to him in the white sections. He worked where he could, sometimes going away for a few weeks or months on a job. He was a more dependable worker, not as lazy as before, but eventually he would end up wanting to fight someone on the job.

He bought a used car just so he could go drinking every night. It was clear to him that he was not welcomed at *La Tacuachera* and he saved all of his bitterness and resentment until Friday or Saturday night. During the week, he would drive by, slowing on the curve, and continue on to Gillette, Yorktown, Kenedy or Karnes City. He drank as usual, becoming drunk very quickly, but he kept quiet there since he knew he was a stranger in these places and no one would take care of him. On the weekends, he would get drunk, leave a little earlier than usual in order to stop at *La Tacuachera* with the single purpose of fighting someone.

He was drunk enough, mean enough, when he arrived so all he had time to drink would be one beer. Tench soon realized that he was beaten more often than not. He gave up fighting Anglos when he received a dozen beatings in a row. He decided the Chicanos were smaller and thus he might improve his chances. The Chicanos who accepted his challenges also beat him. Tench was confused that the Anglos would allow the Mexicans to beat him. He felt that whatever else, Anglos ought to stick together.

When Milly Jones lost her husband in a tractor accident, Tench, who was not a friend of the family, having only known them by sight, attended the funeral. The service over, the casket lowered into the ground, the mourners began filing along the red clay path to where they parked their cars and trucks. Tench stood at some distance away, across the knee-high fence dividing the cemetery between the Anglos and Chicanos. He waited for the widow to leave.

As she was led along the path, leaning on her brother's shoulder with her mother's arm around her waist, Tench, with an obvious hangover and unshaven, walked up to Milly Jones and requested a few words with her. The two women and the man stopped, in their grief unable to anticipate what Tench could want.

"Miz Jones," he stammered, "I know you just lost your husband and everything. I don't expect an answer right away. I really don't. Anyway, what I'm trying to say, I would be glad to drop by your place, uh, if it's ok, tonight, to talk about it."

"Talk about what? Who are you?" Milly Jones asked.

"Ambrose Tench, ma'am. I thought you might know about me."

"No, Mr. Tench. I don't know about you."

Tench curled a corner of his mouth upward in a fiendish smile. "I'm a changed man, ma'am. Anybody will tell you that. And you just lost your man."

The brother tightened his grip on her and said, "I appreciate you trying to comfort my sister, Mr. Tench, but it won't be necessary to come by the house. We accept you sympathies, but it'll just be family at the house tonight."

Tench continued staring at Milly Jones, his head twisted at a nervous angle. "That ain't what I had in mind, ma'am. I mean, I didn't know the deceased except to say hello. I might be sorry for you, but he weren't nothing to me."

"I don't understand what you're trying to get at," she said, confused amidst her bereavement.

"Hell, it ain't that hard to figure out. Shit. Shoot, I'm talking about marrying, ma'am. I had my eye on you for a long time, but you always seemed to be doing all right by the deceased you all just dumped in that hole yonder. He ain't gonna do you no good lying in that hole, I can guarantee you that. Now, I know a sweet young thing like yourself cain't go without it for very long."

Milly Jones' mouth opened, anger colored her cheeks. Tench had prepared his speech, rehearsed it several times, now he was afraid to stop.

"I mean, I seen you walk and shake that behind of yours. Ass like that cain't do without no action for long, shit, I know that. I understand that. Now, I'm kinda known as a real stud. Not around here, of course, not much doing around here. In Houston, that's where, in Houston. They know me as a stud there. Ask anybody in Houston, they'll tell you."

"My lord!" said Milly's mother.

"You're sick!" hissed Milly Jones. She turned to her brother and said, "John, take me home, quickly, please."

The three walked down the path rapidly, almost running. John Jones, when they reached his car, stopped and looked into his sister's face. His anger caused his cheeks to twitch. He turned and started back to where Tench stood, taking long, slow strides.

"She change her mind?" Tench asked.

Through clenched teeth, John Jones said, "If you come near my sister again, I will kill you. You're crazy, an animal!"

He turned away without waiting for a response from Tench. Tench remained where he was, scratching his head. His anger began to rise. Tench ran toward the car just as it went out of the cemetery gate and onto the highway. He punched at a fencepost and said out loud to no one, "God damn it! It ain't like I asked her to shack up. I'da married her. What's the fucking problem?"

He ran to his car which he had not driven into the cemetery, preferring to park it on the shoulder of the highway. He wheeled it around, making his tires screech. He drove straight to Gillette, to a little tavern standing at the crossroads, yelling for a beer as soon as he walked in the door.

At that moment, Chango was driving out of San Antonio on Rigsby Avenue, past Loop 13, where it turns into Highway 87 heading toward Nixon.

150

III

Highway 87 southeast from San Antonio was a ribbon of blacktop, more grey than black, stretching unhurriedly along gentle risings of the terrain which seemed to have begun as hills but were somehow abandoned to become farms and ranches on either side of the road. What remained was a pleasant rising and falling ride flanked on either side by what appeared to be a continuous fence.

Chango left San Antonio early Friday afternoon. He had not been to Nixon for nearly two weeks and at the beginning of the week he faced an urgent assignment which might have to be taken care of that weekend. He waited patiently without receiving further word. When his deadline passed without a commitment on Friday morning, he packed a bag in the event he decided to stay for a few days, had his car serviced, and left after lunch.

Chango drove past the last houses on the edges of San Antonio, driving at a leisurely pace with the windows of his car opened, the wind swirling inside the car twisting his carefully groomed hair in all directions. He was tense and cautious driving the streets of the city. As soon as he saw open country, he leaned back, comfortable and secure, feeling a fresh resurgence of energy as the landscape turned into a quilt of dark brown, green, amber patches. He would smell the clean freshly-turned earth of the farmlands, he could almost taste the sweetness of the green unmowed hay. The air he drew into his lungs was different from that of the city which reeked of exhaust fumes and factory smoke, thick with quarrels and discontent, limp with uncertainties and futures that were only words. The air he now breathed, relaxed and unhurried, was an air of permanence, laden with history and regeneration. It was the air of his boyhood.

The boy hung upside down on the chinaberry tree, his thin legs bent over a branch close to the ground. His arms dangled, lifeless, in imitation of the Christian martyrs in a movie his parents had taken him to see.

The boy did not have brothers or sisters. The nearest neighbors with children his age were too far away to visit by himself. There were plenty of visits by his aunts and uncles who had children his age. By far, though, he preferred to be by himself. In his solitary existence he could invent worlds to entertain himself. He devised all sorts of games, dreaming up as many players as he needed. He planned elaborate excursions into the pasture behind his house, imagining himself at the head of vast armies or leading a safari into the wild and dangerous jungle where he had to shoot lions and tigers, elephants and snakes. When he did see a snake in the pasture, he would follow it for a distance to see it disappear into a gopher hole. He would not tell anyone about it and would return day after day to wait for it to come out again. They never did. He wondered if he had ever seen the same snake twice.

His mother called to him from the back porch as she dried her hands with her apron. It was time to walk the half-mile of dirt road to the paved highway where the yellow school bus stopped for him. He wiggled his legs. They began to slip from the tree, slowly, until they cleared the branch. He landed on his palms in a perfect handstand. With a slight push, his feet dropped to the ground. He jumped up as high as he could and landed straight and tall for his age. He combed his hair with the black pocket comb his cousin Andrés had given him. He inspected himself to see he had not soiled his clothes. His mother was easily upset if he dirtied his clothes before going to school. He never could get her to understand that desert pirates, waving funnylooking swords, had captured him on the hot wind-blown sands. He was lucky to get away in time for school.

The boy picked up a pebble and pitched it at the ancient chicken that somehow managed to escape the dinner table. He did not hit the chicken, nor did he mean to, but she squawked anyway, scurrying under the house.

Inside the house, his mother was not in the kitchen. He looked for her in the adjacent room. When he did not see her, he hurried to the table to drink the remainder of her coffee. His lunch was on a plate on the table, wrapped in a brown paper sack. He found his lunch pail with the color drawing of Roy Rogers and Trigger on top and on the sides. He dropped his tortilla and bean tacos inside it.

After he finished the coffee, he took the cup to the sink and rinsed it. As he did so, he looked at himself in the small mirror on the counter behind the sink. His coloring, which he took from his father, was dark brown, as dark as the soil they farmed. The boy noticed the recalcitrant cowlick sticking in the air behind his head. He wet his hands at the sink tap, plastered it down, but the impertinent tuft of hair refused to stay matted. His cousins made fun of him because of it. When his father took him to Tomás Aguilar for a haircut, he would tell him to cut it all off, to just leave a bald spot. All the men in the barbershop would laugh and he would perspire from embarrassment. He gave up on the cowlick and began to look for the leather book satchel his father had bought for him in Mexico. Upon finding it, he went into the next room which opened on to the front porch. His mother called to him from the bedroom.

"¿Hijo? ¿Dónde estás?" she said.

"Aquí, mamá. Ya me voy. Ahí viene el bos," he said.

"Espera. Tengo algo que decirte."

The boy remained by the screen door, his small fist on the doorknob, turning it to both sides. After waiting a few moments, he grew impatient, afraid he might miss the school bus. He opened the door, craning his head to look for a sign of the bus. Not seeing anything, he closed the door.

"Mamá, ahí viene el bos," he said in a sing-song voice.

Sí, sí. Ahí voy. Espera."

The boy's mother came running into the room. She was as tall as his father, lighter-skinned than he, with long black hair which she braided every morning before doing anything else. When he was younger, she would let him brush her hair, which came down to her waist. As she came into the room, she wore a half-slip and brassiere. Her face was powdered and rouged, but she had not yet applied the red lipstick she used and which his father disapproved of. She smelled of strong eau de toilette. She had unrolled the braids of her hair and one of them slid across her breast like a long black snake.

It was rare for him to see his mother in underclothing. At twelve, he was old enough to be embarrassed. He averted his eyes, stared at his feet.

"Tu papá y yo tenemos que ir para San Antonio," she said. She told him his uncle Samuel was sick and that it would be after dark when they returned.

"Pon atención, niño," she said in a stern voice, "quiero que te vayas a quedar con tu tía Chona cuando salgas de la escuela. Le dices que dije yo que te cuide hasta que vengamos por ti."

The boy turned away from his mother, trying to hide the lump in his throat which made him want to cry. He hated his aunt Chona, hated to be in her house. He felt old enough to take care of himself.

"Yo no necesito a nadie que me cuide," he said sullenly.

"No le hace. Haz lo que te digo, ¿oíste?"

"Sí, mamá."

"Bueno. No se te vaya a olvidar, ¿oíste? Andale, antes de que se te pase el bos."

The boy ran out of the house with his head down, the pent-up tears flowing freely down his cheeks. He dreaded visiting his tía Chona. His father's brother had deserted her, going away to work in the oilfields on the Gulf. After less than a year, he had been killed in an accident and brought home to Wrightsboro for burial in the family plot. His father had felt responsible for his sister-in-law, the grass widow, even before his brother was killed. Afterward, as a true widow in the family, all of his relatives contributed to her welfare. She was old, bitchy, and she smelled. Her whole house smelled of cats and chicken shit as she seldom wiped her feet after feeding the chickens in back. He had stayed with her before and when she fed him, the food was never enough and was seldom fully cooked. She would serve him, almost throwing the plate at him, complaining about how much food cost and how little her relatives, meaning his father, gave her. He begged to stay with one of his school friends, like Frank or Adán, but his father told him it was something only for family.

He wiped his face and started skipping down the road to the highway, swinging his lunch pail in one hand and his book satchel in the other. He saw his father astride the tractor, working a few hours before leaving for San Antonio. The boy yelled at him. The father was furrowing parallel to the highway, going away from the boy. He waved to his father's back, hoping he might turn around and see him. He stopped by the mailbox on the gravel shoulder of the road. When the school bus arrived, he boarded it, but did not join in the yelling and laughing of the other kids. He felt sad.

The La Vernia crossroads were just in front of him, indicating he was halfway to Nixon. The white gravel of the easement hurt his eyes as the sun's reflection hit him. He squinted and slowed the car to negotiate the curve. As quickly as he approached it, he was out of the Lavernia city limit. Two miles away, he crossed the bridge which made him feel he was on home territory.

"Voy a jugar con Mateo, tía." said the boy.

No, señor. Se me queda aquí. Tu mamá dijo que te cuidara y aquí te quedas en esta casa."

The boy sat stiffly in a straight-back chair by the window, gazing at the world outside. Warm sunlight, filtered through encrusted dirt on the window-panes, bathed his face. His aunt sat in a stuffed chair in the dimness of a far corner. He swung his right leg without hitting the chair. He did not want to give her an excuse to scold him. He was suffocating from the stuffiness of the room, the smell of the cats, all of which were in the room, curled about like fur cushions. He could smell his aunt across the room. He stood to go to the room in which he would sleep. His aunt stopped him.

"No sabe usted pedir permiso."

"¿Puedo ir al otro cuarto?"

"No. Vaya a darles de comer a los pollos."

"Ya voy," he said.

He went out the front door, around the side of the house, to the back yard. He was grateful for the fresh air. Even the stench of the chickens and the chickencoop was better than inside the house. He tried to vomit, but could not. He dreaded supper. Whatever it was, he would have to eat all of it. Luckily, she did not serve him much.

"Chango," a voice called from the unpaved street in a mournful sing-song stretching his name to four syllables.

Chango ran to the front yard to meet Mateo. His aunt saw him through the screen door and came out to the porch. Her voice clucked at him.

"¿A dónde vas, huerco travieso?" she demanded.

"Aquí nomás voy a jugar con Mateo."

"¿Y quién es ese Mateo?"

"Mi amigo de la escuela."

"Yo no sé nada de familias que dejan a sus hijos andar sueltos de callejeros."

"Yo no soy callejero, oiga," said Mateo.

"Y malcriado también," she said. "Tú te me quedas en la yarda." With that, she returned inside the house.

"¿Qué pasó, Mateo?"

"Nada, Chango."

They sat on the grass, neither of them speaking. Chango hugged his knees, squinting at a sunflower facing him, bent over, springing from the ditch on the other side of the street.

"Vamos ir a campear tacuache a la noche. Yo y mi primo Julián. Vamos a ir con mi tío Lupe."

"Nomás vas ir a guachar. No te dejan tirar."

"Sí, de veras, me dijo apá que me podía llevar su carabina."

"No te creo, cabrón."

"Sí, a la brava. ¿Por qué no vas con nosotros?"

"Mi tía es muy pinche. No me deja ir. Comoquiera, vienen mis jefes más noche y tengo que estar aquí."

"Pos, mi tío te puede llevar pa' tu casa, tú sabes."

"No le hace. No me deja ir la vieja apestosa."

"Bueno. Entonces vale más irme. Mi tío viene después de la cena. Ahí te miro mañana."

"Andale. Ahí te miro."

Mateo went off, hopping and skipping along the gravel street. Chango finished feeding the chickens and came back to sit on the porch. He did not want to go inside the smelly house. His aunt came to the rusty screen door. She was angry.

"¿Acabaste lo que te mandé? ¿Qué te tardó tanto?"

"Pos, 'taba platicando con Mateo, tía."

"Mira, muchachito, vale más que te portes bien, porque si no, le digo todo a tu mamá que no me hiciste caso."

His aunt's house was on the edge of Smiley. In the distance, he could see the towering grain elevators beside the railroad track. He went inside a room piled with useless furniture, boxes and rags which were once clothes. There was a mattress on the floor with large holes in it from which sprang tufts of coarse cotton. He figured the rats must have chewed on it. There was a small window, partially blocked by some boxes. He started to sit on it, but it would not support him. Instead, he leaned against the wall, staring out into the horizon beyond the trees as the sun set in a bright orange-red ball casting a copper-gold glow over Smiley. Its final streaks were thick and heavy, disappearing in the darkness of the room, turning the blunt objects it contained into distorted, menacing shapes. And then it was night.

There was nothing to do, no one to talk to. The boy remained by the window. He could see a blue-greenish glow over Smiley now coming from the street lamps on the highway running through town. He was hungry but the thought of eating his aunt's cooking made him nauseous. He went into the front room to find her asleep in the stuffed chair. He knew from before that she would sleep there until morning. She had forgotten about supper. Luckily, his parents would take him home before morning. Hungry, and with a longing for something he could not explain, he went back to his room. He settled into the mattress without covers, nudged himself a comfortable valley, pretended he lay on a hammock outside a great house carved from the South American jungle, and fell asleep.

He startled awake, as if from a bad dream. It was chilly and musty in the room. His body inside his clothes was wet with perspiration. He was cold, trembling, his teeth chattered. He thought of getting up to get some of the rags he had seen earlier to use for covers. He thought there might be spiders tangled up in them and did not move from the mattress. As he became fully awake, he trembled more and became colder. The room felt hot in spite of his cold body.

He heard hushed voices somewhere in the house, not voices heard far away in the twilight of sleep, but hushed, purposely low voices. It was pitch dark where he lay and he was frightened. It was only he and his aunt asleep in the front room who inhabited the house. He started to call out to his mother, but he stifled the sound in his throat. Telling himself he was not a little boy anymore, he sat up on the mattress, cradling his head in his hands. He stood up and walked to the door. He opened it, the creaking of it alerting the voices in the other room. They stopped their hushed, whispered conversation to look at him.

The boy entered the light of his aunt's dim living room, his eyes having little difficulty adjusting quickly to the soft light. His aunt sat in the straight-back chair, on the edge of it, her face expressionless, blank, except for the redness of her eyes. She stared at the boy. Neither she nor the two men in the room said anything. All of them just looked at him. He had never seen the two men before. One of them stood a little behind her, with his hand on her shoulder, the other stood by the door, facing him at an angle. He remembered the disarray of his clothes from sleep. He smoothed his hair with both of his hands and then started to tuck in his shirt.

"Ven pa'cá, niño," his aunt said in a tender, soothing voice, unlike anything he had heard from her before.

"¿Qué pasa, tía?" he said, almost in a whimper. "¿Qué pasa?"

"Este es el señor Adames, y éste . . ." She could not finish the introduction. She lowered her head as the silent tears flowed from her eyes.

"Yo soy Pedro Zamora, aquí vivo cerquitas." He lowered his gaze to the floor when he finished speaking.

"Sí, señor."

"Mira, hijo, ven pa' cá," said Jaime Adames.

Pedro Zamora, seeing that the boy was reluctant to come forward, took a few steps from the door toward him. He touched his hand to the boy's cheek. He leaned over until his face was at the same level as the boy's, only inches away. The boy could smell the whiskey on his breath as he started to speak.

"Tu papá y tu mamá tuvieron un accidente."

The boy was too dazed to understand immediately.

156

"¿Dónde está mi mamá?" he cried. "Llévenme a verla."

"Ya traen a los dos, hijito," said Pedro Zamora.

"Entonces, no están muy malos, ¿verdad?"

From behind the two men, his aunt spoke in a firm, though forced voice, pushing back the sobbing that was threatening to erupt.

"Niñito, tus padres duermen con Dios en el cielo."

"Bendito sea Dios," said Jaime Adames.

"Are they dead?" the boy asked in unaccustomed English.

The two men turned their faces away from him, tears welling up in their eyes. The boy was the only one not crying. His aunt resumed her crying, drawing in deep, labored breaths, giving full vent to the grief she had suppressed.

Sutherland Springs, with its one gas station and four houses, was to his right as he went over the horizon. He recalled being stranded there with his cousin, José, when a radiator hose broke. The sulphurous water they drank had reminded him of Smiley. He took the curve easily without having to slow down.

The boy remained with his aunt after the burial of his parents. He continued in school, steadily became accustomed to the smells of his aunt's house. He volunteered to do more and more of the cooking, which was fine with her. One of his uncles brought him his bed and his aunt did her best to fix up the room for him. Freed from the terror of having to stay with her for a day or two, facing the reality that she was now his guardian, she was not as fearsome, nor as bitchy. She became kinder to him, perhaps because he was an orphan or perhaps because she was not as lonely any longer. In any case, he came to respect her and to love her. They shared household duties, although more often than not, he had her share to do as well, but he did not mind. For his part, he was conscientious about what he had to do and for her part she accepted his willingness to be helpful and left him to himself as much as he wanted.

As he now lived in Smiley, he saw more of Mateo, grew very close to his family, especially Mateo's sister, Susana. He was fourteen when he discovered that he was very much in love with her. She was sixteen. At first, she had treated him and Mateo as children, telling them stories from the books she read in high school. Then, when he was not so eager to go off hunting or fishing with Mateo, preferring instead to remain in the coolness of the living room with her, listening to her talk, or just simply looking at her without saying anything, Susana realized he was in love with her. She would look at him and smile.

During the dog-days of August, when it was so hot everyone seemed to move through the harvest season with slow, lethargic steps, the boy went to visit Mateo to plan for the school opening the next week. He was always welcomed in their house and would just walk in without knocking.

The boy entered the house and called for Mateo. From the kitchen

Mateo's mother responded.

"No está. Se fue con papá. Pero espérate, hijo, para que comas algo. Ya mero está la comida."

"Bueno, gracias, pero no tengo mucha hambre."

"Pero vas a comer comoquiera, ¿verdad?" It was Susana.

"I bet I can eat something," he said.

"It won't be ready for a while. Vamos pa' fuera, al columpio."

"Okay," he said.

Susana took him by the hand, led him into the kitchen and out the back door. Her mother smiled at them as they walked by. The back yard had a canopy made from large oak trees. They watered the lawn frequently. The grass was fresh, green and cool. An old tire hung from a thick oak branch, suspended by a long chain. Susana, bare-footed, wearing shorts and a T-shirt, picked up the tire, letting it drop down her shoulders and waist until she could sit on it. The boy dropped to the ground nearby, lying on his stomach, yanking out a leaf of grass to stick between his teeth. Susana swung to and fro, smiling at him each time she caught him looking at her. He would blush and turn his face to the grass.

"¿Por qué no me dices que me quieres, eh?" she said, matter-of-factly.

"Te quiero." He said so quickly, without thinking, surprising himself.

"Yo no sé si te quiero a ti, pero yo creo que sí te quiero."

"What are we going to do?" he asked.

"After what we've just said, tenemos que casarnos. ¿No crees?"

She slid out from the tire and knelt on the ground in front of him. His chest swelled. He could not bear to look at her, hearing again and again the words she had uttered. His forehead touched her knee.

"Mira," she said.

When he raised his head, she kissed him on the mouth.

"Ya," she said, laughing, "confórmate." She jumped up and went back into the house. At lunch, the both of them continued to look at one another, exchanging gestures, being giddy, communicating their secret to each other. Susana's mother noticed their strange behavior.

"Ustedes dos," she said, shaking her head, "parece que andan asoleados."

Mateo began to suspect that he was losing his friend to his sister. He and Mateo still spent as much time as ever together, but Susana was included in more of the things they did. The two of them held hands when Mateo was not looking. Susana would sneak quick kisses, pecking him on the cheek or the lips, but he could not return them for fear of being caught.

After Christmas, Susana began her last term in high school. They had not spoken of marriage any further. He knew he would marry her as soon as he could quit school. He was in the ninth grade, already having more schooling than most of his cousins. He had been working summers, weekends and after school ever since his parents died to take care of himself and his aunt. It was his aunt that would be the problem. The old woman talked of his mother and her wish that he be the first in her family to finish school and go on to college. As his legal guardian she would not allow him to quit.

He would be turning fifteen, he was in love, he wanted to marry Susana, but he knew he would have to wait. One morning he found an important patch of three whiskers on his chin. He felt himself become a man, but because of school and everything around him, he had to continue accepting treatment as a kid.

Susana did not seem to be as impatient as he. Her family, especially Mateo, was more or less understanding of his intentions, and while not approving of them in so many words, they did not object. That was enough for him.

Chango neared Stockdale. The highway veered to the right, by-passing the business district of the town, a block or two of stores. He remembered when the highway went through town. He also remembered that during watermelon season Stockdale would be the nearest place for lunch and cokes, and that the town bustled with trucks and workers—more people than he had ever seen.

"Susana, let's get married. Right away. We can elope."

"You haven't even finished high school," she said, irritated, cross with him.

"I can quit school."

"Don't be silly. You want to work in the packing house or the fields like everybody else?"

"What's wrong with that?"

"Everything. I want to travel, to see things. All I've seen is San Antonio and there is nothing there. Don't you ever dream of New York and Mexico City and Paris, France?"

"Sure, all the time. We might be able to go there some day."

"If I married you, we could never do anything or go any place. We would have to spend the rest of our lives in Smiley. Forever."

"It doesn't have to be like that, Susana. Look, I graduate in May. Tía wants me to go to college in San Antonio. We can have a big wedding, you can come with me and I'll get a job instead."

"I don't know how to tell you this, but I'm already getting married."

"I know we are, but I don't want to wait four more years."

"I'm going to marry someone else."

"We're already engaged."

"Not really. I thought I wanted to marry you, but I don't. I want to marry someone else."

"Why are you doing this to me?"

"I'm not doing anything to you. I want to get away, that's all."

"Then, why don't you go to hell," he said.

The following three months were pure torture for him. He could not bear to visit Mateo for fear of running into Susana with her intended, who now visited her regularly. He saw her mother at the Red and White. She started to say something to him, her face full of sympathy. Instead, she said hello to him and continued on without another word. So much of school was filled with Susana's presence, every hallway, every classroom. He could not go watch football practice in the late afternoons because she had often come from home to wait for him on the bleachers. They would sit, holding hands, not paying attention to the field. As he would not visit Mateo at his home, Mateo came by two or three times to see him. He and Susana had gradually excluded Mateo from their relationship and he realized how estranged he had become from him.

He never saw Susana again after the day she told him of her engagement. It was difficult but he managed to graduate from high school. He was listless, inattentive, almost in a constant daze. He thought of her virtually every minute of the day. After graduation, he left for San Antonio. He attended college for two months, found himself unable to concentrate on his courses and quit. He took a job which lasted six months until he found a better one. Then, the years lost their consecutive quality for him. They became mixed together, the events of his life seemed to have occurred in a random order without his being able to distinguish when a certain event happened and when another followed. Everything was outside the channel of time, coming back to him as the occasion suited, more imagined than real.

He was away for more than seven years. He returned only once in the second year for the burial of his aunt. When he arrived in Smiley, don Pedro Zamora had already arranged for the funeral. Afterward, he did not stay to dispose of her belongings and to sell the house. He quietly told don Pedro to keep what he wanted of her things and to give the rest away. Don Pedro seemed offended at the offer but kept it to himself. On the way back to San Antonio, he had stopped in Nixon, made arrangements with Jim Sturtevant, an attorney, to sell the house and lot, which his father had bought for her, and to forward the money to him.

It was odd, he thought, that he felt no grief at all upon his aunt's death. He had grown to care for her, had continued to send her money and made sure she lacked for nothing. Yet, he could not feel anything. The burial, with many of his uncles, aunts and cousins present, had been a dull, tedious experience. As soon as he arrived in Smiley he had been impatient to leave. After the funeral, his uncle Cipriano asked him to come to his house for the dinner which is almost a ritual commemoration for the deceased. He refused as politely as he could, not wishing to offend, not caring if he did. Before leaving, he drove by Susana's house. He was surprised to find it much smaller and less warm in appearance than he remembered, in disrepair, with a large gaping hole in the porch. It appeared to be abandoned. He could see Susana and himself in the back yard by the swing. The image of her face coming close to his for a kiss was bright and clear. He felt nothing. It was only a picture in his mind that meant nothing. Upon leaving Smiley, he had left a good part of himself, and on that brief return he realized he had lost what he had left behind.

The coldness he felt during his aunt's funeral continued to haunt him in ways he was not conscious of. He drank more, went on his assignments a bit more recklessly than before. He had a succession of girl friends who lived with him for a month to half a year, then they would go away, saying that his coldness and distance was more than they could stand. He stopped seeing women on a regular basis, living alone, enjoying the solitude of his life, realizing the selfishness of demanding companionship but refusing to give it in return.

He received a letter from Jim Sturtevant, the lawyer, informing him that after five years, he had a buyer for his property in Smiley. The offer was for far less than it was worth and Sturtevant felt he ought to confer with him as soon as possible. The house had been rented for years, out of which the lawyer paid taxes, collected his fees, and sent him the remainder. Not wishing to return to Smiley after so many years, he scribbled "SELL" across the text of the letter and mailed it back to Sturtevant.

Two months after mailing the letter, he received an assignment in Victoria. The only way to get there, without chartering a small-engine aircraft, was to drive there on Highway 87. He did not like out-of-town assignments because he did not like being in unfamiliar territory. The one in Victoria was urgent, the fee was better than usual. He agreed to take it. He calculated he would need to spend the night, finish his work by mid morning or early afternoon the following day, and be back in San Antonio by nightfall.

The assignment went according to plan. On his return trip he stopped in Smiley. He had forgotten to eat lunch. Standing outside the Blue Goose Cafe where he parked were a few of his classmates who remembered him from high school. They seemed older to him, darker of skin, but they seemed happy and content with the way life was going for them. He invited them inside the cafe, offering to treat them to hamburgers or whatever the blue plate special might be. They accepted and he felt right at home with them. For a moment it felt as though they had been beside him all along. He was surprised to be wrong, to discover that he did share something with them. After they had eaten, someone suggested they go to Westhoff for a beer. He said he was on his way to San Antonio and told them *La Tacuachera* would be best.

His friends agreed quickly, saying anyplace but someplace. He offered to take some of them in his car and they were impressed by how expensive and new it was. He told them it was rented.

Upon entering the tavern, Jake, the bartender, recognized him. He had worked with Jake one summer at the grain elevators in Smiley. There were others, Chicano and Anglo, who remembered him or his father. Many of them came to shake his hand. He enjoyed a brief celebrity, a homecoming he had not expected. He drank more beers than he had had during the past year, enjoying himself, feeling no compulsion to restrict his drinking. He became maudlin, feeling a lump in his throat, as his friends recounted adventures they'd had together, or as the older men told him stories of his father, events he had put completely out of his mind upon hearing of his death. He found in the people and the land something he had willfully deprived himself of. The past only concerns people who have shared it with you, the land being more resistant to change, serving as a fixture which marks the past. By denying the people with whom he had shared so much, he had deprived himself of his own past, living in the recreations of solitary memory, which is not memory enough. The shared memories had more substance, were confirmations in fact that he had lived whereas alone his life had been a mere suspicion.

From that first time, Chango managed to return every few weeks to spend part of the day and most of the evening at *La Tacuachera*. Often, he rearranged his scheduled assignments so he could have Friday evening or Saturday free for his trips. As he recaptured his past he felt as though he had not been away at all. Some people would say it had been ages since they'd last seen him, but they would have said the same thing had he been gone for only a week or so.

Chango renewed many friendships and made new ones. His manner was even, well-spoken and polite. He was no longer the shy adolescent, as he was reminded, who could not look anyone in the eye. Now he was confident, smiling easily with self-assurance. His English was accentless as was his Spanish. He was not deferential when speaking to Anglos, as were many of the Chicanos. He spoke to them, without defiance, as equals. He did not join in the pretense, carried on by many rural Chicanos, that Anglos are inherently superior. His manner was controlled and no one minded, no one felt threatened by his presence.

There was a mystery about Chango which he would not resolve. He was well-dressed, though not flashy, he was never without money, standing for beer more than his rounds required but less than would be noticeable and embarrassing. When asked what he did in San Antonio, his answer was usually a funny remark, or a joke, or a question away from the subject. When pressed on it, he responded evasively by saying he "worked, had a job." He would not say what kind. Had it been someone else, the mystery concerning what he did for a living might have magnified into a crisis of friendship. There were speculations, ranging from his being a police officer to a master criminal. Don Isidro López settled it one Saturday night when Chango did not come by.

"Este hombre es decente con ustedes y con todo mundo. ¿Qué chingaos les importa más que eso?" he said. It settled the matter once and for all.

Chango liked to talk of the old times. It was not so much that he came to *La Tacuachera* to relive past experiences, or to retell the old jokes and anecdotes, things that are repeated over and over again as a kind of chronicle of life. What brought him back was the sense that here, among these people, his people, a man need never die. He could live so long as these friends remained alive to remember him and to pass on to their children memories of a man they'd never met, just as he knew stories and people long dead before he

162

was born but who were as much a part of him as anyone he knew.

Toward closing time Chango would buy one or two cases of beer to take out. At the appointed hour he would pile the cases in the trunk of his car and drive in the direction of Nixon. About a mile from the tavern, there was a roadside park, with a picnic bench, where he would pull over. Several cars would drive in behind him. He would open the trunk which gave out a dim light and remain drinking there with his friends until the pink of dawn defined clearly and grotesquely the spindly, black, distorted shapes of the mesquite trees on the other side of the fence. Chango never got drunk. He would drink as much or more than most but he remained sober always.

When the last of his friends could no longer take the beer and the late hour, Chango would get into his car and drive back to San Antonio. It did not occur to him to spend the morning sleeping at someone's house. He seldom saw any of his relatives, except when he drove to their homes for brief visits. His cousins his age had moved away and were scattered all over Texas. He could stay with his relatives, but as he did not visit for very long with them, he felt it would be an imposition. Among his friends, he was never invited and he never expected such an invitation. Chango knew the ways of the people, expected them, accepted them, respected them, and was gratified by them. It was something he found dependable, something of which he could be certain.

Coming up the first rise outside of Pandora, he could see the square grain elevator which was the major landmark identifying Nixon. It resembled a cigarette pack with four cigarettes evenly popped out, grey in color, unused for years but too expensive to take down. Chango was a little stiff from the hour's drive and hungry. Within minutes, he turned left at the only traffic light, a blinking red one, and drove to the Main Drugstore to stock up on cigarettes and have a hamburger. Afterward, slightly after three o'clock, he drove on to *La Tacuachera*, arriving there about three-thirty.

It would be nearly six hours before he would have his meeting with Tench.

IV

It was not quite dusk when Ambrose Tench left the tavern at the crossroads in Gillette. With the last of his money, he bought four bottles of beer. Once in his car, he tried to open one but found he did not have an opener. He went back inside the bar for one and discovered he did not have a nickel to pay for it. The bartender told him to take the opener and just leave. Tench pointed a finger at him, as if saying, I will be back, and left.

Tench was not as drunk as he should have been for having started so early. The angry rage over what happened with Milly Jones kept burning within him, preventing him from getting drunk. Midway between Gillette and *La Tacuachera*, he pulled to the side of the road to finish the last two beers. When he finished the last one, he cranked the car but it would not start. In the process, he flooded it. Tench got out, kicked one of the fenders. He stumbled onto the road shoulder to flag a car down for a push. Several cars drove by, their drivers seeing him weaving, and continued on without stopping. He cursed, shaking his fist at them. After waiting and realizing no one would stop for him, he started walking.

Chango had been at *La Tacuachera* since a little before four. He sat with a group of friends, talking, laughing, drinking beer. Tench walked two miles to *La Tacuachera*. When he arrived, he had sobered considerably, he was tired and sweating. He kicked open the door so violently that it shook on its hinges. The door swung to and fro. Tench remained standing, framed by the doorway, waiting for a comment from someone, anyone. Not receiving one, he took a step forward, raised his leg, coiled it around the door and shut it loudly with his foot. It slammed with such a noise that all conversation stopped. There was no longer the hum of human voices to be heard above the metallic, grating, music of the jukebox.

Ambrose Tench walked slowly to the corner of the bar. He surveyed all those in front of him. His eyelids drooping slightly, giving him a reptilian appearance, he swayed from the Chicano side to the Anglo side and back again. On the Anglo side, some stared at him, others grimaced and shook their heads. Most of the Chicanos bent their heads over their beers. Chicanos and Anglos alike had never seen Tench as he was. They knew the trouble he wanted was more than a fistfight would satisfy.

Chango had never seen Tench before. For all his trips to *La Tacuachera*, he had never been there to witness Tench's belligerent goading of people into fights. Apart from the bravado of kicking the door open, slamming it shut, and leaning with his back against the bar, Chango did not pay particular attention to Tench. Chango continued telling a series of new jokes he had heard in San Antonio. In the silence of the bar as the men watched to see what Tench would do next, Chango's voice sounded louder than usual. Tench fixed his gaze on Chango's table, watching as Chango told his new joke, moving his head in a circular motion to address each person at the table.

Ambrose Tench's jugular veins popped out like the terraces in the fields outside. His neck skin stretched tautly making his scar seem even more hideous. His jaws were clenched, his face turning into a sickly, discolored red, crisscrossed by white lines that made him look old and ghoulish. The narrow ribbon that was his mouth turned a pale, deathly white from the pressure. His eyes bulged forward deep from within their sockets as he stared at the Mexican he had not seen before. Chango's neat appearance and bright, even, teeth, which he could see in the gloom of the bar, became the focal point of all the reverses of his day.

Tossing his words over his shoulder, Tench yelled to the bartender in a loud voice to make sure everyone in the tavern heard him.

"Give me a god-damn beer, Jake. It better be a cold one, too, because I want to enjoy a real cold beer before I start kicking shit out of that Meskin' sitting over yonder."

Jake opened the beerbox and went deep for a cold one, wiping off the frost with his bar rag. He set the bottle on the bar within reach of Tench's arm. He knew there was no way to pacify Tench. Chango appeared to be in good condition as though he could take care of himself. Jake stepped back to watch. There was little else he could do. He did not even charge for the beer.

Ambrose Tench picked up the beer bottle by the neck, holding it between his thumb and forefinger, swinging it slightly, his eyes not turning for an instant away from Chango's table. With a strange, almost delicate motion, Tench raised the spout to his mouth, speaking before he took a drink. His voice had a hollow, echo-sound, as part of it reverberated inside the bottle. He was speaking in Chango's direction, although Chango appeared not to be paying attention to him.

"Take a good look at me, Meskin'. I'm the one that's gonna chug this beer and then I'm the one that's gonna take you outside and beat the hell out of you. Just 'cause I don't like your fucking face. What d'you think about that?"

Chango was still relaxed, not being able to take seriously the buffoon and the scene in front of him. He detected a mixture of fear and embarrassment throughout the building. All the Anglos were looking at him as if encouraging him to do something. A few of the Chicanos lifted their heads to look at him. These are blank, expressionless faces, speaking from roots Chango understood only too well. Thus far Tench had not said or done anything that a man had to respond to.

Chango thought Tench must be crazy. There could not be any seriousness in any of it. The people around him seemed concerned over something that was obviously a practical joke. At best, he thought, this man must be the community idiot, the person that no one pays any special attention to and the one who is tolerated so long as he does not lay a hand on anyone. Chango looked at Tench briefly and went back to telling his jokes, trying to draw his friends into more conversation when they did not laugh. From the expression on the faces around him, he slowly came to realize that something was about to happen.

"Parece que está loco. No le hagan caso," Chango said, annoyed.

"N'ombre, Chango, tú no lo conoces. Es muy desgraciado. Se ha puesto con varios aquí y les ha metido una chinguisa no más por ser cabrón. No sueltes el cabrón hasta que no lo dejes tirado. Cuídate."

Chango spoke up cheerfully.

"Saben que me he puesto con mejores que él. Tiene cara de puro cabrón. Ladra pero no muerde. No pica el baboso. Es uno de esos que les gusta hablar, es todo." Chango laughed confidently.

"Vale más que te salgas de volada, Chango, antes de que se acabe la vironga." The man who spoke was in earnest, fearing for his friend from San Antonio.

"N'ombre. No hay pedo. Si toca que se viene el puto, pos aquí traigo para él y para su abuela también." Chango intended the last to be funny, but no one laughed.

Tench finished the beer without moving it from his lips. He brought the bottle down to the bar with a loud dull thud. He burped obscenely, wiping his mouth with his sleeve. His eyes retained the same wild look as before when he first noticed Chango. Even as he had his head tilted back while drinking the beer, he had not taken his eyes off Chango. Ambrose Tench stretched his body to its full length.

"All right, Meskin', let's go. You and me, outside."

"Chango!" someone said, "¡córrele a la puerta!"

"No vale la pena, amigo," someone else said.

Chango brought his head up to look at Tench as if seeing him for the first time.

"Were you talking to me?"

"God-damn right I'm talking to you, Meskin'!"

"What do you want?" asked Chango, softly.

"What do I want? You, fella. You're the one I'm gonna kick around the parking lot. I feel mean. Kicking shit out of a Meskin' makes me feel so god-damn good! Come on, now, let's go. Outside."

Chango still had not been insulted beyond what he could easily dismiss. These were his friends, though. They might understand him running out the backdoor close by, but he would never be able to face them again. He had run away from Smiley once before. He had turned his back on these people a long time before and now he was back, making himself one of them again. He could not run. Yet, he could not afford to fight and draw attention to himself.

Tench and Chango kept staring at each other. Chango's face remained impassive. It was impossible to tell what went on his his mind. He knew that the least flicker of his eyes, twitch of his face, movement of his hands, and it would begin without his being able to do anything about it. The Anglos leaned forward in their chairs, watching the stagnating scene intently.

The fury that spit out his first words was subsiding from Tench.

"Don't think you can run out that back door, Meskin'. I'm already real mad. Now, if you make a try for it, I'm just gonna have to run right after you and I'm gonna catch you. You know I'm gonna catch you."

A small group of Chicanos started edging toward the door.

"Hold it right there, you! Sit the fuck back down. Nobody moves."

Jake kept polishing the bar, circling the same spot on the bar with his left hand. In his right hand, he held a piece of lead pipe covered with electrical tape. He hoped Chango would take Tench outside. The Chicanos sat down again.

"I just want to beat some shit out of you now, Meskin', but if you up and run on me, well, when I catch you, boy, when I catch up with you, it's gonna be a whole hell of a lot worse for you. I might just kill you, you know that? I don't think I ever killed anyone."

Chango still had difficulty believing what he was hearing. Suddenly, Chango's brown eyes fastened onto the wild, animal eyes that seemed suspended outside of Tench's face. Both men were unable to drop their glances. Chango's face became a mass of taut skin and nerve. Without breaking the trance which held his eyes fixed to Tench's, Chango began to rise slowly, evenly, from his chair.

He rose smoothly, gracefully, until he was firmly on his feet. Chango was taller than Tench. He stared down at an angle at him. He drew in a deep breath, expanded his chest, causing a slight strain on his tailored shirt. For what appeared to be a full minute, Chango, arms at his side, continued to face Tench. When he spoke, he was not angry or tense. He spoke evenly, in a measured voice.

"Don't push your luck."

"He talks," said Tench.

"I said, don't push your luck, redneck."

Upon hearing "redneck," Tench stepped forward and sidekicked a chair, sending it reeling, crashing, into a cluster of tables and chairs in the Anglo area, next to the dance floor.

"Go to 'im, Chango," someone said.

Tench turned in the direction the voice came from.

"You're next, motherfucker, you're next!" he shouted.

"Knock the shit out of him, Chango," said an Anglo.

"I'll be getting you, too, bastard!" said Tench.

"Cálmala, Chango," said an older Chicano. "Comoquiera pierdes."

Chango had not heard a word. It was only he and Tench in the bar. His mind and body waited for the right gesture to spring onto Tench, to tear him to pieces. Tench was a combination village idiot, maniac and bully. He had broken the peace and good feeling he came to *La Tacuachera* for. Tench spoiled the only tranquility he had enjoyed in many years. He had never wanted to rip another human being apart as much as he did now, as he realized this would be his last trip. If he ran, he could not face anybody here again. If he hurt Tench, they would forever be afraid of his violence. Tench was threatening to end what he enjoyed most in his life. As it was over in any case, the more he thought about it the more he wanted to hurt Tench, the more he wanted to yank Tench's arms from their sockets, to beat his brains out of his head with them.

"Dale en le madre al puto," yelled El Cucuy Sánchez.

"I heard that, Meskin'. You talk English around me, understand? I might decide to kill you, too!" said Tench.

Tench took another step forward.

"Come on outside, Meskin'," he said to Chango.

Chango did not move. He continued to stare at Tench.

"Redneck, you don't want to fool with me. You've run off at the mouth long enough."

The fury that was subsiding in Tench returned full force. No one had ever stood up to him in his manner. He yelled at the top of his voice, in a pained, weird, animal squeal.

"I'll kill you right here, in front of your friends! You can't talk to me that way! Never!"

Seeing that Tench was no longer in his senses, Chango saw immediately that it was not to be a fight. The entire confrontation had suddenly changed. He saw that Tench was merely a bully trying to scare him. Chango could see now that he had been wrong about Tench's face. There had been no anger there, no hatred, no fury.

Chango now knew that it was fear in Tench's face. He had matched words with him and in doing so he had already beaten him. Tench was now terrified about what to do next. Chango knew Tench would fight and would get himself beaten senseless, perhaps killed. The one thing Tench could not stand was to be made a fool of. He had started a fight and it was over without any blows exchanged. Seeing Chango begin to relax his body, Tench became more terrified. He took another step toward Chango, with only the table separating them. Chango's friends had moved away.

"Redneck, I can wipe the floor with your face, except you'd probably dirty it. You're a loud-mouth, a bully. I guess these people around here always thought you were serious. You're yellow through and through. So, relax. If you promise to behave, I'll buy you a beer. There's no use trying your bullshit anymore, you're finished."

Chango returned to his seat, relaxing his gaze, turning it away from Tench. He picked up his beer and began drinking it slowly, smiling over the rim of the bottleneck, showing everyone his white teeth set in the dark brown face. He took a small sip, then tilted it up higher to take a larger draught. When he lowered the bottle to the table, a droplet of beer coarsed down his chin. He took a handkerchief from his hip pocket to wipe his mouth. When he finished wiping his chin, Chango started to laugh.

Tench was confused. His hands were still pressed together into impotent, useless, fists. He could not tell why Chango laughed. Chango looked up to become aware of the confused expression on Tench's face. He laughed all the more as if someone were tickling him, lifting one knee under the table.

Soon, a few of the Chicanos in the immediate area of Chango's table also started to laugh. The laughter began cautiously, more from the contagious nature of Chango's laugh. First, one Chicano snorted, unable to suppress the guffaw that swelled in his chest. Before long, two or three more Chicanos started to laugh, not knowing exactly why. At first, only Chango laughed openly and freely. The quiet, cautious laughter, begun more as a nervous release, gave way to uninhibited, uncontrollable belly laughter and the sound of it filled *La Tacuachera* on the Chicano side.

They laughed and pointed fingers at one another. Some covered their gaping mouths to conceal missing teeth, but they still pointed. When they realized how Chango had finally punctured Tench's puffed-up reputation, they pointed, first at Tench, then at Chango. With each pointing of a finger, there came a resurgance of laughter. The sound of the laughter was mixed with coughing.

Tench leaped in front of a small, elderly Chicano who held his sides in laughter. Tench yelled at him at the top of his lungs, trying to be heard above the laughing, making the meanest face he could muster.

"Old man, I'll kick the shit out of you."

Upon hearing this, the old man laughed even harder, placing one hand over his mouth to cover up his bad teeth. He pointed at Tench and as he did so, everyone started laughing again. Tench ran out the back door, his face contorted in what appeared to be anger, yelling something drowned out by the laughter.

Chango motioned to Jake to bring beers for everybody in *La Tacuachera*. When he approached to pay, Jake told him it was on the house. Again and again for the rest of the evening, someone would be unable to suppress a guffaw and *La Tacuachera* was sent into gales of laughter.

ARTE PÚBLICO PRESS BOOKS

La Carreta Made a U-turn, by Tato Laviera.	ISBN 0-934770-01-8	$5
EnClave, by Tato Laviera.	ISBN 0-934770-11-5	$5
La Bodega Sold Dreams, by Miguel Piñero.	ISBN 0-934770-02-6	$5
On Call, by Miguel Algarín.	ISBN 0-934770-03-4	$5
Mongo Affair, by Miguel Algarín.	ISBN 0-934770-04-2	$5
Nosotros Anthology (Latino Literature from Chicago).	ISBN 0-934770-06-9	$7.50
Latino Short Fiction, eds. Dávila & Kanellos	ISBN 0-934770-07-7	$7.50
The Adventures of the Chicano Kid and Other Stories, by Max Martínez.	ISBN 0-934770-08-5	$7.50
Spik in Glyph?, by Alurista.	ISBN 0-934770-09-3	$5
Mi querido Rafa, by Rolando Hinojosa.	ISBN 0-934770-10-7	$7.50
Mujeres y agonías, by Rima Vallbona.	ISBN 0-934770-12-3	$5
Thirty 'n Seen a Lot, by Evangelina Vigil.	ISBN 0-934770-13-1	$5
El hombre que no sudaba, by Jaime Carrero.	ISBN 0-934770-14-x	$7.50
Kikirikí: Stories and Poems in English and Spanish for Children, edited by Sylvia Peña.	ISBN 0-934770-15-8	$7.50

Send Orders To
Arte Público Press
Revista Chicano-Riqueña
University of Houston
Central Campus
Houston, Texas 77004